DIRTY LITTLE MIDLIFE (FAKE) DATE

HEART'S COVE HOTTIES
BOOK 9

LILIAN MONROE

Cover design: Qamber Designs
Editing: Shavonne Clarke
Proofreading: Jane Beyer

Published by Method and Madness Publishing PTY LTD
PO Box 168 Subiaco, WA, Australia 6008

Print ISBN: 978-1-922986-49-8

ONE
MIA

THEY SAY that when it rains, it pours. In my case, when it rains in my shower, it pours in my kitchen. Wonderful.

"Okay, turn it off!" I call out.

My daughter dutifully shuts the shower off, but the puddle of water on my linoleum floor keeps growing inch by inch. Bailey comes stomping out of the bathroom and stands at the mouth of the hallway, her lips bunched to the side, her hands on her hips. "It's leaking," she points out.

I glance at her above the spreading water, unimpressed. Bailey rolls her lips inward to hide her grin.

My daughter is nine years old—soon to be ten in a few short months—and she is my life. Wearing an old graphic tee with a picture of the Ninja Turtles paired with loose, faded black jeans, her hair in a no-nonsense ponytail, Bailey surveys the damage like she's an expert plumber about to tell me how to fix it. She has a way of looking completely comfortable in any situation. She's confident, exuberant, active, and totally hilarious. She's the best kid in the world (I might be a touch biased).

I, on the other hand, feel like I'm about to have a nervous breakdown.

Standing there watching the growing lagoon for a moment, I allow myself two or three short seconds of despair. I don't need this. I'm already struggling to come up with next month's rent money for this two-bedroom apartment and the attached barbershop. It's the fifteenth of September, which means I have two weeks and a day to come up with more money than I have right now.

But worse than my money woes is the fact that this leak means I'm going to have to call my landlord, and that's an item on my to-do list I could *really* do without.

I grab an old towel from the stack on the kitchen table I'd prepared. I toss it haphazardly on the floor and watch it quickly saturate with water. It's not enough, so I toss another towel down. Bailey grabs an old tea towel from the oven door handle and creates a dam on her side of the lake.

"Where are we going to shower tonight?" Bailey asks, shoving the tea towel farther into the kitchen. A rivulet of water escapes to the side and she yelps, trying to catch it with her hands, then her shirt, then her legs. Finally, she decides to lie on her side to act as a human barrier. Water absorbs into her clothes, drenching her all the way down her front and side. "There." She beams at me, satisfied—and soaked.

I drop my shoulders, lips twitching.

Bailey gives me that impish grin—the one I can never resist.

"You did that on purpose," I accuse.

"I didn't want the water to get onto the carpet in the hallway!"

"And your clothes are better?"

Bailey bites her lip, leaning her head on her hand like she's lying on a chaise and not a puddle of dirty kitchen floor water. "Yeah," she says simply.

I click my tongue and give in to the giggles. I probably shouldn't. I always feel like I'm doing wrong by Bailey, like I've never been able to be the mother she needs. But when Bailey gives me that look with her sparkling hazel eyes and messy blond hair, it's impossible for me to resist laughing.

She does it on purpose, the little hobgoblin.

"I'm going to call Mr. Thomas," I say, tossing another towel on the floor, finally absorbing the worst of the water. At least the puddle isn't growing. I glance at my daughter. "You go get changed and ready for bed."

"No shower?" Bailey stands, dripping everywhere. Despite her best efforts, the hallway carpet won't be saved—not even a little bit.

"Wash in the sink," I say, feeling like a terrible parent. Not only am I struggling to make rent, but I can't even make sure my daughter has the facilities to keep herself clean.

"Okay." Bailey wrings out her tee onto the wet towels on the floor, then disappears down the hall.

With no other choice, I grab my phone. Time to call my stinking, rude, arrogant, good-for-nothing landlord and tell him to fix this dump if he wants to get his precious (extortionate) rent payment.

Not that I'm bitter or anything.

. . .

THE DOORBELL RINGS HALF an hour later, when I've just shut the door to Bailey's room, leaving her tucked into bed with a book. I glance down at my own appearance—messy hair, old tank top, yoga pants—and curse.

A snicker from behind the door tells me Bailey heard it, and once again, I wonder what kind of mother I really am. It's been the two of us against the world for so long, I wonder if I'm blind to all the ways I'm failing her.

But I gather my pride around me like armor and head for the door. I have a plumbing problem to sort out and a big, bullish landlord to confront.

My apartment is a two-bedroom, one-bathroom residence that occupies one story, tucked in behind my barbershop. It's accessible from a door at the back of the barbershop that opens onto Cove Boulevard, the main road through town, or via an entrance on the back lane.

Through the frosted glass of the back door, I spy a very large shadow, and I wish I were wearing something that didn't scream, "I'm a hot mess." But hey—this is me, and if Desmond Thomas doesn't like it, well, it's no skin off my nose. I don't like him either.

I pull the door open and glare. I can't help it. The man has that effect on me. He's so big and broad, he makes me feel small. His hands are the size of dinner plates. If he held my hand—which, *no, thank you*—it would probably feel like my palm was being completely engulfed in his flesh. Gross.

Worse than his size, though, is the way he looks at me. He's always serious, hiding behind that shuttered expression, looking at my little kingdom like it's the most pathetic thing he's ever seen. When he first walked into my barbershop all those weeks ago, slapping a new lease on my desk and telling me he was raising the rent, I could just *feel* the disdain leaking off him, like oil spreading over a pristine body of water. He polluted my sanctuary. I wanted to punch him.

The feeling hasn't gone away.

Listen, I know I'm a single mom and what I can provide my daughter isn't the best. But it's *my* best. I don't need some massive thug reminding me of all my inadequacies.

My landlord is wearing olive-green pants and a white T-shirt. It's the first time I've seen him in anything but a button-down, and the sight of it does something strange to my stomach. I feel like I'm witnessing something I'm not supposed to. This is too intimate. His own gaze coasts down my body and back up again, taking in my outfit, but his expression gives nothing away. His dark eyes are just as black, his jaw just as hard.

I'm sure he thinks I'm a slob.

"Hello, Mia." Desmond's voice is deep and rumbly, and it sets little explosions off in the pit of my stomach. Don't ask me why; I don't know. My hindbrain sees a threat, and some wires are getting crossed somewhere because my body is reacting with... arousal? The best I can tell, it's some sort of fight-or-flight response.

Being me, I choose to fight. "There's a leak," I start. "The shower is unusable. If this place isn't livable, I don't know how you get off charging this much rent for it."

Pow, pow! Mia lands an uppercut on Desmond's jaw...and breaks her hand in the process.

Desmond watches me for a moment, those dark, dark eyes steady on mine. He blinks slowly, like a lazy cat, and sweeps a hand to indicate that he'd like to come inside.

Why did that make my nipples tighten? Honestly, what is *wrong* with my body? This fight-or-flight response is whack. I glare at him for as long as I can stand it, then pull the door open wider.

He smells amazing. I get a big whiff of it when he steps past me, sandalwood and the hint of something fresh and citrusy.

Glowering, I shut the door gently and follow him into the kitchen. He looks gigantic. The room seems to shrink around him, like some sort of doll house. If he stretched his arms on either side, he'd almost be able to touch both walls.

I don't like having him in my space. Not one bit.

He stands with his toes just touching the first towel, which I've clumped up into a big mess of wet terrycloth on the kitchen floor. Then he crouches, peering into the cabinet where the water was leaking. It's soaked, of course, with what looks like old water damage on the back of the cabinet.

Before I can stop him, Desmond reaches inside and yanks the back of the cabinet apart. The particle board disintegrates in his hands, and he opens a huge hole up to look inside. Wet gypsum board comes off next, the damaged materials growing in a pile next to him.

He's *strong*. Even with the water damage, I doubt I would've been able to pull the wall apart with my bare hands. He just did it like he was tearing a wet piece of newspaper. I watch his shoulders bunch and release as he widens the hole. His legs flex as he leans forward, his whole body coiling with strength.

I wrap my hands around my chest and rub my puny biceps, wanting him to leave.

"Hmm." Desmond goes to lean forward, but the mountain of soaked towels is in the way. He shoves them aside with a frustrated grunt, his forearm flexing with hard, corded muscle while he does, then kneels on the floor in front of the cabinet. The position gives me an unobstructed view of his butt, which is nice.

No. No, it's not nice. Well, yes, the butt itself is nice, but the fact that I have a view of it is *not*. Sure, his pants fit perfectly, and he obviously works out enough that he has some junk in his trunk, but I should not be staring at it right now.

"Looks like this has been leaking for a while," he says, his voice muffled.

I tear my gaze away from his ass, but the only other thing to look at is the breadth of his shoulders, which take up the entire space inside the cabinet. I didn't know humans could get so big. It's unnatural. "Oh?"

"Maybe I can figure out where the leak is..." He pulls his upper body out of the cabinet and glances at me. "Can you turn the shower on?"

"I'll do it!" Bailey says, her head poking around the corner of the wall, then disappearing again.

I jump, staring after her, wondering how long my daughter was watching me stare at my landlord's butt. Again, this begs the question: What is *wrong* with me?

"*Okay, I'm here!*" Bailey yells from the bathroom. "*Hot or cold?*"

"Start with cold," Desmond answers, ducking his head back into the cabinet. "Go ahead!"

The pipes bang as Bailey turns the shower on full blast, and for a second or two, nothing happens. I imagine the water is leaking, because Desmond hums thoughtfully. He shifts his weight and shuffles deeper into the cabinet, his knees spread wide on the floor, his big, thick thighs hard against his dark-green pants.

Then there's a noise, like a big crack, and water blows through the cabinet in a violent spray. Desmond yells, jerking, and bangs his head into the countertop. With an awful snap, the laminate counter cracks, jumping slightly, and Desmond comes tumbling out of the cabinet.

Water sprays out of the bottom cabinet so hard I stumble back. It soaks me from head to toe while Desmond rolls on the floor at my feet, groaning. He's clutching his head, swearing as he crawls on the ground toward the cabinet.

"Whoa..." Bailey stares at us, eyes wide, while the water comes pouring and pouring and pouring in.

"*SHUT THE WATER OFF!*" I scream, my hands straight out in front of me in a useless attempt to stop the spray.

Bailey springs, and a moment later, the fountain stops.

There's a pause, with the only sound in the room being a steady trickling of water. I lift my bare foot up and place it back down, unable to see a single spot of dry land. Everything is covered with an inch of water.

Desmond lets out a sigh and lifts himself up so he's sitting on the floor, one arm curled around his bended knee. He's drenched. His white tee clings to him, completely see-through. I can see the shadow of chest hair, the hard pack of his muscles. He runs a wet hand through his hair, causing it to tousle oh-so-perfectly. Then he lets out a sardonic little chuckle. Like he thinks this is fucking funny.

It infuriates me. I don't know why. Maybe because he's wealthy, and successful, and rude, and he has a gorgeous body. It just isn't fair. He waltzed into my life, raised my rent, and brought me to the brink of homelessness. Now he's sitting in my kitchen like he just won a wet T-shirt contest, staring at the waterfall still coming out of the cabinet like he didn't just wreck my home.

This home isn't much. My barbershop isn't much. Most people would walk in here and think it was too small, or too cramped, or too dark. Years ago, my mother tried to shame me into moving back in with her and Dad, because she said an apartment like this was no place to raise a daughter. Her words burned me like hot coals. I hated it—hated feeling inadequate. Hating knowing she was right.

But this place is *mine.* I made a home here for me and my daughter out of *nothing.* My ex-husband left me when I got pregnant because I wouldn't give up the baby. I put myself through cosmetology school, I built my business, and I gave Bailey everything I could.

And now this oaf, this *blockhead,* this rich *asshole* is sitting in my kitchen, staring at the water damage, not understanding that *he just ruined my life.*

Anger winds through me like a flame, licking at my insides, coiling around my limbs.

Desmond lifts his gaze to me, taking in my sodden sweatpants and the old pink tank top clinging to my upper body. Heat and cold go to war inside me. My skin feels cool, but just below it, my blood burns.

When Desmond's slow perusal stops on my face, he has the audacity to frown and say, "Are you okay?"

"Am I okay?" I seethe. "Am I *okay*?"

He unfolds his long body and stands before me, towering above me like some hulking meathead. "You're trembling." His giant hands come to rest on my upper arms, thumbs stroking the front of my shoulders. They're so warm, I almost allow myself to enjoy the touch.

Then I knock his hands away and take a step back. "Look at what you did!" I stomp my foot in the inch-deep water so it splashes us both. "Why? Why did you have to turn the water on? Wasn't it enough to see the evidence of the leak? Look at this." I splash my way to the countertop and point at the cracked laminate. "How am I supposed to use this kitchen now? Your stupid, hard head *broke my countertop*."

It's the silliest thing to be upset about. I should be mad that every single one of my towels is in a wet clump on the floor, and that there's an inch of water everywhere. I should be mad that my shoes, which had been stored by the back door, are now floating by the kitchen table. I should be mad that neither I nor my daughter can bathe, cook, or live in the only home she's ever known.

I should be mad about a lot of things, but I'm finding myself staring at the countertop that came up against Desmond Thomas's hard head—and lost. And that's making me very, very angry.

Desmond lifts his hands. "Mia. Calm down."

The words hit me like bullets. "Calm down," I repeat, a trembling starting in my toes and slowly making its way up my legs. I spin slowly, trying to burn a hole through my landlord's forehead with my gaze. *"Calm down? Did you just tell me to calm down?"*

"Mom..." Bailey clings to the corner of the wall, staring at me with worried eyes.

"Bailey—" It comes out too harsh, so I take a deep breath. "Baby, can you go to your room and pack up some clothes for tomorrow? We're going to sleep in a hotel tonight." It's not like I have any other options. My parents sold their home and took off on a round-the-country RV tour in their retirement, and my sister lives on the East Coast.

I have friends now, sure, but I just met them after years of keeping to myself. I can't exactly call them up and ask to crash on anyone's couch. The thought of asking for a favor gives me hives.

Bailey doesn't move, just flicks her gaze between me and our landlord. Then she nods.

"Don't forget your toothbrush and your gym class uniform," I tell her after she's disappeared down the hallway. My voice is full of tension, but at least I can breathe again.

I turn back to the landlord who's made my life infinitely harder than it needs to be. His lips are pinched and a muscle feathers in his cheek as he stares at the destruction in the kitchen. He stands with his hands clamped on his hips, tension written in every line of his body.

Good.

He should be tense. He should feel guilty. He should feel like the worst person in the world right now, because he basically is.

Who says they need to call a plumber, then proceeds to cause a geyser in their tenant's kitchen? Who makes someone's home unlivable, then *laughs*?

I can't even look at him right now. I turn my back on my gigantic, hot idiot of a landlord and grab my phone from the table. Thank God it was on the table. If I'd had to shell out money for a new phone on top of everything, I would've lost it.

Well—I would've lost it more than I already have.

There's only one hotel in town worth staying in, and that's the Heart's Cove Hotel. It's run by two elderly ladies, the twins Dorothy and Margaret. They're probably not at the hotel right now, but I'm sure whoever's manning the front desk will be able to help me.

Unfortunately, my phone's touch screen is having a hard time registering my wet fingertips. I growl in frustration, poking at my phone, then finally give up and use a voice command. "Call Margaret."

"Mia, wait." Desmond takes a step toward me, sloshing through the water from the geyser he created, and stops when I lift my hand.

"Don't come close to me. You've done enough damage."

"Hello?" Margaret's voice sounds strangely echoey over the speakerphone. "Mia, is that you?"

"Hi, Margaret. I'm sorry to call you so late."

"What's wrong, dear?" There's a shuffling sound and a man's voice. Then Margaret says, obviously to Hamish, her partner, "*It's Mia. I don't know why she's calling. Let me ask her.*" More shuffling. "What's going on, honey?"

"There's been...an incident...at my house," I say, glancing at the manmade lake both Desmond and I are standing in. "Water damage. I need somewhere for Bailey and me to stay tonight."

Desmond plucks the phone from my fingers before I can even squeak in outrage. "Margaret, it's Des."

Margaret's voice warms. "Oh, Des! I'm glad you're there. I just spoke to your grandmother this morning and she said you were settling into town just wonderfully. Is everything okay? I can call up the hotel and reserve a room if—"

"That won't be necessary," Desmond growls. "One of my grandparents' condos is available on Seventh Avenue. I'll put Mia and Bailey in there until we get the water damage fixed."

"Oh, you're a dear," Margaret croons, and I wonder if she and I know the same Desmond Thomas. I would never, ever, not in a million years, call him "a dear." "I'll still call the hotel to warn them, and if Mia needs a place, we can put her in one of the cabanas out back. I think the one Candice stayed in is free, and we've just renovated all the bathrooms."

"Thank you, Margaret," Desmond says, and his voice loses the edge of tension it usually has with me. "It's really not necessary. I can take the girls over to the condo tonight. It's furnished, and it has two bedrooms."

Excuse me—"the girls?" Did he just call me and Bailey "the girls?" Are you freaking kidding me? Since when does he have the right to refer to us like that? That sounds...it sounds...*intimate*. Like the three of us belong together. Like he has some sort of ownership over us.

I do *not* like that. Not one bit.

Margaret doesn't seem to notice, though. She just says, "All right. I'm glad you were there to sort things out. Ta-ta!"

The call ends, and I snatch my phone back. "You had no right to butt in. I'm taking Bailey somewhere safe, and you can't do anything about it."

Desmond's face gains a neutral expression. "Legally, I have to provide you with livable accommodation, but you're free to refuse it. Since we have the condo on Seventh Avenue available, if you decide not to stay there, you'll be out of pocket for the hotel room."

My throat burns. I clench my phone in my hand and I think it might be to stop myself from punching that solid chest of his. Once again—just like when he raised my rent—Desmond is using money to try to push me around.

The worst part is, I think I might have to accept. I can't afford a hotel room, and I have nowhere else to go. I could probably call Georgia, my new friend and neighbor, but we barely know each other. She's glamorous and beautiful and I'm too proud to show up at her doorstep like a bedraggled beggar-woman.

Desmond is offering me a two-bedroom residence, free of charge, until my own place is fixed. It would be stupid and irresponsible of me to refuse.

"Fine," I sneer at him. "Text me the address, and I'll let you know when we're on our way."

"I can drive you."

"Yes, but then I wouldn't have my car with me, would I?" I sound snippy and awful, but I can't help it.

Desmond's jaw tics. His shirt still clings to every carved inch of him, his pants drenched so they look almost black. A droplet of water runs down his bicep and onto his forearm. He would be sexy if he weren't such a dick.

I widen my eyes. "Goodbye, now. Thanks for nothing."

My landlord has the audacity to grin. It's devastating. Men shouldn't be allowed to be that attractive and that dickish at the same time. *Ugh!*

It's not until the door closes behind him that I take a full breath, gather myself together, and go check on my daughter.

TWO

DES

I DON'T REMEMBER the drive from Mia's place to mine, but I realize I've made it when I pull into the parking spot reserved for me.

Stumbling to the elevator, I make my way to the condo on the third floor, dripping water the whole way. I can't stop thinking of Mia. The way her eyes flashed with anger, how her cheeks flushed with red. As I close the door and strip off my sodden clothes, I picture how she looked standing there, furious, her nipples poking through her wet shirt.

My cock aches for her. I'm so hard, it's doubly difficult to take off my pants. I strip them off and let them land with a wet smack on the bathroom floor, then turn on the shower to heat it up.

I wanted to kiss her. The moment she opened the door, I wanted to tug her close and crush my lips to hers, then throw her over my shoulder and carry her somewhere safe. I'd kill to feel her soften against me, to have her hands plowing through my hair, to feel her whimper and sigh at the taste of my lips.

My hand wraps around my throbbing flesh, and as the bathroom fills up with steam, I lean against the bathroom sink and stroke my cock at the thought of that little blond firecracker who hates my guts. She's wound up so tight, I bet she's dying for release. If I could lay her down on the bed, spread those sweet thighs, and find nirvana between them, I'd die happy.

When she yells at me, furious and tense, all I can think about is how badly I want to slide my cock between her lips. It's wrong. It's depraved. I'm a complete degenerate for wanting her that way, but I can't fucking help it.

As my breaths become jagged, I think about that evening two weeks ago, when I saw her at the Art's Cove gallery opening. She looked like sunlight incarnate in a golden gown, golden jewelry, and golden hair. Now, I imagine what would have happened if she were mine.

That night, I would've tugged her gown up to her waist and worshipped her body. I would've made her scream my name while she came on my tongue with her thighs wrapped around my head. I would've gathered her limp, sated body in my arms, pressing myself down on top of her until she moaned my name, then spread her legs wide with my knees and buried myself in her wet heat.

My movements become jerky, almost spasmodic, as my fist tugs up and down my shaft. When I think of Mia on my bed, splayed out before me, moaning my name, pressure builds at the base of my spine. I've wanted her from the moment she glared at me when I walked into her barbershop. I've wanted her every way I can imagine. I've been dying to taste the honey between her legs.

She'll never let me have her—but mercy, I want her bad. Thinking of that pink tank top clinging to her curves, and how much my mouth was begging to latch onto her puckered nipples, I come in thick lashes into the sink. Panting heavily, I grip the edge of the vanity in an iron-hard grip.

The mirror is fogged, so I don't have to look myself in the eye as I clean up the mess and go take a shower.

BY THE TIME I'm dressed again, Mia still hasn't texted. Part of me is worried she won't message me at all. Maybe she'll decide the hotel is the better bargain, even though I'm offering her something nicer, free of charge.

Staring at my phone doesn't make her text me, so I open the dating app I joined last month. It's called Blind Date, and it's supposed to allow people to forge deeper connections before they can exchange pictures or even names.

The only woman who's remotely interested me on it has the username of NaturalBlondie. We've exchanged a few messages over the past couple of weeks, mostly just light flirting and one-liner jokes by legendary comedian, Mitch Hedberg. We haven't made any plans to meet or even exchanged names. When I mentioned coffee, she didn't answer for a full day, and then she changed the subject. Neither of us knows what the other does for work, or much beyond what we've put on our profiles.

It's low stakes, but we've talked every couple of days for a few weeks. As far as dating goes, for me, that constitutes a success.

Now, as I stare at my silent phone, I wonder if I should put more effort into it. Have I been avoiding NaturalBlondie because I'm obsessed with a different blonde? What happened just now, in the bathroom—that isn't the first time. I've jerked myself off to the thought of Mia so many times, I should be ashamed of myself. When I first met her a few months ago, she lifted her chin and challenged me. She literally called me a B-movie goon in a cheap suit. Half of me wanted to laugh, and the other half wanted to bend her over one of her barber's chairs and take her right then and there.

I've been crazy for her ever since.

Unfortunately, I'm the guy who raised her rent and made her life exponentially more difficult. She hates my guts and has made it plainly obvious. And I guess a part of me thinks I deserve it.

I'd explain to her that my grandparents have been ripped off by their property manager for the past fifteen years, and I've got a hell of a job ahead of me to fix up the mess, especially with my grandfather's medical bills piling up. But my grandparents don't deserve their business spread around town like that. I can be the bad guy to Mia and everyone else—I'm used to being on the outside, used to not belonging. Been that way since I was eleven years old.

I open the Blind Date app and look for my messages with NaturalBlondie. If I can't have Mia, I might as well distract myself with the only other woman in my life who seems remotely interested. But before I can do anything, my phone lights up.

I groan, letting it ring a couple of times. Finally, with a sigh, I swipe to answer. "Vince," I growl.

"Hello, *brother*." In Vince's voice, the word "brother" sounds like an insult. It's a subtle jab to remind me I'll never *really* be his brother. Technically speaking, we're cousins by blood, brothers by adoption. He doesn't call his actual brother by that particular nickname.

"What do you want?"

"It's ten weeks until Thanksgiving. Caitlyn and I were just admiring the Thomas Trophy and looking forward to another victory this year. Thought I'd call and ask if you'd found a date, or if you'll be paired up with Grandma Maude again?"

Very few people have the ability to rile me up. Mia is one; a single look from her, and I want to either fight or drop to my knees and worship her. My brother Vince is another. One word, and the urge to punch him is too strong to ignore.

"Your gloating is pathetic."

Vince laughs. "Is it? That's three years in a row I've won the race, Des. No one's ever won it four times. I could make family history."

"Wow," I deadpan. "Making family history by winning our yearly Thanksgiving three-legged couples' race. You should be so proud."

"Every time I look at the trophy, I am."

I can just imagine his smarmy smile, and it infuriates me. I know, I know—I'm forty-one years old. I shouldn't care about petty things like a yearly family tradition. It's a three-legged race; it's hardly the Olympics. I shouldn't care that Vince is harassing me over two months before the big event.

But damn it, after going over to Mia's house and feeling just how much she dislikes me, knowing she'll never be mine no matter how much I want her, Vince's taunting gets to me. It's just a race, but I've never won it. I've been paired up with our grandmother every year just so she can participate. I should rise above Vince's taunting, but I *can't*.

"Is that all you wanted? I'm busy, Vince."

"Whoa, whoa!" Vince laughs. "No need to get crabby with me. Is there something more going on? Are you upset about the trophy, or are you still bitter about me and Caitlyn?"

I take a deep breath. This is a familiar pattern between me and Vince. He's the baby of the family, and my aunt's—his mother's—favorite. In my childhood years, he was my biggest bully, but it was hard to convince anyone of it since he was four years younger and much smaller than I was. He tormented me, made me feel like an outsider in my adoptive family, then pursued my high school girlfriend just to prove that he could win her over. Then he did—and he married her.

"I haven't been bitter about Caitlyn in twenty years, Vince."

"Could've fooled me. Right, baby?" He hums. "Caitlyn agrees. She says this should all be water under the bridge by now."

"I have to go."

"See you at Thanksgiving. You and Grandma Maude make a great team. Always good to know who's going to come in last place."

Click.

I stare at the phone and fume. As I grip the device between my fingers so hard my knuckles turn white, I realize something: I don't care about Caitlyn. I was telling the truth when I told Vince I'd moved on twenty years ago.

But I *do* care about our stupid yearly three-legged race.

How crazy is that?

If Vince and Caitlyn win it four years in a row, I'll never hear the end of it. The thought of putting up with Vince's gloating for a whole other year... *God*, that makes my blood boil. I can't let that happen.

Does it make me petty? Probably. Does it annoy me that Vince can still nettle me so easily? Hell, yes.

You know how much Vince riles me up? There's a guy in town who kind of looks like him—same hair color, same build, similar features—and when I met him, I immediately disliked him. His name is Sebastian, and he's dating one of my grandparents' tenants, Georgia, who just opened an art gallery in one of their vacant commercial properties. He's fine. He's a nice guy. But I can't look at him without feeling vaguely annoyed, because he reminds me of Vince. I even flirted with Georgia because I could tell it bothered him. That's how much Vince irritates me. It's completely irrational.

I'll be damned if I show up to Thanksgiving without a date and end up being paired up with my grandmother again. I'm *not* coming in last place. I'm not watching Vince swan around with the trophy under his arm all weekend. I'm not listening to twenty more years of him gloating about this stupid race, his wife, and all the ways he's better than me.

I'm bringing a date to Thanksgiving. I have ten weeks to find one, and she's going to be lifting the Thomas Trophy above her head by my side.

Mia would be competitive enough to want to win.

The thought pops up, unbidden, and I smack it clean out of my head. Mia hates me. She's not going to go to my family's Thanksgiving reunion just so I can win some stupid race.

Enough messing around. The only woman who's remotely interested in me is NaturalBlondie, and we haven't even exchanged names. If I'm going to find a date, I might as well find out if she's even an option. I open the Blind Date app and type a message.

TallDarkandHandy: Fun fact: Donald Duck's middle name is Fauntleroy. What's yours?

I stare at the message for a while, but no response comes from her—or from Mia.

Where *is* Mia? How long does it take to pack up a few things and drive across town?

Pacing my living room, I grab a set of keys off the hook and duck across the hall. The vacant condo is tidy, modern, and bright. I glance through kitchen cupboards to make sure Mia and Bailey will have everything they need, then duck over to my place to bring over some coffee, filters, milk, and sugar. The only breakfast foods I have are instant oatmeal and a couple of bananas, so I bring those over with a full gallon of milk.

Other than that, the condo is furnished. My grandparents had been renting it as a short-term rental through the property manager, who had skimmed almost all the profits from them.

When they fired him, my grandparents bought all new furniture for the place before running the numbers and deciding it would actually be better to sell it.

Now, I have the job of getting this place ready for sale, along with mine across the hall. They're mostly ready; my grandparents have no personal possessions, and all I've got is what was in my suitcases. The furniture can either go to the buyer or be sold/donated as quickly as possible.

My real estate agent told me to leave furniture and other items, in case people opened cupboards. It allows them to picture their life in the condo more easily. The beds are covered with brand-new sheets I bought for staging, and the kitchen is stocked with the basics. Mia and Bailey will be comfortable here—if they ever show up. Twenty minutes pass, and I still hear nothing from NaturalBlondie or from Mia.

Finally, I glance in the bathrooms and frown. There aren't any towels. I duck across the hall and grab a few clean towels, hand towels, and washcloths, and set them down on the master bed.

The phone in my back pocket vibrates. It's Mia, telling me she's outside the building. *Finally*.

My heart feels like it's being squeezed in a vise, and I grit my teeth to get a grip on myself. Then I buzz her into the building and head for the elevator. It takes forever for it to arrive, close, and go down to the ground floor. Finally, when the doors slide open to reveal the lobby, I get a glimpse of Mia and Bailey.

Bailey has a backpack on and a little wheelie suitcase, while Mia has a massive purse over her shoulder and a full-size suitcase. Dark smudges under her eyes betray her exhaustion, and she doesn't even get that usual bulldog expression on her face when she sees me.

She looks...defeated.

I hate it. It's wrong. Mia is made of spitfire and attitude. This woman with hunched shoulders and bags under her eyes isn't Mia. She's some stranger who snatched her body.

Holding the elevator door open, I usher them inside and clench my hands into fists to stop myself from reaching for the woman standing on the other side of the elevator, as far from me as she can get. Every cell in my body wants to wrap her in my arms and tug her into my chest, but what right do I have?

Instead, I just stare at the display above the door, counting the numbers to the third floor. When we get there, the girls follow me down the hallway to number 312. I open the door and lead them inside.

Bailey immediately rushes in, drops her bags, and says, "Whoa! Look at the fridge! It's silver, just like the one at Georgia's house. Ours is old and white. Can we get a silver fridge when we move back in, Mom?" Bailey glances at Mia, then shakes her head. "Or not. It's probably super expensive."

Mia cringes, like she's embarrassed, then hides it behind a smile. She kisses Bailey's head, then squares her shoulders and faces me. "Thank you. Do you need anything from me? Need me to sign anything...?"

I shake my head. "No. I'm right across the hall, so if there are any issues, just knock. Or call. Or text." I clear my throat. "I'll call a plumber tomorrow, so we'll be at your place in the morning. Is that okay?"

Mia stares at me for a beat, then frowns. "You're right across the hall?"

I point at the door marked 309. "That's me."

She seems taken aback but recovers quickly. "Okay. That's fine about the plumber, go in whenever you need to." We stare at each other for a while. I'm not sure how long; I lose track of time. Finally, Mia's eyes widen slightly and she says, "Well... goodnight."

Right. Knowing when I'm dismissed, I take one big step so I'm on the other side of the threshold, then watch the door close with a soft snick. After a pause that seems almost thoughtful, the deadbolt slides home.

THREE
MIA

SIPPING a coffee after I come back from dropping Bailey at school the next morning, I do a thorough inspection of the condo Des provided.

Resentfully, I admit to myself that it's nice. The beds boast pillow-top mattresses, the sheets are silky-soft, and the towels are fluffy. This place is *much* brighter than mine. There's a big, leafy tree outside the living room windows, with its leaves all different shades of green and yellow, and it gives the September sunlight a golden glow. The appliances are brand new, and the furniture is solid and well-made. There's artwork on the walls that looks relatively generic and inexpensive, but still tasteful.

Bailey loves it. I had a heck of a time getting her to bed when she wanted to explore every nook and cranny in the place. This morning, I woke up to the sound of kitchen cupboards opening and closing with steady bangs, and Bailey exclaiming at the fact that there was even milk in the fridge for us.

I walked into the kitchen and saw her staring at the distorted reflection of her face in the dishwasher's stainless-steel front.

Oh, yeah—there's a dishwasher. I haven't had one of those since I moved out of my ex-husband Colin's house.

I smiled at Bailey and made her some breakfast—she opted for some oatmeal that she'd found in one of the cupboards instead of her usual bowl of cereal that I brought from home—but all the while I felt like I'd let her down. Bailey should have the best of the best. She shouldn't be amazed by a dishwasher.

I felt like I'd failed her in a thousand new ways, and I was just waiting for her to realize it too.

Now, as I sip a coffee and glance around the space, the hardwood floors, the abstract geometric rug under the leather couch, the shiny appliances, I still feel the same inadequacy. Bailey deserves all this and more, but I haven't been able to provide for her. I've given her the bare minimum, and she's turned into the best kid I could ask for.

What if I'd given her a home with a yard and a dog and... Gosh, a *father*? What if she didn't have to choose between soccer and basketball, and I could afford to pay for both?

A buzz from the intercom pulls me out of my torrent of self-flagellation. Frowning, I head for the little white box by the front door and press the button.

The box lights up, and I see Georgia's face in the little grainy screen. Two more heads poke into view—Simone and Fiona.

"Georgia?"

"Hi, girl," Georgia answers, smiling. "We come bearing coffee and pastries."

"How did you find me?"

Simone elbows her way to the front. "Mia. Stop talking. This almond croissant smells delicious, and my stomach is growling. Let us in."

Grinning, I press the button to unlock the door. Then I prop my front door open and flutter my hands near my chest. I haven't had guests in a long, long time. I rarely have people over to my home, because it's so small and dingy that I'm embarrassed.

Before I can do anything, though, the three women enter the condo and chorus with *oohs* and *aahs*.

Georgia wraps her long, slender arms around me in a tight hug. "We heard about the plumbing issues. How are you holding up?"

"Des to the rescue," Simone notes, opening the fridge to peek inside. "This place is great!"

"I'm fine," I answer Georgia, accepting a coffee from Fiona with a smile. My own mug is on the kitchen table, but the coffee from Four Cups is far, far superior, so I dump the tar I made and opt for the new stuff.

"Sit," Fiona commands, pulling a chair at the kitchen table. "Eat." She takes one of the brown paper bags while Simone finds a plate from the kitchen, and a beautiful croissant stuffed with almond filling slides toward me. Powdered sugar falls like snow over the plate when I pick it up.

"Margaret said you called last night," Georgia says. "She came by the gallery this morning while I was taking the delivery of some paintings and told me all about it. She said Des had put you up here, so I called Maude for the address."

"There are no secrets in Heart's Cove," I answer with an arched brow. All those years of keeping mostly to myself, and now I'm finding myself drawn into this community of women who have taken our small town on the Northern California coast by storm.

As they bustle around me with their own plates, pastries, and coffees, filling the empty room with laughter and chatter, I can't bring myself to be angry about it. Maybe I've been *too* isolated. I've carried shame over not being able to provide for Bailey, and I've been so scared of being abandoned by the people that should care about me...but this feels good. Having these women here to talk about what happened last night feels comforting in a way I haven't experienced in a long time.

"So," Fiona prompts. "Tell us what happened!"

I do just that, and the ladies prove to be an amazingly receptive audience. They gasp and laugh at all the right places, and for the first time since the leak first started last night, my shoulders start to relax. Things aren't as bad as I thought they were. I have a place to stay, and my landlord will fix the leak. Bailey and I are safe...and everything is all right.

"Okay, back up," Simone says, setting her coffee cup down. "You said the water sprayed everywhere. Did it spray Des?"

I nod.

"So you had Desmond Thomas in your kitchen, soaked... What was he wearing?"

For some inexplicable reason, my face turns hot. "A T-shirt." I clear my throat. "A white T-shirt."

Cackles echo in the space. Simone bangs the table and points at me. "You were holding out on us! Come on, details. I want a full mental image of what that looked like. Did you take a picture?"

"What? No! Why would I take a picture?"

"Why would you—" Simone stares at me, then at Georgia and at Fiona, who both laugh. Simone just shakes her head. "Girl."

"You're all ridiculous," I grumble, picking up a few croissant crumbs with the tip of my finger. I put them in my mouth to hide my smile.

"Margaret told me he was *very* insistent that Mia come stay here," Georgia informs the group. Her eyes glimmer. "Margaret offered a room at the hotel, but he patently refused." She leans in. "And apparently, Des lives in this building too."

Right across the hall, in fact. But I'm not going to mention that right now.

I narrow my eyes at her. "Just a few short weeks ago, you were complaining to me about the gossip around here," I accuse. "Now look at you."

"Yes, but it's so much more fun to be on this side of it," Georgia says with a laugh. "Besides, it worked out for me, didn't it?" She wiggles her left hand, where her new—or should I say old?—diamond ring glitters.

"Enough about Des," Fiona says. "What about the Blind Date app? Didn't you tell us there was someone interesting on there?"

I blow a breath out through my lips, then get up to grab my phone from the kitchen counter. "He messaged me last night," I admit, "but I haven't answered."

"Why not?" Georgia swirls her coffee mug to check how much is left, then tips it to her mouth.

I slide back into my chair and open the app. "He asked me for my middle name. I think he might be getting impatient with how slow we're going."

"You haven't even exchanged names?" Simone frowns. She leans back in her chair and lets out a sigh. "Man, I'm glad I don't have to date anymore. I do *not* have that kind of patience."

"Not helping," I singsong.

Simone laughs. "Well, come on. Show us the messages."

Three heads crowd around my phone to read through the history of messages between me and TallDarkandHandy. When they're done, they all lean back with pensive expressions on their faces.

My anxiety ratchets up. "So?"

"I think you should go for it. See where it goes. Meet him in person," Fiona proclaims. "Look, here—the messages from two weeks ago. You guys were bantering back and forth when you admitted you hadn't made it to a third date in over a decade, and he joked that he felt almost sad to break your streak. That's chemistry."

"Chemistry?" I repeat, unconvinced. "More like pathetic."

"Plus, if there isn't physical chemistry, you don't want to waste weeks or months on someone that you aren't attracted to." Simone purses her lips. "I agree. I think it's better to meet in person as soon as possible."

"You should answer right now." Georgia pushes my phone across the table toward me. "We'll help."

My heart thumps. I've been on so few dates since I split with my ex-husband that the thought of meeting someone new makes my palms sweat. But I stare at the screen and type my middle name: Edith.

"It was my grandmother's name," I explain, then I type that too.

I hit send before I can reconsider.

Simone claps. "Yay! Okay, tell us when he answers. We'll start a group chat and you can put screenshots in there. And any pictures of hot men in wet T-shirts you might happen to take."

I most certainly will *not* be doing that.

Georgia grins. "Are you going to work now? We can walk over with you."

I glance at the time and nod. "Yeah."

"Well, pop by the café if you have a free minute." Fiona smiles at me, then walks around to my side of the table to give me a hug. "We're glad you're okay."

The four of us leave together, and I manage to avoid looking at the door across the hall for longer than a few seconds, thankful that my three friends don't notice the lingering glance.

MY BARBERSHOP IS A TINY, two-hundred-square-foot space with checkered black-and-white tiles, red vinyl chairs, and a small reception desk I got off the side of the road and restored myself. The mirrors have big black frames around them, and my little espresso machine and refrigerator are tucked into the back corner. As I walk in, I take a deep breath and let my lips curl into a smile.

It ain't much, but it's all mine.

The shop is pristine, so the only thing I need to do to open up is grab my laptop from the safe and fire it up, warm up the espresso machine, and check that all my instruments are sanitized and ready to use.

Then I hear a noise from the back, behind the door leading to my apartment. Another, louder bang follows.

Frowning, I unlock the door and cross into my old living space. A short hallway leads straight to the kitchen, where Des is mopping up water from the floor and a portly plumber is wedged under the cabinets.

"I thought I'd cleaned everything last night," I say, nodding to Desmond's mop. "Did I miss some?"

He turns to face me, eyes sweeping from head to toe and back up again. "Mia."

Everything inside me turns electric, then tension steals over me. I hate that every time I'm in the same room as Desmond, it feels like I'm losing control over my own body. But the ladies are right—he did put me up in a nice condominium. He provided coffee and the basics for breakfast. He's been a good landlord, if I ignore the massive rent hike. I should really try to be civil, and that means ignoring this strange tension gripping my body and treating him as a tenant would treat a landlord.

I wave. "Hi. Did it leak overnight?"

"No, the floor was pristine when we came in. This is my doing." He lifts the mop. "But it does explain why it took you so long to arrive last night."

I frown. It was just over an hour between the time Desmond left and I showed up at the new condo. That's hardly an eternity. Why does it sound like he was worried? Maybe he was just annoyed to be waiting.

The plumber removes his upper body from the cabinets and turns his head toward me. "Ma'am."

(Side note: I hate being called that.)

I nod. "How's it looking?"

"Completely fu—messed up." He rests his hands on his thighs and lets out a breath. "Looks like it's been leaking for months, if not longer. There's water damage as far as I can see."

Desmond frowns in my direction. "Did you not notice the leak before yesterday?"

I plant my hands on my hips. "Are you blaming *me* for this?"

Desmond swivels to face me fully, his brows lowering. "What's with the attitude? I was just asking a question."

"Oh, he was just asking a question! Ex-*cuse* me. I must have been mistaken. I thought you were telling me that *your* plumbing issues were *my* fault."

How. *How* can this man take me from zero to furious in 3.2 seconds? It's just his, his, his... It's just *him*! He's so big and menacing, and he thinks he can intimidate me. He's the reason I'm in financial trouble. He's the reason I had to move my daughter across town way after her bedtime. He's the reason I have to open the barbershop for longer hours and why I'm also looking for a part-time job.

And now he's blaming me.

My father has a name for my temper: he calls her the dragon. I hoard my hurts like gold and jewels, sleeping on them until someone wakes me up. Then, when she's awoken (for example, by a big clod of a man), the mythical beast spreads her wings inside my body, scales scraping against the inside of my skin, reminding me of all the reasons I'm angry.

Desmond Thomas has a special knack for waking up the dragon. One dark look from him, and I'm ready to breathe fire.

"Listen, Mia," he says with false patience, which just annoys me more. "Leaks often cause damp smells. Stains. I was just asking if you'd noticed anything. I wasn't accusing you of anything. There's no need to get prissy."

Prissy. He just called me *prissy*.

"No. I hadn't noticed anything. Oh, wait." I give him a grimace of a smile. "Apart from the mold in the bathroom, which I called the property manager about...oh, a dozen or so times? Someone finally came by to slap a lick of paint over it." I start counting off on my fingers for emphasis. "Then there's the fly screen in my daughter's bedroom that never got fixed, so I had to do it myself, and got yelled at in one of the yearly inspections. There was the exhaust fan above the stove that stopped working, and I never got *any* response about that either. That cost me nearly five hundred dollars to replace, and when I informed the manager I'd take it out of the rent, he threatened to take me to court. It wasn't until I asked Mr. Thomas about it during one of his haircuts that I stopped getting threats of lawsuits. So my apologies, Desmond, for being *prissy*. If I didn't love your grandparents so much, and if there was *anywhere* in this town that I could afford that wasn't a total dump, I would move. Unfortunately, some *asshole* just hiked my rent so much that I no longer have any savings."

Desmond's chest heaves. His nostrils flare. Dark, dark eyes stare at me across the space. "If you'd told me any of this—"

I put up my palm. "Terribly sorry, sir, but it isn't my responsibility to inform you of the history of *your* properties. Go ask that useless property manager for the records before you start coming at me, blaming me for all kinds of things that aren't my fault. I've put in countless maintenance requests over the years, and most of them went ignored until I spent my own money on them. I've been threatened with court so many times, I came to expect it. This apartment would be in shambles if I didn't put my own funds and time into it. I've spent *thousands* that never got reimbursed." I suck in a deep breath, fuming. He has the *audacity* to come at me with accusations, to make me feel small and powerless and weak. Gah! *I hate this man.* "And you know what? Fuck you."

"Mia—" He takes a step toward me.

The plumber whistles. "You guys need me to leave the room? Give you a little privacy?" Fuming, I glare at the man, who grins. "Sorry, ma'am."

Ugh! I'll ma'am him. I'll ma'am him right in the face!

Spinning on my heels, I stomp back through the short hallway and slam the door. Back in my barbershop, I turn in a circle looking for a pillow or a blanket or something soft that I can shove against my face to muffle my scream. Not finding anything, I march to the front door intending to flip my sign over and unlock the door to open the shop. Who knows, maybe my cheery personality will attract new customers.

And the lights go out.

I pause, standing in the middle of the room, waiting for them to come back on. A loud swear comes from the apartment out back, moments before the door opens. Desmond strides through, stopping short when he sees me staring.

"The power went out," he says, stating the obvious.

I blink. "Do you think I'm an idiot or something?"

"Why are you being so—"

"Choose your next words very carefully, dickhead."

"I'm trying to be nice!"

"Nice? You're trying to be *nice?*"

Des shoves a hand through his hair and turns his back on me. His shoulders heave as he takes a deep breath, hands dropping to fist at his sides. Another deep breath, and he lifts his head to the ceiling.

The dragon inside me huffs, sending ash and smoke swirling around me.

Desmond spins slowly, meeting my gaze with his own black eyes. "You'll stay in the condo on Seventh Ave for as long as you need to," he informs me. He points over his shoulder at the back door leading to my old apartment. "I'm going to make sure all the issues in this place are fixed. If you could send over a list of the maintenance requests that still haven't been addressed, and a record of what you've paid, with receipts if possible, I can make sure everything is sorted out and you get what you're owed. I'm sorry your experience with the old property manager was so poor. You weren't the only one who has a long laundry list of complaints, and I'm sorry it's taken so long to fix it."

I sip in little shallow breaths, waiting for the other shoe to drop. People don't usually apologize like that without some sort of qualifier.

Desmond stays silent, watching me.

I rock back on my heels and give him a nod. "Okay."

"I'll get the power back on as soon as I can. Might take an hour or so. Is that going to be a problem?"

I shake my head. My first scheduled cut and shave isn't until eleven, which is two hours from now. "That's fine. I can go grab a coffee at Four Cups."

"I'll message you when the power's back on." Des gives me a quick jerk of the chin, then heads to the door. Pausing in the doorway, he turns to face me again. His eyes lift to meet my gaze. There's a bit of scruff on his cheeks that my fingers itch to feel, especially when he clenches his jaw so tightly it looks diamond-hard, even from across the room. "Mia," he grates, "I'm sorry for calling you prissy."

His shoulders are so wide they almost brush either side of the doorway. He stands there, staring at me with those unreadable eyes, and I feel my stomach simultaneously knot and loosen while he watches me. Gripping the headrest on one of my chairs, I try to keep myself steady as I lift my chin.

The dragon falls down on her pile of treasure with a huff, exhausted. "I'm sorry for calling you a dickhead."

Des exhales. "I was being one. I'll text you in a while." His eyes look sad as they linger on mine, then he turns and disappears through the door.

I lock up, hands trembling, needing to put some distance between me and my stupidly handsome, stubborn, annoying, rude, infuriating landlord.

Then my phone buzzes.

TallDarkandHandy: I have my dad's name as my middle name. Allen. Ready for first names?

A cool wind blows down the street, ruffling my hair. I shiver, pulling my cardigan tighter. The air tastes fresh on my tongue, but soon it'll turn colder. At least Bailey and I have somewhere to stay, and I'm guessing the condo has better insulation and heating than our old place behind the barbershop.

I glance through the darkened windows of my business, then look at my phone again. The last thing I want to do is go on a date. I'd rather crawl under my blankets and fall asleep until the next ice age, especially after that argument. I feel *tired*.

But maybe the girls are right. I should embrace the flirtation and move this along with Mr. Handy. Otherwise, I might get caught up in another man's orbit—someone big and strong and dark-eyed, who somehow makes me want to simultaneously rip his head off and fall on my back with my legs spread.

Maybe in my past life I was a praying mantis. The urges feel familiar.

NaturalBlondie: How about a date instead? Let's take the spirit of this app all the way...a true blind date.

I send the message, feeling oddly guilty and a little bit disappointed, like I'm doing something wrong. My heart isn't really in it. But what else can I do? Indulge in this awful, contentious relationship with my landlord? Continue to live my life on my own, until I blink and my daughter's all grown up and I'm completely alone?

I need a distraction. I need to feel attractive. I need *sex*, damn it.

And even though my body hasn't got the memo, I will *not* be having sex with Desmond Thomas. Ever.

So, marching across to the café, I find Fiona behind the till and show her my latest message. "I did it," I announce. "I asked him out."

FOUR

DES

A TRUE BLIND DATE.

I read the message over a few times, bitterness coating my tongue. I like this woman—I do. She's the only person that's made me laugh in my many attempts at online dating. Going out with Blondie is a good idea. Intellectually, I know it is.

But...

God, the way Mia stared at me. The way she deflated when I apologized, like all the fight just went out of her. Every cell in my body is begging me to gather her up in my arms and hold her close. I want to protect her from all the demons she's had to fight. I want to crack her open like a walnut and see what she's hiding behind that tough exterior, tell her I'll fix everything for her. I'll make everything okay.

That's never going to happen, though—and I need a date to my family's Thanksgiving reunion. Last night, after I got home from showing Mia and Bailey the apartment, I got a text from Vince. It was a picture of the trophy, gleaming under the lights of his kitchen island.

I'm not going home without a date this year. No freaking way. I'll hire one if I need to.

TallDarkandHandy: How about the new Italian place opening up in town, Dolce Vita? Say, Saturday night?

Shoving my phone back in my pocket, I turn to Bill, the plumber. He's grumbling to himself incessantly and finally stands up beside me. "We're going to have to pull all these cabinets away from the wall. There was no waterproofing done in the bathroom. The damage is extensive. You'll probably have to replace all this drywall, rip out the shower, and maybe do the floor in the bathroom. I can fix the leak, but it won't be enough."

"All right."

The electrician I called pokes his head out of the hallway. "Power's good to come back on. Fuse blew. The whole board isn't up to code, though. It's too small for the number of circuits you've got, and you should really update it. Could use some whole-house surge protection while you're at it. And the barbershop should be on a separate board entirely."

Nodding, I tell the electrician to send me a quote and his availability. This feels like my old life in Colorado. I started working for a builder when I was seventeen. Then I got a degree in project management, moving up the ranks until I was the second in command in the whole company. The old man was ready to hand me the keys to his kingdom—then it all fell apart. Not long after, my grandparents called, admitting that they'd been swindled by a scummy property manager, and here I am.

He flicks the power back on, and I take out my phone to text Mia. There's a message from Blondie.

NaturalBlondie: Can't do this Saturday. I'm free next week, though. My kid has a playdate at a friend's house. Friday?

TallDarkandHandy: Works for me. Looking forward to meeting you (and finding out if your username is true).

NaturalBlondie: Even if it isn't, you'll never know 😜

Huffing a laugh, I close the app and find Mia's number.

Desmond: Power's back on. Safe to come back.

Mia answers within a second.

Mia: Ten-four.

I wander to the front, through the barbershop, in time to unlock the door for Mia. She's holding two coffees and hands me one with a tight smile.

"Olive branch," she explains.

My throat shouldn't be this tight. It's just a coffee. I nod, popping the lid to check the contents. Large cappuccino, and judging by the markings on the lid, it includes an extra shot of espresso. My usual order. "Thanks, Mia."

"Don't mention it." She holds my gaze. "Seriously. Don't mention it. It's hard for me not to get annoyed at you on a good day."

I can't help the laugh that falls from my lips. This woman is something else. Even with her temper, her teasing, she makes me feel like I'm part of something. Like I belong here, if only to make her angry.

"Hey—you got time for a shave?" I rub the scruff on my beard. If I were being honest with myself, I might admit that I'm using this as an excuse to spend more time with Mia, to enjoy this slight detente between us.

Mia blinks, something flashing across her face so fast I can't quite read it. Apprehension? Nerves? Embarrassment?

I wish she'd let me in. She's so guarded, it makes me crazy. I want to know everything about her. For just a moment, I allow myself to imagine what it would be like to bring Mia to my family's Thanksgiving. She'd charm everyone, of course. She'd be fast friends with my cousin Katie, who's just as spirited as she is. Vince and David, my adoptive brothers, would be insanely jealous. I already know my grandparents love her. Even the thought of showing her off on my arm in front of the whole family makes me want to puff out my chest.

But that's a pipe dream. Ain't gonna happen.

"Sure," Mia says. "I've got time for a shave. Take a seat."

I slide into the chair, vinyl creaking under me, and then the barbershop phone rings. Mia excuses herself with a pat on my shoulder—a casual touch that makes my whole body buzz—and sways those perfect, petite hips toward the front of the shop. She has a fantastic ass, and those jeans look like they were made for her.

"You've reached Blade Barbershop; this is Mia speaking. How may I help you?" Her voice is bright and professional, just this side of friendly. She's never—not once—spoken to me like that, but somehow I don't mind. When she's slinging insults at me, it feels more real.

Then Mia's whole body goes solid. "Colin. How—what do you want?"

I frown, spinning the chair around toward her. She's got her back to me, but I can see from here that she's gripping the edge of her desk so hard her fingertips are white. Her shoulders are hiked up near her ears.

"Oh," she says. "No, it's fine. It's just unexpected, is all. It's been nine years. Why now?"

I lean forward. I don't like this. Not at all. I don't like the way Mia's voice got thin, or the way her leg jiggles anxiously.

There's a long silence until she says, "This is...quite a shock."

Another long pause. "I don't know. You made it very clear that you wanted nothing to do with her when I was pregnant. I won't have you waltzing in and out of her life. She deserves better than that. You're either in or out until she's old enough to decide for herself." Mia glances over her shoulder, sees me watching. Her eyes are tortured, and it kills me not to be able to comfort her. "Listen, I can't talk. I'm working. Send me an email, I still have the same address. Yeah. Uh-huh. Okay, bye." She places the phone in its cradle harder than necessary, then takes a moment to gather herself. I watch her take a deep breath and let it out slowly.

When she turns around, Mia is perfectly composed.

"Is everything okay?"

She snorts. "Is everything ever okay?" Shaking her head, she puts up a hand. "Sorry. I'm being horribly unprofessional. Coffee? Tea? Water?" Her eyes flick to the coffee cup in my hands, and she gives me a sheepish smile. "I guess I already covered the drink, didn't I?"

"You sure you're okay?"

Mia's hip shoots out to the side, head cocking. "What, afraid I'll get prissy again?" She stops herself, closes her eyes. "Sorry. That was uncalled for. I must sound like a lunatic to you right now."

"I'm used to it," I answer, the corner of my lips twitching.

Mia huffs, like she wants to smile but won't allow herself to do it. We watch each other in silence for a beat, until Mia nods toward the phone. "That was my ex-husband. He wants to meet Bailey." She sweeps a cape over my shoulders and ties it behind me, her fingers cool against the nape of my neck as she does the snaps up one by one. Each touch sends a shiver coursing down my spine. I sip my coffee to hide my reaction.

"He hasn't met his own daughter?" How could someone stay away from their own kid? How could a man choose to walk away and not look back? If I had a kid, I'd be there every single day. I would make sure that child had everything I had for the first eleven years of my life—and never felt as alone and abandoned as I did for the next thirty.

Mia lets out a bitter laugh. "No, he hasn't met Bailey. Not once in the nine—almost ten—years she's been alive. Why call me now? Maybe he knows that I'm clinging onto sanity with the edge of my fingertips."

I gather these hints about Mia like a crow collecting shiny objects, treating them like the precious gems they are. It's like a doorway has been shoved open a tiny sliver, and I get a glimpse at the woman inside.

In the mirror, Mia meets my eyes...and flicks up a gleaming straight razor. "Now that we've established my tenuous hold on my mental health... Clean shave, was it?"

I laugh. "Very scary."

"Honey, you have no idea." Even though I know it means nothing, having Mia call me a pet name sends warmth unfurling in my chest.

Ridiculous. I'm ridiculous.

She puts the razor down and starts lathering shaving cream on my cheeks and jaw. The brush moves in smooth circles over my skin, and her body presses into my side. I'm keenly, intensely aware of the shape of her breast against my upper arm, the warmth of her leg near mine.

Then she moves away, and I take a deep, silent breath. I watch her duck her head over her tools, her hands shaking. She closes them into fists for a moment, gathers herself, and picks up the razor once more.

When she brings the edge to my skin, her movements are steady, precise. Her armor is back on, the door to her inner self slammed shut.

LATER, when I've paid and left through the back door into Mia's apartment, I feel strung out and jittery. I can't stop thinking about that phone call. Her ex, wanting to weasel his way back into her life. Has he finally realized the amazing woman he left behind? Why does that make me want to burn this place to the ground?

Oh, right. I know why. It's because I'm fucking obsessed with her.

Pathetic.

I find the plumber in the bathroom, his head stuck under the sink. He's knocked another hole in the wall beside the shower, and I poke my head in the wall to see the massive amount of water damage we're dealing with.

"We're going to have to rip this wall out," I note.

"Yep," Bill replies.

"I'll get started, call you back when I've stripped the walls. Is there anything you can do in the meantime?"

"Not until we have it opened up."

"Leave it with me."

I head back out to the living room and pull out my phone. My grandparents' old property manager had connections with a contractor in town, but who knows if they were legitimate or if they were ripping us off as well. I tap my phone against the side of my leg. I'd have to research contractors, call references, get a quote...that all takes time.

I *could* do a lot of the work myself. It would be quicker, and Mia needs her home back. After what she told me she endured with the old manager, I'm not going to give her back her apartment in anything other than tip-top shape. Plus, the sooner she's out of the condo, the sooner I can sell it and give my grandparents some financial breathing room.

Turning toward the kitchen, intending to start ripping down the wall myself, I stop short as something catches my eye in the living room. There's a frame on the wall about the size of a piece of printer paper, with a cross-stitch of a cartoon foot. Below the foot, the words, "A severed foot is the ultimate stocking stuffer," are written in cursive stitches.

My blood runs cold. I take a step toward the frame, heart pounding. I know that quote. It's comedian Mitch Hedberg's joke, and I saw it on a dating profile on the Blind Date app.

Not just any profile.

On NaturalBlondie's profile.

My breaths come out staggered, sawing through my lungs.

She—

No. Oh, no. This is bad. This is so bad, it's not even funny.

The woman I've been texting, flirting with...that's *Mia*? The woman who makes me chuckle with messages every couple of days, the one who wants to take it slow.

I've organized a date with Mia for next Friday night.

I turn my head to look at the closed door separating the apartment from the barbershop. She's just beyond it, cutting and shaving and primping the men of Heart's Cove. And she has no idea.

Before I know what I'm doing, I'm halfway to the door—and I stop short.

If I admit that I'm TallDarkandHandy, she'll cancel the date. There's no question in my mind, no doubts whatsoever. If I walk in there and I tell her that she's going out to dinner with me, it'll never happen.

Blood rushing in my ears, I stand still in the hallway, not knowing what to do.

Suddenly, my date on Friday is much more exciting. I could sit across from her, in a candlelit restaurant, drinking wine, making her laugh...

I want that.

God, I want that so much.

I want to see her dressed up, with her golden hair curled around her face, and I want her to look at me like I mean something to her.

Maybe...maybe if I don't tell her about the date, she'll show up...and stay?

No. I have to tell her.

The image of Mia on my arm at my family's Thanksgiving reunion pops into my head again. Now it doesn't seem so far-fetched. I'll take her out, wine her and dine her, let her know that I never meant to make her life difficult. I raised the rent on her place because my grandparents' finances were in bad shape and they needed cash. My grandfather's medical bills are mounting, and although they have five properties in town, they're remarkably cash poor. The previous property manager stole so much money from them and left most of their properties in such disre-pair that I *had* to raise all the rents just to try to generate some money to be able to fix the Seventh Ave condos up for sale.

I'll explain this to Mia. She'll understand.

A dinner date is the perfect time to do it.

FIVE
MIA

TODAY WAS AWFUL. By the time Bailey is in bed, I feel like I've been up for thirty hours or more. My body aches, my eyes itch with tiredness, but I can't quite get myself to relax. I already know I won't be able to sleep.

Instead, I brew a mug of peppermint tea and snuggle on the leather couch in the living room. Unfortunately, the remote is way over on the coffee table, so it looks like I won't be watching any television right now. As a poor substitute, I stare at my phone —specifically, I stare at the little red notification on my email icon.

Colin didn't waste any time. I saw his name pop up on my screen when Desmond left the barbershop after his shave, and I almost threw my phone through the front window. I'm not entirely crazy, though, so instead I just swiped to ignore the notification and pretended it didn't exist, like the rational adult I am.

Bailey came home in a whirlwind, excited by her third week

of school, telling me she'd decided to play basketball again this year. Then she frowned at me and asked if we'd have enough money for her to participate, and my heart just shattered into a million pieces. She shouldn't be worrying about that stuff.

I feel absolutely pummeled by life right now. Today was just one reminder after another that I haven't provided my daughter with a good life. First, there was the old, crappy apartment. It felt good in the moment to sling insults at Desmond, watch them land against his big, muscular chest. In my anger, I loved telling him about everything that was wrong with the home I'd made for me and Bailey...but in the end, all it did was remind me of everything I've put up with over the years.

Then I had a big, fat reminder that my daughter grew up without a father—and she's already worried about money.

That's all my fault.

Bailey deserves better. She deserves not to worry about money. She's a *child*. She should be able to play sports and go to school and learn an instrument and do whatever she wants. And even though I'd like to delete Colin's email without reading it, I know that my daughter deserves the chance to at least meet her own father.

So, I open the email.

Mia,

First of all, I'd like to apologize. I walked away from you and Bailey a decade ago, signed away my parental rights, and thought I'd never look back. I'm sorry for putting you in that position. It was selfish.

I find myself looking back now. My brother just had his first kid, a boy, and I'm realizing how much I missed. All those years, and I didn't even realize what I gave up.

I'd like to meet my daughter, get to know her. I know I don't have the right to demand that from you, but I'm asking, Mia. Please.

You can contact me on this email, or at the phone number in my email signature.

Colin

I lie back on the couch and stare at the ceiling. The worst thing about getting that email is the reminder that Colin isn't a bad man. From the start, he was clear with me that he didn't want children. When I got pregnant, that didn't change. He wasn't nasty or cruel or abusive. He just signed away his rights, and that was it. Our split was devastating for me, but relatively amicable. He didn't want kids, and I discovered I did.

It was awful in the simple finality of it. I was pregnant, heartbroken, and alone.

How could I refuse him the right to meet his own daughter?

Answer: I can't.

Hauling myself off the couch, I leave my now-cold tea behind and pad to Bailey's room. She cracks her lids open when I peek through the door, and I find myself slipping through the doorway.

I climb into bed beside her and wrap my daughter in my arms, holding her tight.

"Are you okay, Mom?"

"Just needed some snuggles," I whisper.

Bailey squeezes me in response and promptly falls asleep. I watch her steady breathing for a while, combing my fingers through her dark-gold hair, counting the fine, long eyelashes resting against her cheeks. She's so perfect. My precious daughter, growing up faster than I ever thought possible.

Later, when I finally feel my lids getting heavy, I untangle myself from my daughter's limbs and head for my own bed. The sheets are cold, and the moonlight sneaks past the edges of the blinds. I fall into that space just beyond the shallowest edge of sleep, and my mind fills with familiar images.

Bailey, a few months old, colicky, crying and crying and crying. A shadowy figure coming to take her away, accusing me of not being able to care for her. Running and going nowhere, my feet stuck in a sticky black substance. Being so awfully alone, screaming, searching for my child.

I bolt awake, drenched in sweat. My whole body trembles as I claw the covers off my body, swinging my legs over the edge of the bed. I gulp down deep breaths, trying to clear the images from my mind.

I haven't had that nightmare in many, many years—but it seems it still has the same effect on me. Scrubbing my hands over my face, I leave the bedroom with its unfamiliar shadows. I can't quite resist checking on Bailey, and I find her sleeping peacefully. The kid could sleep through an air raid siren.

The clock on the microwave tells me it's nearly three o'clock in the morning. I dump my old peppermint tea and make a new mug, then sit back on the couch, spreading the fluffy blanket over my lap.

My fingers have a mind of their own; they lead me to the Blind Date app. Maybe I just need some distraction and thinking of going on a date is sufficiently terrifying so as to brush away the last sticky cobwebs of my nightmare.

NaturalBlondie: How will I know it's you on Friday? You'll have to tell me what you're wearing.

To my surprise, I get a response right away.

TallDarkandHandy: If you want to know what I'm wearing, all you have to do is ask.

A flush creeps over my cheeks. This is a new kind of tenor to our conversation. Nothing has been even slightly sexual between us so far, but... Yes, this is good. Flirting, teasing...that's a good distraction.

NaturalBlondie: What are you wearing?

NaturalBlondie: And why are you awake?

TallDarkandHandy: Dark-gray sweatpants and socks.
And I couldn't sleep. Too excited about our date.

Yeah, right. It's just a line, but it still makes me smile to read it.

TallDarkandHandy: Your turn.

For a moment, I allow myself to picture a man wearing gray sweatpants and socks...and nothing else. Unfortunately, I have no idea what my mystery date looks like, so the face that pops into my head is Desmond Thomas.

He would look sexy as hell wearing nothing but sweats and socks. That big, muscular body with coarse, curly chest hair and bumpy, solid abs. I can just imagine a trail of dark hair disappearing behind the elastic waistband of his sweats. Des is solid everywhere, muscle on muscle on muscle. I could curl up into a ball in the crook of his arm and feel completely protected by his warmth, his size.

Mentally slapping myself, I refocus on the man on the phone. There's no way he's as hot as Des. Literally no way. I've never met *anyone* as attractive as Des (the jerk) so imagining him right now is pointless. And counterproductive. I don't even like him.

Maybe TallDarkandHandy is solid and muscular from working on his hands, but a bit soft around the edges. That can be sexy too. A big bear of a man.

But then I imagine a big bear of a man with Des's face, and I'm right back to square one.

TallDarkandHandy: You still there?

I bite my lip and glance down at myself. I'm wearing sleep shorts and an old T-shirt with holes in the neckline and under the arms. There are half a dozen stains down the front and on the shoulders, and it's soft from being washed a thousand times. It's so threadbare, it's mostly see-through.

Now, I may be clueless when it comes to dating, but I'm pretty sure you're not supposed to tell a prospective lover that you're wearing an old T-shirt that has nuclear-yellow stains with origins dating back to your daughter's infancy. I couldn't tell you which end of Bailey each stain came out of, but I'm pretty sure most of them originated from inside her body. The rest of the stains are coffee.

Mm, yes, I'm a sexy, independent woman wearing a decade-old T-shirt that wouldn't be fit to wash the windows.

Yeah—that'll go over well.

NaturalBlondie: I'm awake because I had a nightmare. I'm wearing a nightie. It's my favorite one: light-blue silk with a little bow at the front.

A crash occurs from across the hall. I bolt off the sofa, the blanket sliding off my thighs to puddle at my feet. Tiptoeing to the front door, I press my ear against it. Did that noise come from Des's condo?

There's another noise, his voice, and it sounds like a curse. Should I go over there?

My phone vibrates.

TallDarkandHandy: You can't put images like that in my head, Blondie. It's dangerous for my health.

Vanity, thy name is Mia. I spin around to lean my back against the door, resolving to put my landlord-cum-neighbor out of my head. If he's swearing, he's probably okay. I wouldn't want him to accuse me of caring about him. Showing up at his door at three o'clock in the morning because I heard a worrisome noise is *not* on my list of most desirable activities.

Plus, there's another man talking to me who actually makes me laugh, instead of only infuriating me. Maybe my date with this man could actually go well? Oh, please let him be attractive. I think I might actually like him—he's funny and clever, and now (because of my little white lie), I feel a little bit hot and bothered. I need *something* good to happen. Or at least, I need a man to think about other than Desmond freaking Thomas.

NaturalBlondie: You don't even know what I look like. How could a nightie be bad for your health?

TallDarkandHandy: I have a vivid imagination.

Before I can think up a suitably flirty (but not too sexual) response, he messages again.

TallDarkandHandy: What was your nightmare about?

NaturalBlondie: Same one I used to have when my daughter was a baby. I can't take care of her properly and she gets taken away by some nightmare shadow creature. I try to run after her to get her back, but the faster I try to run, the slower I go. I end up completely alone, my feet encased in this disgusting black goo. It's silly.

TallDarkandHandy: Doesn't sound silly.

NaturalBlondie: That's nice of you to say. It feels ridiculous to have nightmares as a full-grown adult.

TallDarkandHandy: Do you have Netflix?

I frown. That's an abrupt change of conversation.

NaturalBlondie: Um. Yes?

TallDarkandHandy: There's a new David Attenborough show on. You want to watch it with me?

Oh, this man is good. Please, *please* let me be attracted to him when we see each other. If there's no spark, I'll be so incredibly disappointed. I find myself smiling at my phone, then with one last press of my ear against the door to make sure there aren't any more noises coming from my landlord's residence, I head back to the couch. Flicking to the app on the TV and finding the show, I message him back.

NaturalBlondie: Ooh. Big cats. My fave.

TallDarkandHandy: Press play in three, two, one...

I press the play button, snuggling deeper into the cushions and pulling the blanket over me again. A small smile plays over my lips. Yes, I'm still alone in this unfamiliar home, but knowing that someone on the other side of this phone is watching this show at the same time as me...it feels like a small, tenuous connection to someone else. I'm not *quite* so alone.

TallDarkandHandy: The quality of the cameras they use is insane. You can see every single muscle on that lioness's body.

NaturalBlondie: And every hair on the male's mane.

I watch the big animal on the screen as he stalks around his pride's latest kill, taking the choicest pieces of meat for himself.

The way Desmond moves reminds me of a big, predatory cat—like when his eyes drop to half-mast and he watches me, circling me like that lion, deciding what pieces of me he likes best. Or when he gets up from a chair or a crouch, unfolding that long body in slow, graceful movements. Or when he combs his fingers through his hair, tousling it slightly.

Even when he's wearing a button-down and slacks, he can never quite hide the power beneath the polished veneer.

Then my phone buzzes—a message from a different man. I shake my head and answer his message about the show, trying to push my new landlord out of my mind. One man is more than enough. I don't need two. I certainly don't need to feed this silly, annoying attraction to Desmond Thomas. I don't even *like* the man, for crying out loud. Better to focus on the guy currently texting me. I may not know his name yet—or whether or not I'll be attracted to him when we meet—but at least I know we have things in common, and he's here, with me, if only virtually.

I WAKE up on the couch with the throw blanket pulled up to my chin. Bailey pokes me in the cheek and says, "We're out of milk."

I rub my eyes and sit up. "Okay. Give me a second."

"Okay." Bailey saunters out of view behind the couch.

What time is it? When did I fall asleep? The TV is on, but the screen is blank, so I flick it off while a yawn makes my jaw crackle and pop. I turn to squint at the time on the microwave, but the numbers are blurry. I claw at the cushions around me to find my phone and tap the screen. Seven o'clock in the morning. Jeez. I don't even remember falling asleep.

That's when I hear Bailey's voice in the direction of the front door. "Hi. Do you have any milk? We ran out and I want cereal for breakfast."

A deep voice rumbles in response. "Um. Sure. I'll bring it across. Give me a minute."

I jump off the couch like I've just been electrocuted.

"Are you a Lakers fan?" Bailey asks, her voice rising in excitement. "You like basketball? Where did you get those socks? I'm a Golden State Warriors fan, but I don't have any socks with their logo on them. Those are really cool."

A chuckle. "Thanks. Maybe Santa Claus will bring you some for Christmas if you're nice."

"Santa doesn't exist, silly. Don't you know that yet? I figured it out like two whole years ago. Aren't you like, really old?"

Another laugh, deeper this time. "Not that old. How'd you figure it out?"

"The handwriting on the tags from Mom was the same as Santa's."

"Clever," Des replies, the smile evident in his voice. "Let me get that milk and I'll be right over."

Jarred out of my stupor, I take one step toward the door, and get my feet tangled in the blanket. I kick the blanket off my toes.

Bailey, in true Bailey Abbott fashion, completely ignores Des's request and keeps talking. "What happened to your coffee table? Why is there a big bag of broken glass next to the door?"

I stop moving, frowning. Was that the crash I heard?

"It broke," comes the deep response. "Be careful. It's safety glass, but I don't want you to touch any of the pieces. You could still cut yourself, and your mom already dislikes me enough as it is."

"Okay. She doesn't dislike you, by the way. She just gets all red and jittery when you're around, and she doesn't like feeling that way. It's kind of funny."

Ha-ha. My kid is freaking hilarious. I need to get her back here, *now*. I take another step toward the door, on top of the blanket this time.

"How did the table break?"

Desmond clears his throat. "An accident."

I pause, curious.

"What kind of accident?"

"If you keep asking me questions, I won't be able to get you any milk for your breakfast."

"I want cereal."

"You mentioned that. I'll be over in a second, okay? Go back home."

"Home is behind the barbershop. This is just temporary."

"You know what I mean, kid."

Bailey comes striding through the door again and beams at me. She jabs a thumb over her shoulder. "Des is bringing milk over. I want cereal for breakfast this morning."

I gape at my daughter, mouth opening and closing like a fish. Through the open doorway, I see the door across the hall open, and Des strides through. He's wearing a black T-shirt, purple LA Lakers socks, and gray sweatpants, and yes, he looks great in them.

Damn him.

He knocks on the doorframe and lifts a gallon of milk like it weighs nothing. "I got milk." His eyes snag on me, on the bird's nest of my hair, then on my awful, stained, hole-ridden tee. Surprise lights his eyes, followed by a teasing, satisfied smirk.

My landlord's gaze coasts down to my tiny sleep shorts that are barely any bigger than my biggest panties (which, to be fair, are pretty big), and his face takes on an expression I can't read. He stares at my thighs for long enough that heat starts to build between them.

Des's gaze lifts to my chest, and his body goes completely still. I glance down. My nipples are fully erect—and fully visible—through the fabric of my shirt. Naturally, I slap my hands over my breasts to hide the evidence. Then I try to kick the blanket up so I can wrap it around my mostly exposed chest, but I ram my toes into the corner of the coffee table on the way up.

That's how I end up hopping around, saying, *Ouch, ouch, ouch*, with my hands cupped over my boobs.

"Mia!" Des starts crossing the space toward me.

"Don't come any closer," I say, breathing fire, still holding my tits. I drop onto the sofa and shimmy down so I can grab the blanket from the floor. Then I drape it over my chest and let out a long sigh.

I can't believe this. This is Bailey's fault.

It would be a lot easier to hate Des if he weren't so hot. Or maybe I hate him *because* he's hot? I can't tell. It's confusing.

"Thanks, Des," Bailey says brightly. "Can you bring the milk over here?" She's in the kitchen, pouring cereal out and probably getting at least eighty percent of it into her bowl. I can hear pieces of cereal dropping onto the floor, but that's the least of my worries right now.

I peek over the back of the sofa and wrap the blanket around my chest. But when I try to stand up, the edge of the blanket gets caught under my foot and I accidentally yank it down to the floor as I straighten, so I have to grab my breasts again to prevent another nipple emergency.

"Um." Des tears his gaze away from me and hesitates in the doorway, then quickly strides across. He plonks the milk on the kitchen counter so hard it sloshes in the plastic jug. Then he nods at my kid, gives me one more lingering glance as I debate the merits of just saying, *Fuck it*, and dropping my hands to let the nips fly free—then Des walks out, flicking the door closed with the tips of his fingers.

I'm still rooted to the same spot on the ground, nipples poking out of my old tee and pressing against my palms, goosebumps prickling over every inch of my skin, face flushed, heart pounding.

Bailey starts humming, not a care in her perfect nine-year-old world. She glances up. I drop my hands.

"I'm taking a shower," I announce. I stride to the bathroom and pause before entering, turning back to face my daughter. "You can't just knock on people's doors at seven in the morning, Bailey. I told you I'd get you some milk."

She frowns, unscrewing the lid on the milk. "No, you said, 'Give me a second.' And plus, Des told us to knock on the door if we needed anything. I heard him with my own ears."

"I don't think he meant milk," I growl.

Bailey blinks. "Oh. What did he mean?"

"Never mind. Don't knock on strangers' doors, okay?"

"But Des isn't a stranger."

"Bailey." I use That Special Voice, and my daughter lets out a dramatic sigh.

"Fine. So should I keep this milk? If I can't knock on the door, I can't give it back when I'm done with it."

Flustered, I just wave my hands at the fridge. "Put it away when you're done. I'll deal with it."

Then I stomp to the shower, turn it on cold, and do my best to strip the heat from my skin.

My toe is really, really sore.

SIX
FIONA

FOUR CUPS IS BUZZING by the time the very early swarm has given way to the post-school-drop-off horde. I watch over our most recent trainee, Alicia, who's a whiz on the computer system, then move to bus a few tables when I'm satisfied she can handle the rush.

As I wipe down the table nearest the door, Mia walks in. Her cheeks are flushed, her hair is pulled back in a messy bun, and she looks like she just ran a marathon.

"Morning. Everything okay?" I ask, straightening.

"No." She crashes to a halt beside me and slices her hands through the air. "Everything is a disaster."

"How come?"

"My ex-husband contacted me, wanting to meet my daughter, I have a date next Friday for the first time in months, my apartment is in shambles, and my landlord is now my neighbor, and this morning, Bailey thought it was appropriate to knock on his door first thing in the morning and ask him for a cup of milk. Which he then brought over before I'd had time to put on a bra. And you know what I did when I noticed my nipples were poking out? I cupped my breasts, Fiona. I stood there with a *hand bra* on, then I accidentally hit my toe on the coffee table so I was hopping around holding my boobs until he left."

I cackle. "Lucky Des."

"Don't start." She slaps her hand over her forehead and lets out a long sigh. "I need coffee."

"You need coffee and a debrief," I amend, following her to the register. To Alicia, I say, "Mia's coffee's on the house. I'll be upstairs for a while if you need me."

"No problem," the teenager says with a smile. She turns to Mia. "What can I get for you?"

While Mia orders, I gather the troops. And by troops I mean girlfriends. There's one thing I've learned over the past few years, and it's the power of a good gab. Ducking my head into the kitchen, I see Jen busy frosting a cake.

"You have time to come upstairs?" I ask.

She frowns, eyes still on the cake. "Just need to get the crumb coat on and I'm putting this cake in the fridge. Fallon, will you be okay in the kitchen alone for a bit?"

Fallon smiles at Jen in that special, soft way, then nods. "I'll be fine, Jen."

Simone is already upstairs working on her laptop, so I give Trina, Candice, Lily, Nora, and Georgia a call one by one. When I hang up with Georgia, who comes striding out of her art gallery, I link arms with Mia and guide her out of Four Cups.

We walk the few steps to the shiny red door to the side of the café's plate glass windows. The door leads to the space above the café: our private sanctuary, library, romance novel haven, and emergency conference center.

As I hold the door open for Mia, a honk draws my attention to a passing truck. I wave at my husband, who winks at me and gives me a little two-finger wave over his steering wheel. Smiling, I turn back to the door and see Mia watching me with a pensive expression on her face.

"How did you meet Grant?"

"Um." I laugh. "Well, funny story..."

When I get to the part when Grant dropped his robe and I saw...everything...Mia is in stitches, sitting in one of our comfy armchairs, the tension draining away from her shoulders.

Simone accepts one of the coffees I brought up for her with a grateful smile. "Grant just would *not* keep his clothes on in those first couple of years. It was awful." She winks.

"What Simone isn't telling you is that the first few times she met Wes, he wasn't wearing much either." I grin at my best friend, then touch the rim of my coffee to hers.

Over the next twenty minutes, all of our friends enter the library with various drinks and snacks, and we all sit down to catch up. These eight women came into my life at a time when I'd given up on life—and they showed me that I was far from done. In fact, I can honestly say my forties have been the best years of my life. I'm more myself than ever, I care less about what other people think, and I'm not afraid to go after what I want. I can't quite help the warm buzz in my chest as I look over my friends, knowing they made this town mean so much more to me than it could have otherwise.

"Well?" Lily says, looking happier and healthier every day. "Why the call? What's the big news? Is someone pregnant?"

"God, no," Simone exclaims. "That was all you, girl."

Lily laughs.

"Mia?" I glance at our newest member.

She puts her coffee cup down and rubs her hands on her thighs. "I'm struggling, ladies. I'm completely overwhelmed, and I don't know what to do."

She proceeds to tell us about her week—the flooded kitchen, the move, the ramped-up flirting with her mystery man, the upcoming date, the contact from her ex, the look in Des's eyes when he saw her fondling herself—to the absolute delight of every other woman in the room.

"Gosh, it's so much better to be on the other side of these types of situations," Nora says, bright-red lipstick shimmering on her smiling lips. She arches a brow at me. "You all must have really enjoyed watching us all suffer over the years."

"Girl, you have no idea," Simone quips, laughing. She turns to Mia. "A word to the wise: Just bang him and get it over with."

"Which 'him' are we talking about here?" Mia answers suspiciously.

Simone just giggles.

"Well, first things first," Trina cuts in, "let's figure out your outfit for the date."

"They're going to Dolce Vita," I supply.

"The new Italian place? Dorothy told me it was divine," Nora adds.

"They have great cannolis," Jen says. "I'm going to drop off some pastries next week and see if the chef will give me any hints about the recipe."

"How does Des feel about you going on a date with another man?" Simone asks, eyes sparkling.

Mia sips her coffee primly. "Des and I aren't dating, so whatever his feelings are, they're not relevant."

"Sure they aren't," Simone says with a laugh.

"Outfit, ladies, outfit!" Trina brings us back to the matter at hand. "What are your options?"

Mia shrugs. "I don't know. I'm guessing I don't want to look like I'm trying too hard?"

"What are we, twenty-two years old?" Georgia waves a hand. "Wear whatever you want. Try hard. Look fab. Show up in a freaking ball gown if you feel like it. Life's too short to worry about what other people think."

"Hear, hear!" I call out.

"Finally, you ladies are on my level." Trina laughs. "There's no such thing as being overdressed. I think you should try to look as hot as humanly possible."

"But something loose enough that you can stuff your face with pasta and cannolis and you won't bust any seams on the way home," Simone adds. "Plus, vigorous sex requires adequate nutrition."

Mia's face breaks into a smile. She shakes her head. "How did it take me so long to befriend you all? I needed this kind of cheerleading years ago."

"We can come over on Friday afternoon and help you get ready," Trina offers.

"I'll go over to my old apartment and grab some options," Mia says, nodding. She grins at us all in turn. "Thank you. I feel much better."

Candice pats her knee. "Glad to help, Mia."

"Gives us something to gossip about," Simone adds. "So it's a fair trade."

When we finally break apart, heading to various homes and businesses around town, I wave at Mia and watch her head across to her barbershop.

Simone bumps her hip against mine. "You coming to Candice's tonight for yoga?"

"Yeah," I answer. "You think Mia's okay? We didn't even talk about her ex-husband contacting her out of the blue."

"I got the feeling she'd rather talk about outfits and Italian restaurants," Simone answers, "but I hope she'll open up about the rest of it when she's ready."

I nod, then follow my best and oldest friend into our coffee shop with one last glance as the newest member of our group disappears behind her barbershop door.

SEVEN

MIA

DESMOND IS IN MY APARTMENT, wearing old jeans and a flannel button-down. He's ripping the wall apart with his bare hands again, tossing bits of wood and drywall into a pile of debris in the middle of my kitchen (technically, he's wearing gloves, but he's still ripping the wall apart with his freaking hands). He looks like a big meathead, grunting around using his strength to push his way around. Ugh. It's awful.

And yes, I get that he's helping me. No, I don't want to think about the tightening below my belly button. I dislike him. Period. Whatever's going on in my body is some hormonal imbalance, not an actual, genuine attraction to the man. There's a medical explanation for all this—probably. Maybe. Don't quote me on that.

Des wipes his forehead with his forearm and glances my way when I enter the room. "Hey."

The tightening spreads through my stomach, darting like little lightning bugs flitting through my veins. How dare he do that to me. "Hi." I clear my throat. "Thanks for the milk."

His lips tip into a tiny smile, and for a brief moment, I wonder what it would look like to see him smile fully. Not that he ever would, because he's grumpy and arrogant and annoying, and the only time he ever chuckles is when he's mocking me. Yesterday, when I flicked my razor out and cracked a joke, he laughed, but I could tell he was holding back. Maybe he's incapable of truly laughing.

His face softens slightly. "No problem."

"I'll bring the rest of the gallon back this evening."

"Don't worry about it." He pulls off work gloves from his hands, tugging each finger one at a time.

I watch, fascinated. Then I realize what I'm doing and walk jerkily toward the hallway. "I'm just here to grab a few things. Don't mind me."

Not waiting for an answer, I make it to my bedroom and start throwing clothes into a big tote bag I fished out of my closet. I have a never-ending supply of large purses. It started when Bailey was a baby.

I pack dresses that have been barely worn, shapewear, a leather skirt that I bought on a whim and then decided wasn't age-appropriate, but now I'm not sure exactly what "age-appropriate" really means anymore... I walk to my dresser and tug open the top drawer, grabbing handfuls of lacy things.

And I stop.

I used to wear beautiful underwear all the time. I loved having something sexy on under my clothes—and Colin never complained about it either—but at some point, that part of me disappeared. I don't even know if any of these bits of lingerie will fit anymore. Most of them I bought before I had Bailey.

Those first few years—when she was little and I was on my own—were tough. In fact, "tough" doesn't even come close to describing the absolute hell I went through. I kept telling myself to enjoy those precious years, to try to appreciate the wonder of my new baby, my toddler, my precocious growing child, but I struggled more than I care to admit. It's only in the past couple of years, when Bailey has become a bit more independent, that I feel like I've got my feet under me again.

Motherhood became wrapped up in shame for me, because I was supposed to be glowing and thriving on little to no sleep, but in reality, I was isolated, alone, and perpetually on the verge of a breakdown. I went through a divorce, a pregnancy riddled with medical issues, and a horrendous birth. My vagina was sliced open. I peed myself for months. My house was a mess. I couldn't keep up with basic grooming. I didn't have anyone to talk to. Anytime I even whispered about struggling to my parents, my mother would try to convince me to move back home, until they bought their RV and she started trying to convince me to find a man.

Maybe I was just too proud to realize she was trying to help me. Those first few years of Bailey's life exist in my memory blanketed in haze, punctuated by the highs of loving my daughter and the lows of being solely responsible for her health and upbringing —and feeling like I was failing.

Is it any wonder I stopped wearing sexy underwear?

There's a red satin teddy I wore for my first wedding anniversary. Rubbing the fabric between my fingers, I try to remember how it felt to slide it on over my skin, knowing that I looked amazing. On some level, it's the same way I felt when I put on my yellow dress and went to Georgia's art gallery opening.

Maybe the girls are right; this date will be a good thing for me. Maybe it doesn't matter if TallDarkandHandy is attractive. Maybe the point of this is for *me* to feel attractive, for me to remind myself of the woman who bought lingerie on a whim and wore it under yoga pants and hoodies just because she felt like it.

That woman is still me. She's in here somewhere.

I pull out a see-through demi bra made of black lace and hold it up against my chest, frowning. Were my boobs really that much smaller before Bailey? I wonder if I loosened the straps, if I could—

"Oh—" Des clears his throat and spins around, facing away from me. "Sorry. I didn't—"

I snatch the lingerie off my chest and stuff it into my tote. My face is on fire. "Can I help you?"

His voice comes out low and rough. "I wanted to ask about the layout of the kitchen. It's really long and narrow, but since I'm taking the wall down, I could expand it into the dining room and swap things around." He glances over his shoulder, sees that it's safe to turn around, and faces me again. "But I wanted to ask you for your opinion."

Begrudgingly, I admit that it's a nice thought. The kitchen hasn't exactly been functional. I had to buy a trolley on caster wheels and screw a plank of scrap plywood on top to get enough counter space to work in it. I'd gotten used to it, thinking that having a bigger kitchen was a pipe dream.

I shove down my embarrassment and elbow the drawer full of

lace and silk until it's mostly closed. "I see. Thank you—that's a good idea."

Desmond nods, his eyes sliding down to my tote bag. "Hot date?" His voice sounds like he swallowed a truckload of gravel.

I like the sound of it. It rattles through me, sending more shivers and lightning bugs bouncing around my body. But letting him see that would be giving him power over me, and he's got quite enough of that already.

"That's none of your business, Desmond."

His gaze rises to meet mine, and it feels like he wants to say something. The moment hangs between us, an unspoken confession dancing on the tip of his tongue. I can almost feel it vibrating between us.

The dragon cracks an eyelid, making me stand up straighter. I'd *love* for Desmond to say something. Is he going to tell me off for not having milk at the house? For sleeping on the couch? For letting Bailey run wild to go over to his house this morning? Maybe he'll mock me for my stupid hands-on-boobs stunt this morning. He'll say something snarky about me dating. I narrow my eyes at him, challenging.

He rocks back on his heels and tips his head toward the kitchen. "Can I show you what I have in mind?"

I deflate, then nod and follow him down the hallway. That's when I notice little cuts on the backs of his arms, and I want to ask if he's okay. He said he broke his coffee table—but how? And did he disinfect the cuts? Were any of them worse than the little scrapes I can see?

My pride holds me back. Or maybe it's fear—fear that if I let this man get any closer to me, I'll actually let him in. He's already proven to me that he can raise my rent with no thought to how much I'll struggle. He's merciless, mercenary, and rude. I shouldn't care about minor injuries that he brought on himself.

So there.

As it turns out, Desmond's ideas are great. He wants to rearrange the layout of the kitchen and living/dining rooms so they become connected in a larger L-shape. It's a clever use of space and the living room will end up slightly smaller, but we both agree it'll be worth it.

When I head for the barbershop door, Desmond calls out my name. I turn to see him leaning a shoulder against the wall, watching me. "This is the first time we've been able to have a conversation without fighting. Feels momentous."

I snort. "Quit while you're ahead, buddy." I zip my fingers over my lips and mime throwing the key over my shoulder.

Des laughs, then—a true belly laugh. I watch, fascinated, at the movement of his chest, his throat, his shoulders. When I feel my own lips tilt up, I shake my head and turn around, throwing him a wave over my shoulder.

By the time I'm safely in my barbershop tending to my first client of the day, there's something strange going on in my chest. Despite having a terrible day yesterday and feeling like my life was going down the toilet quicker than I could blink, I'm starting to feel *hope*.

Hope that I'll get my home back, that things will work out, that my date will go well. Hope that my life from now on might actually get easier, instead of harder. I'm no longer that frazzled woman hanging on by a thread who pees herself whenever she sneezes. I'm a lingerie-wearing, confident, sexy, dinner-date-attending babe.

Unfortunately, Lady Hope is smiling at me, beckoning with one hand—while the other is bent behind her back, hiding a very sharp knife. I should know the stab to the gut is coming. Things in my life rarely ever get better.

EIGHT
DES

I HAVE to tell Mia that she's been talking to me on the Blind Date app.

It must have been some kind of delusion that made me think I could actually show up on our date without confessing to her. She'll kill me. She'll never speak to me again.

God, even the thought of hurting her makes me sick. I've got it so bad for this woman, I can hardly think straight. I broke my fucking coffee table by falling off the couch at the thought of her wearing a blue silk nightie.

And it turns out, she wasn't wearing one at all. When I saw her the next morning, I wanted to laugh and tackle her to the ground, maybe redden her ass with my palm for teasing me like that.

I *have* to tell her it's me.

I knew I shouldn't have taken the conversation anywhere flirty that evening, but the anonymity of Blind Date seems to allow her to open up in a way she won't in person. I'm so desperate for a crumb of her attention that I'm not willing to let that go. Not yet.

I stare at the stud wall separating the kitchen and bathroom, cursing myself. She's right—I'm an ass, a total piece of shit. I'm *lying* to her.

It's now Saturday, which means our date is in six days. I've spent all week at her old apartment, trying to fix things up. Work is progressing, and the plumber's scheduled to come back on Monday. I've just finished the last of the demolition, with the kitchen completely stripped and all the debris cleared away. That's all I can do for today.

Now I have more work to do at another house, so I get in my car and drive across town.

I pull up to my grandparents' place and see the net curtains twitch. I cut the engine and wave as my grandmother appears in the doorway, beaming. She spreads her arms like she wants me to run to her for a hug.

"Des!" She turns her head to yell inside. "It's Desmond, Arthur!"

"Hey, Grandma." I hop up the three steps to the front porch and give her that hug. "Looks like the leaves need to be raked already. I can mow the lawn while I'm at it."

"You're a darling." Grandma Maude pats my cheek. Her face is lined with deep wrinkles around her eyes and mouth, evidence of a life full of laughter and joy.

"Anything else that needs to get done around here?"

"Oh, I'm sure I can put you to work." My grandmother winks. "Come on in. I was just going to put a pot of coffee on."

I walk inside and wave at my grandfather, who's got his legs up in his favorite brown armchair. "Hey, Gramps."

"Desmond!" he yells. "Maude, put on some coffee!"

"She's already on it," I shout back, making sure to lean toward his left ear, which is slightly more functional than his right.

"Huh?"

"Grandma is making coffee!" I shout.

"Tell her to make some," my grandfather yells back. The TV blares in the corner, *Wheel of Fortune* playing an old rerun. Even if my grandfather's hearing was perfect, I doubt he could hear me over the noise of the show. I sit down on the couch next to my grandfather.

He shifts to look at me. "Maude said there was a leak at Mia's place?"

More like a geyser, but I just nod.

"I'm working on it," I answer.

"Good." He nods at me, and I wonder how it is he can understand me perfectly when I'm not even trying.

I give him a thumbs-up. "I'm going to go check on Grandma!"

"Go see your grandmother," he tells me, gaze returning to the TV. "She's probably in there making coffee."

Down a narrow hallway to the back of the house is the old kitchen. Nothing in here has changed since my grandparents moved in. The same curtains hang in front of the window above the sink, once-white fabric with lemons and leaves dotted over it, now faded to a dull beige after years of sun exposure. The oven and microwave are relics. The table in the corner is scarred and stained.

It's always felt like home—which is a rare occurrence for me.

"Here, honey," my grandmother says, placing a mug of hot coffee in front of a chair at the table. "Sit and drink that. We'll let your grandfather watch his show. He'll be asleep in a minute, anyway."

"How did the doctor's appointment go yesterday?" I ask.

My grandmother waves a hand, not meeting my eyes. "Oh, you know. We're two old farts now. Your grandfather is going to be ninety-five next February. I'm not far behind." She's turning ninety next year.

"You don't look a day over seventy-five, Grandma."

She laughs, sliding into the chair at the head of the table. "Sweet talker." She squints. "Now. Have you found a nice woman yet, or what?"

"Grandma," I groan.

"I'm just asking." She pats my forearm. "You're a handsome, smart young man. I don't understand why you haven't found anyone yet."

"Maybe I'm not as handsome and smart to other people," I answer. "And I'm forty-one years old. Does that still count as a young man?"

"Don't be ridiculous." My grandma sits down with her own mug of coffee. She watches me over the rim. "Does that mean I'll still have my usual partner for the Thanksgiving race?"

I sip my coffee to buy myself some time. "Hmm. Maybe."

Her eyes gleam. "Maybe? Does that mean...maybe not? You might be bringing someone?"

If a certain blonde deigns to continue speaking to me after I reveal who I am.

Instead of committing to bringing a date, I decide to change the subject. "How did the three-legged race start, anyway?"

My grandma leans back, grinning. "It was a Thomas tradition that your great-grandmother started. Arthur's mother. She was competitive as all heck. She made the trophy and declared that every year, we'd get all the adults racing for it. It started as an egg-and-spoon race, then a sack race, and finally evolved to a three-legged race around the time your father was born. I won the race the year I was pregnant with your uncle Reggie."

"He was three years older than Dad, right?"

"That's right." Grandma Maude smiles. "Reggie, then Wendy, then your father. The year I won was the last sack race. Everyone was up in arms about a pregnant woman participating, never mind taking the trophy home. Well. I showed them, didn't I?" She grins. "But we decided to try a three-legged race the next year to welcome your great-aunt Martha into the family, and the race has been a couples' affair ever since."

I smile. "And now it's tradition."

"Now it's tradition," my grandmother repeats with a nod. She holds my gaze and gives me a small smile. "But you know, darling boy, I'm getting older. I don't know that I'm quite up to it this year. If there's someone special you'd like to bring to race by your side, I'm happy to give up my place of honor beside my favorite grandson."

"You're not actually supposed to have favorites, Grandma."

My grandmother's eyes twinkle. "I'm nearly ninety years old, Desmond. I can have whatever I please."

Tension slips out of me as our conversation continues, the familiar sounds and smells of my grandmother's kitchen settling over me like a comforting blanket. My grandmother moves slowly, though, and I notice that she needs to steady herself on the table and counters a little bit more than she used to.

Not for the first time, I'm angry at that property manager who stole from them. My grandparents refused to sue him, saying they were too old to be dragged through the court system. But now, they're left with a bunch of run-down assets and very little cash to actually pay their bills. They're *old*. I never thought I'd say it, because my grandparents have always been full of strength and vitality, but I can see the years weighing both of them down.

I have to fix it. I have to help. As much as Mia hates me for it, I *had* to up her rent to current market value. I have to hurry to fix it up so she can move back in and I can sell both condos on Seventh Avenue.

"Desmond, honey," my grandmother says, placing her hand on my shoulder. "Stop frowning."

"I was just thinking about everything I need to do to fix up the properties. I want to get them sold as fast as possible."

"This is why you're my favorite," my grandmother says, pecking my cheek. She smooths my hair back and smiles at me. "I'd like to see you happy before I leave this earth, darling boy. Man or woman, if there's someone you care about, bring them to meet the family this year. Do it for me."

My throat grows tight.

Grandma arches a brow. "If that's not enough motivation, do it to beat Vince in this year's race. I can't *stand* his gloating, and I'm too slow to give you a chance."

I bark out a laugh. "All right, Grandma." I throw back the rest of my coffee and stand. "I'll get started on the yard work. Holler if you need anything."

"I'll have some food ready for you when you finish." She hobbles to the refrigerator, and I head outside to get to work.

THAT EVENING, as I enter my condo, I glance at the door across the hall.

The right thing to do is to tell Mia that I'm the man she's been speaking to on Blind Date. But if I tell her, I'll lose my chance at a date with her. After my conversation with my grandmother, the thought of Mia next to me at my family's Thanksgiving is like a thorn under my skin. I want it so badly, I can hardly think of anything else.

Maybe if I explain everything when we're at the restaurant, Mia will understand. The way I see it, the only chance I have of her hearing me out is when we're not in our usual situation, our usual dynamic.

And, selfishly, I *want* to take her out to dinner. I want to treat her, spoil her, romance her. What if my only chance at a date is through this app? What if I blow it before it even begins?

It's a risk, but as I cross the threshold, I make a decision: I'm going through with the date. It might be the only one I ever get, and I'm not losing that opportunity.

NINE
MIA

ON FRIDAY, after dropping Bailey at a friend's house for a sleepover she was invited to last week, I head home and proceed to have a miniature panic attack. For some reason, this blind date feels different from my previous forays into dating as a single mom. Maybe because TallDarkandHandy and I have been speaking for weeks, while I used to try to get the first date out of the way as quickly as possible. I actually *like* this man. There's a hum in my blood, anticipation and fear and nerves all mixed into one.

It was the Netflix night, I realize. For him to take the time to calm me down after a nightmare means a lot. Maybe he even sensed that it wouldn't be right to flirt too sexually, that even our talk of nighties and sweatpants was making my heart thump. This man has never met me—doesn't even know my name—but he seems to *know* me. He can sense my moods, my needs.

And that scares the ever-living crap out of me.

I've been alone for a long time. Colin leaving me ripped a hole in my heart—and my confidence—that I'm only now realizing never really healed right. I'm terrified that TallDarkandHandy is too good to be true. I'm afraid that even if we do have a physical spark and I'm willing to pursue him, he'll turn his back on me too. Being abandoned once was hard enough; I don't want to go through it again.

Thankfully, having a bevy of women take over my home and ply me with snacks and alcohol is enough to bring me back from the edge. With my new friends in my home, it doesn't feel like I'm jumping off the edge of a cliff by going on this date. It feels like the stakes are much, much lower. I'm just meeting a man, having a meal, and seeing what happens. That, I can do.

"Okay, ladies," Trina says, stepping into the living room like she's Tan France and I'm some unfortunate, bedraggled sod nominated for Queer Eye: Heart's Cove. "This is option one. Come on out, Mia."

I hobble over on spike heels borrowed from Trina, wearing a black pencil skirt and a silky cream-colored top. It has a delicate cowl neck and fluttery sleeves. It's pretty and feminine, sexy without being revealing.

"Hmm," Fiona says.

I straighten. "'Hmm?' What does that mean?"

"It's a bit...corporate," Simone says, a glass of wine dangling between her fingertips. "Maybe it's the pencil skirt. I feel like you're about to call me into a boardroom for an interview."

"It's hot, though," Candice adds. "But I agree. Not first-date material."

"Dang," Trina says, tapping her lips with a manicured finger. "I thought the sheer tights with the line down the back would up the sex factor."

"Oh, they do," Simone says. "She looks very bang-able—"

"'Bang-able?'" I arch a brow.

"—if you were going to bang her in her corner office," Simone finishes, not paying me any mind.

"No one's banging anyone tonight," I say.

"Keep your options open, girl," Simone says.

"You're saying I should have sex on the first date?"

"I'm saying you shouldn't say you *won't*," she answers, tilting her head from side to side. "Just see how it goes!"

"Agreed," Fiona adds with a decisive nod. "But not in that outfit."

"Okay. Back in the room." Trina ushers me into the bedroom and directs me to the second outfit. This one is a chunky sweater with tight jeans and lots of gold jewelry. She shows the ladies, gathering my hair up in a ponytail to give them an idea of the rest of the styling.

This is also shot down, this time for being too casual.

"We want this guy to lose his mind," Fiona complains. "She's not going out for coffee. She's going to a candlelit dinner. Give us cleavage, Trina!"

"I like this outfit!" I protest, throwing my hands out. "It's comfy. And I can wear my gold hoop earrings. I love these earrings."

"You can be comfy with him later," Simone informs me. "Right now, you need to be a bombshell."

"Hmm," Trina says, eyes narrowing on me. "Maybe Simone is right."

"Of course I'm right!"

"I like this outfit," I repeat. "These boots are comfy. Those other heels are a broken ankle waiting to happen."

My protests fall on deaf ears as Candice looks at her sister. "Trina, you can do better."

Trina hums. "I know." She looks at me with narrowed eyes. "I've been giving your opinions too much weight, Mia."

"*I'm* the one wearing the clothes! I would hope you'd listen to my opinion."

"Hush. You're throwing me off my game."

Laughing, I head back in the room with Trina. She expertly flicks through my closet, stopping on a dress I haven't worn in a *long* time. It cost me more money than I care to admit, and every time I've done a purge of my closet over the years, I haven't been able to get rid of it. Deceptively flattering with thick fabric and cleverly placed seams, the dress is brilliant in its simplicity. It has thick shoulder straps, a subtle sweetheart neckline, and a body-con silhouette with a touch of ruching around the hips. It's insanely flattering.

"Little black dress," Trina says, touching the fabric. "Can't go wrong."

For some reason, my heart picks up. As Trina leaves me to get dressed, I look at the black fabric lying across the bed and take a deep breath. Wearing this dress is really putting myself out there. There's no way to pretend that I'm not trying hard, or that I see myself as old and over the hill and undesirable. If I put this dress on and go out on a blind date, I'm telling everyone who sees me that I think I'm sexy, and I'm not afraid of showing it.

Do I think that? Can I still wear this dress?

Throat tight, I grab seamless undies and hesitate. I'm wearing my same old nude bra—the one that's worn around the edges and a little bit stretched out in the band. It would be wrong to wear ugly undergarments beneath *that* dress. So, I strip my bra off and find one of the lacy numbers I brought over from my old apartment. I have a subtle push-up bra with lace trim that will work. I dress quickly, slip my feet into the borrowed stilettos, and walk out into the living room.

Conversation stops dead. I smooth my hands over my hips, breathing deeply, and meet my new friends' gazes.

Simone whistles. Fiona beams. Candice claps.

Trina has literal tears in her eyes. She clasps her hands at her breast and shakes her head. "Gosh, I'm good."

I laugh. "I'm guessing this is it."

"That's it," Simone confirms.

"Simple pendant," Trina says, zeroing in on me. "Something that hits right between your gorgeous collarbones. Hair in a ponytail with curled tendrils. Earrings. A fabulous bag." She squeals, doing a little jig. "Your date is going to need a shovel to pick his jaw up off the floor when he sees you, Mia."

Laughing, I allow myself to be swept along into these new friendships, and when it comes time for me to make my way to the door of the condo, my nerves have been almost entirely replaced by fresh confidence.

I'm forty years old, and I'm sexy as hell. These things will never be mutually exclusive.

"Remember to use protection," Simone whispers in my ear as she hugs me goodbye.

"Oh, shut up," I answer, laughing, and then I get in my old car and drive myself to the restaurant for the first real date I've had in a long, long time.

TEN
DES

STRAIGHTENING my fork with one hand, I smooth my shirt down over my chest with the other. Then I swap hands to smooth the other side of my shirt and straighten the knife. My knee jiggles, and I glance at the door to Dolce Vita for the millionth time since I got here ten minutes ago.

This was a mistake. I'm such a colossal idiot. I can hardly believe it.

I should have told Mia as soon as I saw the cross-stitch in her living room. But now...

Now, it's too late.

I can't stop thinking about how she looked the morning after our Netflix show, rumpled and sleepy. If I woke up to her like that beside me in bed just *once* in my life, I could die happy, silky nightie or no.

She's driven me mad. It's torture being in her apartment,

renovating it, knowing she's just beyond the barbershop door. Ever since I walked in on her picking through her lingerie, I haven't been able to get that image out of my mind, either.

Her short, tight body clad in black lace, ready to be unwrapped like a present.

I close my eyes, then open them and adjust the pink pocket square in my jacket pocket—the item of clothing I told her to look for.

I've had so many opportunities to come clean, and I've ignored them all. She's going to hate this. It's going to be a disaster.

But what if it isn't? What if this is your one shot to take this woman out for dinner?

The restaurant door opens, and I hear the hostess call out a greeting. Mia's voice answers, and the hostess guides her into the dining room.

My heart stops.

She's the most gorgeous woman I've ever seen. Her body—her *body*. God. I've never seen anything so beautiful. Her black dress leaves almost nothing to the imagination, sculpting her curves like it was made for her, but I still want to tear it off and worship her. She takes a couple steps, and I have to suck in a hard breath at the sight of her shoes.

Patent leather stilettos click on the restaurant's wooden floorboards. I want to fuck her in those shoes. Those shoes and that black bra she was fondling in her bedroom, and nothing else.

Get a grip, Des.

Mia's gaze sweeps over the dining room, a slight frown drawing her dark-blond brows together. There's something shimmery on her cheekbones and eyelids. Her hair is curled softly, falling from her ponytail in a golden wave.

She dressed up for me. She put those clothes on, those shoes, she did her makeup—for me. I'm the luckiest man in the world. This woman is a goddess.

Her eyes land on me, then drop to the pocket square. Mia freezes.

No, I realize. Mia didn't dress up for me; she dressed up for TallDarkandHandy. She dressed up for someone who, in her mind, was another man. A man who isn't me.

Jealousy tears through me, like the claws of some beast rending my flesh to strips. Completely irrational. I'm jealous of a man that doesn't exist. Or am I jealous of myself? I don't know, but I feel like flipping this table and watching all the glassware smash into tiny, sharp shards.

Mia jerks back, frantically scanning the rest of the restaurant. Her gaze catches on couples laughing intimately, a young family in the corner, a table of three women sharing a bottle of wine and laughing. Panic pulls her features tight as she glances at me again, the hostess saying something to her as she gestures my way.

I'm the only single man in the restaurant. The only person wearing a pink pocket square.

I stand.

Mia drifts toward me in a daze. Comprehension finally slaps across her features, along with outrage. Her hands curl around the back of her chair while the hostess realizes something's wrong. The young woman frowns, glancing between us, then backs away slowly.

"Mia," I say, every speech and line I'd prepared flying out of my head.

Her face is beautiful and terrible. She's so, so angry.

I'm a complete moron. Did I really think this would work? Did I really think she'd sit down and have dinner with me?

I must have lost my fucking mind. I just messed up so badly, it's not even funny.

I should have told her the moment I knew it was her on the other side of the phone.

"How long?" Mia asks through clenched teeth. Her chest flushes red and the tendrils of hair framing her face start trembling. "How long have you known it was me?"

"Sit," I grate, panic mounting in my chest. "Please, Mia. I can explain."

"*How long?*" The words come out as a hiss, and the couple at the table next to ours glance over. The woman whispers to her husband, staring at us. Mia's knuckles are bloodless as she grips the back of the chair.

I shift my gaze down and to the side. "A week or so. I saw the cross-stitch of the foot, and I put two and two together."

"Before you asked me out?" She tries to swallow, but it looks almost painful. Her eyes are wide and wild.

I shake my head. We're standing on opposite sides of the table, and all I want to do is go over to her, touch her. "No. I didn't know it was you when I asked you out."

"Before the—the nature documentary?"

I nod. "Yeah. I knew it was you that night."

She sips in little breaths. It isn't only anger in her eyes, I realize—it's hurt. Embarrassment. I'm so fucking ashamed of myself. I can't believe I let this get this far. What kind of delusional idiot thinks *this* is the best course of action?

I put that look on her face. I hurt her. I embarrassed her.

Of course I did. Have I ever been the kind of guy who does things right?

Mia opens her mouth to say something, then reconsiders. I watch as her defenses are shored up, her spine straightens, and her eyes turn shuttered and cold. She clamps her lips together without saying a word, turns, and walks away.

No. I can't let that happen. I fucked up—I know that. But, but—

"Mia! Mia, wait!"

I catch up to her just as she steps outside and keeps walking.

"Mia!"

"Do *not*"—she whirls around, sticking her finger in my face— "do *not* speak to me."

"I'm sorry."

"What did I *just* say?" She snorts and turns her back on me. Her hips sway as she crosses toward the small parking lot.

"I should have told you as soon as I figured out who you were."

"Ya think?" Her keys jingle.

"Mia, I was *glad* it was you."

She pauses at her car, turning to frown at me. "Well whoop-de-doo for you, Des. I'm glad I don't disgust you, and you still deigned to go on our date, even when you knew it was me."

What? No. Is that what I said? My heart is pounding so hard I can't think straight. "That's not what I meant."

"Do you have any idea how humiliating this is? You *lied* to me, Desmond. You texted me pretty words, let me tell you about how long it's been since I've been on a date and how long it's been since I've had sex, and then you looked me in the eyes and asked me where I wanted to put my new kitchen, and oh, by the way, remember that rent is due next week. What the fuck?"

"I never reminded you about the rent."

"How could I forget about it, when you are who you are?" She spits the words at me like they're venom.

"It wasn't like that." I shove my hand in my hair, desperate to make her understand. She needs to know that she's special, that from the first moment I saw her—

But how could someone like me ever deserve someone like her? I've been on the outside since I was eleven years old. I never belonged to my family, never found my place in my hometown. Even now, with the only woman who's interested me in years, I only manage to push her away.

My claim to fame is being my grandmother's favorite. Whoop-de-doo indeed.

"Is this some sort of joke to you, Desmond?" Her eyes gleam under the streetlights, and I realize with cold, dawning horror that it looks like she's going to cry.

Because of me. She's going to cry because of what I did. I put those tears in her eyes.

I close the distance between us. "No, Mia. Never." I lift my hand to her cheek. "Please, just listen to me."

She trembles, closing her eyes, but she doesn't push me away. Her skin is soft as silk as I hold her face, afraid to move, afraid to breathe, in case I mess this up any worse than I already have.

Her lip wobbles. I did that to her. Fuck—oh, oh...fuck.

"Ever since you walked into my barbershop, you've done your best to make my life more difficult. Why, Des? What is it about me that makes you want to humiliate me like this?"

"You want to know why?" I grate, dropping my hand, suddenly frustrated. "You want to know what my problem is?"

"Please." She wipes her cheeks with angry movements then crosses her arms, scowling.

I clench my hands into fists, huffing a bitter laugh. "Mia, I'm insanely, unbelievably attracted to you. I've wanted you since I first laid eyes on you. When you walk into a room, I can't fucking think straight. Things come out all wrong, because—" I clamp my lips shut. I've said too much. She'll see right to the core of me, and she'll see that I don't belong beside her.

Mia watches me for a beat, then rolls her eyes and snorts. "Right. You humiliated me and lied to me because I'm just *so* hot. That's a good one. I'm going home." She turns to open her door, but I put my hand on it to keep it shut.

"You don't believe me?"

Facing me once more, Mia cocks a hip and arches her brows at me. "What, that I'm so irresistible that I turn you into this, this..." She waves her hand up and down my body. "This rude, arrogant ass? Please. You walked into my life, lifted my rent so much I can hardly make ends meet, then had the audacity to blame *me* when that dump finally started falling apart. The only reason you offered me the condo on Seventh is because you didn't want to pay for a hotel. You got off on manipulating me into this date because... I don't even know why! Maybe you wanted to have yet another opportunity to shove all your money in my face. You wanted to wave your credit card around and treat me to a meal, because you know how fucking poor I am."

"I just told you why I wanted to take you out. It has nothing to do with money."

"Give me a break. I don't buy it for a second. I think you're just an asshole who gets off on making other people miserable."

"Mia, the last thing I want you to be is miserable."

At my words, her eyes flare. There's a hint of disbelief in her expression, and that just kills me. This woman is going to drive me insane—well, *more* insane. I just told her how crazy she makes me, and *she doesn't believe me.*

Her eyes narrow, and she lifts her chin. "You're telling me that the reason you're such an asshole is because you're so attracted to me it makes you stupid."

"Yes," I grate.

"That's the most ridiculous thing I've ever heard."

"It's the truth."

Suspicion rolls off her in waves. She searches my gaze, lips pursed, body tense. After a long moment, she seems to come to a decision. "Yeah?" Her voice is soft, menacing.

"Yeah, Mia."

"Prove it." The words pop on her lips, the challenge hanging in the air between us. A cool breeze makes goosebumps lift over her arms and sends her ponytail fluttering over her shoulder. Leaves rustle in the trees around us, a few of them falling to the ground and scraping over the asphalt of the parking lot.

This isn't what I wanted. All the times I've imagined Mia in my arms, she hasn't been angry and defensive. She hasn't been slinging challenges at me like insults. If I had any hope of helping the situation, I'd back away, beg for forgiveness, and ask her to start over.

But this woman doesn't want anything from me. I've messed it up from the moment I looked at my grandparents' affairs and decided to raise her rent. I walked into her barbershop, thinking I was doing the right thing, and the force of her hit me like a rogue wave. It knocked me down, dragged me under, and I've been drowning ever since. I've been a jerk and an absolute, unbelievable idiot.

She'll never be mine, but if this woman wants me to prove how much I want her? Well that, I can do.

With one step forward, I cage her against the driver's side door of her car. My hand coasts over her cheek, curling around her nape. The other notches into the curve of her waist, gripping tight. Her lips fall open on a gasp.

She fits in my arms like we were made for each other. My soul sings, my body hums, and I feel like I've finally come home. Breaths sawing in and out of my lungs, I dip my head toward hers, then let my lips hover just above her mouth.

It feels wrong. We shouldn't be coming together for the first time this way, with animosity and hurt built up like stone walls between us. Once again, a voice in my head tells me I'm doing it all wrong, but it's too late. I've had her in my arms now, I can feel her breath against my lips. There's no going back.

A trembling sweeps through Mia's body, and her hands curl into the lapels of my jacket. "What are you waiting for?" she whispers, taunting. "I thought you were all hot and bothered because of me."

If only she knew. I tighten my grip on her small body, committing it to memory. "This might be the only chance I get to kiss you, Mia. I want to enjoy it."

I tighten my hold on her nape, slide my other hand down to her ass, tug her tight to my body, and crush my lips to hers.

ELEVEN

MIA

WELL. I asked for this, didn't I?

Sandwiched between my car and Desmond, I have nowhere to go. All I can do is cling onto his bulk and hope I survive the ride. His lips conquer, claim, devour. He slides his tongue against mine and licks into my mouth like he wants to taste every bit of me. He nips at my bottom lip, letting out the sexiest, deepest moan I've ever heard.

My body goes wild. Liquid heat pools between my legs as I lose the ability to stand on my own two feet. My grip on his jacket tightens, then goes slack as I curl my hands around his neck. An explosion detonates somewhere in the pit of my stomach.

I've never been kissed like this. I didn't even know it was possible. Suddenly, being so much smaller than Desmond doesn't annoy me. I love how big his body feels as it circles mine. I love feeling like he could pick me up and carry me to bed. I wonder how it would feel to have him inside me.

That big hand on my butt squeezes, and I let out a gasp. Oh, my. It feels amazing to be held like this, to be kissed, to be touched. Des drops his head to my neck, inhaling deeply before running his tongue down the line of my pulse.

My pulse, incidentally, goes into overdrive. I pant heavily, arching my back into his touch, mindless with the need to kiss and kiss and kiss. I'm unraveling, forgetting all the reasons I hate this man. He's unspooling me, spinning me around and around and around until everything is a kaleidoscopic blur of light and color and lust.

Then, abruptly, Desmond tears himself away from me. He pulls me tight and tucks me into his chest, leaning his chin on my head. The spinning stops and I'm left clinging to him, off-balance and out of breath. Disoriented, I stare at the slice of parking lot I can see past his chest, not understanding what the hell just happened.

What in the world possessed me to ask him to prove his attraction? How did I ever think that was a good idea?

Blame the dragon. That beast has a mind of its own. I was hurt and humiliated, and he was giving me all these ridiculous reasons for his actions. But now…

Is he attracted to me? Is that what's going on between us?

I've never felt this kind of animal desire for a man. I've never had my body be so at odds with my mind. But which is right? Physical needs (of which there are many), or mental safety?

Gently, I pull away from Des's embrace and clear my throat. I need to regain some kind of control over this situation, over my body. I don't like the heat sweeping under my skin, the urge to lean into him again and beg for more.

When I want things—like sex, or affection, or support—from men, I know how it ends: they leave. It was a harsh lesson to learn with my ex-husband, but it sank in deep and grew roots. Now, faced with the force of nature that is Desmond Thomas, I know what I'm looking at. He wants me on his terms. His kiss proved his attraction to me, but he still used money and manipulation to get me here. Colin tried the same when I fell pregnant, lording his fancy job title and his big salary over me to remind me how much I'd struggle without him if I decided to keep the baby—and lose him in the process.

I was strong enough to make it through those early years with Bailey on my own, and I'm strong enough to resist this lust I feel for Desmond. As the haze clears, I know what I need to do: erect a tall, impenetrable barricade between me and Desmond Thomas... then walk away.

"I'm not having dinner with you," I grit out through clenched teeth.

My words don't seem to surprise him. He watches me, a palm lifting up to rub the side of his jaw. "All right."

"I still don't like you."

Desmond looks...resigned. For some reason, that makes my chest ache. He takes a breath, his broad chest heaving. "That makes sense. I don't like myself right now, either."

Squinting, I meet his gaze. "I'm angry that you lied to me about who you were. That was a really shitty thing to do."

His shoulders drop. "Yeah."

"I'm not going to have sex with you."

There's a tiny catch of his breath when I say the word "sex," but Des hides it with a nod. "I wouldn't expect you to."

"While we're confessing our darkest sins, I might as well tell you mine. I don't have enough money for rent next month. I'm going to be late. I'll pay the barbershop rent, but I can't make the rent on the apartment. I'll get you your money eventually, but I might be a couple of days late. I would...appreciate it if you gave me some grace."

His eyes are unreadable as they search mine, inky pools in the darkness of the night. He says nothing, but I sense anger from him. I see it in the sudden tension of his shoulders and the clench of his jaw.

After all that—his big song and dance about thinking I'm the hottest thing since a country bonfire—he's still angry he's not going to get his money. Figures.

I try to brush it off, but the realization that I'm just a dollar sign to him hurts more than I'd like to admit.

With nothing else to say, and a desperate need to get away, I unlock my car and slip inside. I feel his eyes on me the whole way out of the parking lot, and I don't take a full breath until I'm safely behind my own apartment door.

What a freaking disaster.

The disaster continues an hour later, after I've ordered way too much Chinese food and I hear a knock on the door. Thinking it's my food, I open the door without checking the peephole.

Desmond is standing on my welcome mat, holding my bag of takeout. "I ran into the delivery guy in the lobby," he explains.

"Oh. How much do I owe you?" I grab the bag from him and peek at the foil and cardboard containers inside. They gave me three sets of plastic utensils, which is hilarious.

"That's actually what I wanted to talk to you about."

I squint at him, not understanding.

"Can I come in?"

Hmm, let me think about that. Having the guy who lied to me, led me on, then gave me the kiss of a lifetime after revealing his secret identity enter my home while I'm here alone. How about: "No."

Des nods, like he was expecting it. "I have a proposition for you."

Shock rips through me, quickly followed by outrage. "A *proposition*?"

"Not that," Desmond hurries to say. "It's something else. Look, I know I raised your rent pretty steeply."

"Pretty steeply?" I arch a brow. "Try exorbitantly."

His jaw tightens. "Do you remember the old property manager my grandparents used?"

"How could I forget," I deadpan. "He was the worst."

"He stole tens of thousands of dollars from my grandparents."

I blink. "Oh. I had no idea."

"No one knows. Even my grandparents don't know the extent of it. He pocketed all the money for maintenance, took an extra-large cut of commission, and screwed so many tenants out of their damage deposit. He took almost all the profits from the Airbnb he convinced them to run. He was pond scum."

Understanding dawns. "You're cleaning up the mess."

"On paper, raising your rent made sense. The new rate is in line with the market, and you hadn't had a rent increase since you moved in. We needed cash to get the two condos ready for sale, and the plan was to raise the rents to market value on the two commercial properties, sell this place"—he waves a hand to the apartment behind me—"and try to get the books back in order."

I chew my lip. I should have known something was going on with the old property manager. And as much as I hate to admit it, I know I was getting an amazing deal on my rent. Maude and Arthur have been charging me a decade-old rate for the barbershop, and nothing at all for the two-bedroom apartment out back. The rent increase is a shock, and I can't exactly afford it, but it's not that bad for Heart's Cove. With all the increased tourism, the town's been getting more and more expensive these past few years.

"I should have talked to you first," Desmond says. "But I walked into your barbershop, and..." He rakes his fingers through his hair. "Look. I want to make it right. I need a favor, and in exchange, we can talk about a rent discount."

My eyes narrow. "What kind of favor?"

He tugs at his collar. "So, here's the thing." He pauses, and the silence stretches. And stretches. And stretches.

"Desmond. Rip off the Band-Aid. Just tell me. What's this proposition?"

He holds my gaze for a long moment. Long enough for me to huff and start closing the door in his face.

Finally, he says, "I need a date to my family's Thanksgiving reunion."

I can honestly say that I'd rather roll around in human hair and set myself on fire. "No," I answer, and slam the door in his face.

TWELVE

DES

I STARE at the door for a beat, eyes level with the brass numbers, and almost start laughing. Then again, I guess I deserved that reaction from Mia. I deserve a lot worse.

But I also need to wipe Vince's smug smile off his face at this year's family Thanksgiving. And, more importantly, I need Mia to not hate my guts.

It would probably be smart to let her cool off and approach her later. When she told me she didn't have enough money to pay the rent, I was so fucking mad at myself for putting her in that position. Not only did I humiliate her tonight, but I also made her life unbearably difficult by raising her rent before I knew her situation. She's hurting because of me.

The last thing I should do is push my proposition on her when she's already irate. But she's just on the other side of this door, wearing a gorgeous black dress, looking like a goddess at whose altar I want to serve. It's physically impossible for me to move my legs to walk myself across the hallway and into my condo. I'm tethered to this spot, as close as I can get to her without breaking a hole through the door to get to the other side.

Screw it. I knock on the door.

No answer.

I knock again. "Mia!"

The door swings open. Mia stands in the gap, brandishing a plastic fork like it's Excalibur, a hunk of orange chicken pierced on its tip. "What."

"Please, just hear me out."

She pops the chicken in her mouth and chews, moving the fork in a circular "let's hurry this up" motion.

"I'm sorry," I start. Then words just—stop. She's so beautiful, and so fearfully angry. I want to kiss her again. It was a mistake to indulge in the parking lot. Now that I know how she tastes, I think I'll die if I don't get to do it again.

Mia takes her time to swallow her bite, then shakes her head gently. "Is that it?"

"No. I'm just trying to get my thoughts together."

"Herculean task, I gather." Her snark snaps against my skin, and my cock swells. Not the right time. So not the right time for me to get hard, but what am I supposed to do?

My voice is gravelly when I speak again. "How about half off your rent for November in exchange for attending Thanksgiving with me."

The silence between us is thick as soup. Mia lifts her chin slightly, eyes narrowing. Then her face clears, anger fading away, and my heart sings. Yes, I want her to look at me like this forever. I want to wake up to that face. I want to kiss those lips for hours.

"Des," she says softly.

"Yeah?" My upper body leans forward. Her lips are my own personal siren song. I want to crash my ship against her rocks, then crawl out of the surf to get a taste of her again. Just one taste.

Her lids lower slightly, and her hip curves out to the side. Her body is so beautiful. So small and lithe and perfect. She leans toward me, a mirror image of myself, her upper body just poking out of her front door, close enough to touch. Her scent wraps its soft, feminine fingers around my chest, squeezing, squeezing.

Then she whispers, "You're fucking delusional," and slams the door in my face—again.

This time, I do laugh.

THIRTEEN
GEORGIA

FALL IS MY FAVORITE SEASON. This morning, as my steps crunch over dry leaves on the sidewalk on my way to my new art gallery, I snuggle into my softest cashmere scarf and sip my delicious sugar-filled coffee. The air is crisp, the trees are a riot of color, and I get to wear ankle boots and layers of cute clothes. What else could a girl want?

Happiness warms me from within. Life couldn't be better right now.

Then I see Mia's face.

She hasn't spotted me yet, so I get a few seconds to observe her peering through the windows of her own barbershop, eyes narrowed, gigantic purse clutched in both hands. Her shoulders are tense and her knuckles are white, and I can already tell that Something Happened.

"Hey, neighbor."

She jumps, a hand flying to her chest. "Oh. Georgia. Hi."

"Is everything okay? You look stressed."

"Everything is a disaster. I'm beyond stressed." She closes her eyes. "I sound like Bailey. I'm sorry; everything's fine. I'm just being dramatic."

Hmm. I haven't known Mia for very long, but she's not someone I'd call dramatic. Time to get my CIA on and probe her for information. "How was your date last night? I'm sensing you didn't get lucky."

Mia's face darkens. "I don't want to talk about it."

"Definitely didn't get lucky, then." I tap my lip with my index finger. "What was his issue? Was he not attractive? Did he give you weird, creepy vibes? Did he talk about his mother the entire time?" I wrinkle my nose. "I once had a guy call his mother *during* the date so he could tell her how it was going. He literally recapped our entire conversation with me sitting right across from him. It was horrifying."

Mia lets out a little chuckle, then shakes her head. "Georgia —" She stops herself, smoothing a hand over her head and tucking a few flyaways back into her ponytail. Her eyes dart to the barbershop then back to me. "My date was *Des*."

If she'd told me her date was with the President, I couldn't have been more shocked. We stare at each other for a minute. I blink. She blinks. Then I lean in and say, "The guy from the app?" Why am I whispering? Why is my heart thumping?

Mia nods, cheeks flushing. Her jaw clenches and fire sparks in her gaze. "And he knew it was me."

I slap a hand across my mouth. "No."

"Yes."

"Holy crap. Is he still alive? Did you stab him with the stem of a wine glass after smashing it over his head?"

Her lips tremble, wanting to smile, but her eyes are glassy. "Where were you last night? I could have used the inspiration." Mia's voice is wry, but there's an edge of hurt around the edges. "No. I...basically just went home."

Basically. I wonder what that means, exactly.

I nod to my gallery. "You have time to chat about it for a few minutes? I could call the girls, see if they're free."

Mia sighs and shakes her head. "I have a full day of bookings today," she says. "Which I should be happy about, but really it's just making me more tense. Maybe this is for the best. I really don't have time to date."

"I'll come by in an hour or so with a coffee from Four Cups," I tell her. I hesitate, then say, "And I won't tell the girls if you don't want me to."

She meets my gaze with stormy blue eyes and dips her chin in a slight nod. "Thanks. I need a bit of time to think."

"Okay."

Mia smiles, then seems to gather her courage to finally enter her barbershop. I take a quick peek inside, but there's no evidence of our large (lying bastard of a) landlord anywhere in sight.

"Whatcha doin' there, Sweet Peach?"

I jump at the sound of my husband's voice. His hands slide over my hips, and he presses a kiss to the back of my neck.

Even within the confines of my own mind, calling Sebastian my husband sends little trickles of warmth and happiness buzzing through my body. It took twenty-five years, but I finally feel like I've found my way home—to him.

"Or should I call you Peeping Tom?"

Laughing, I spin in his arms. "Quiet, you."

"I should be the one saying that to you," he growls near my ear, and I know he's referring to my, uh, vocalizations this morning in bed.

We kiss, right there on Cove Boulevard in view of every Tom, Dick, and Dorothy, and I fall in love with him all over again. I can't believe I'm wearing a diamond ring on my left hand again. I can't believe I'm Sebastian Finch's wife.

"Better stop now," Seb says, not pulling away from me at all. "Otherwise I won't be able to fix the wobbly stair tread in your gallery without spending some time locked in your office together first." He pulls me tighter, grinning that roguish grin. "But on second thought, being locked in the office with you for an hour sounds like a mighty fine idea."

"I have to open the gallery," I protest weakly.

Sebastian makes a big show of glancing up and down the street. "I don't see any customers waiting to come in."

"Stop it." I laugh, extricating myself from his hold. I unlock the door to my gallery and when we're both inside, I see none other than Desmond Thomas getting out of his car and heading into Four Cups.

Sebastian sees me watching him and frowns. "Don't like that guy," he states.

"Join the club."

My husband's brows jump. "When did that change? I thought you were best friends. Dinner dates and everything." His voice is rough by the end of the last sentence.

I can't help the smile stealing over my lips. "Are you talking about that evening at Taqueria? It wasn't a dinner date, and you know it. He only sat down at my table because he could see it pissed you off. Plus, how could it be a date when my sister was there with her kids, and Trina and Mac had joined too?"

"Still don't like him."

Glancing at the empty street outside, I reach over and flick the lock on my door. Then I turn to face Sebastian. "Maybe you should take me to the office and show me how you feel, precisely," I tell him, voice husky.

I squeal when he hauls me over his shoulder, cowboy boots stomping on the hardwood floors. "You shouldn't ask for trouble, Sweet Peach," he says, depositing me on the edge of my desk. His eyes are very, very dark, glittering under the fluorescent lights in my office. "You know what happens when you get in trouble."

I sure do. Must be why I like trouble so much.

AN HOUR OR SO LATER, after I've pulled myself together and scrambled around to find what's left of my brain, I make my way to Four Cups and order two coffees.

Fiona glances at my order and arches her brows. "Recon mission? Have you spoken to Mia yet?"

"I ran into her quickly," I admit. "She seems shaken up."

"Hmm." Fiona purses her lips, then nods to the barista, who starts my order. "Let me know if you need anything."

With my fresh coffees in hand, I make my way across Cove Boulevard, under the canopy of red, orange, and yellow leaves, and over to the barbershop.

Mia is poring over her computer, pen poised over a notebook, brows drawn. She looks up when I push the door open with my hip.

"Hello, hello!" I call out.

Her shoulders drop, and she lets out a sigh. "Hey."

"Ready to tell me what happened?"

"No. Yes." She pauses, accepting her coffee. "No."

Laughing, I sit down in one of the spinning barber's chairs and give Mia a few moments to begin her tale of woe. And—whoa. When she gets to the kiss, I nearly fall out of my chair. When she tells me what Desmond proposed on her doorstep, I have to use an industrial-strength winch to haul my jaw up off the floor.

"And the worst part is, I could actually use the rent reduction really, really badly." She angles her head to the now-dark laptop screen. "I was just balancing my books, and honestly Georgia, things are grim."

"How much do you need?" I answer. "I can lend you money if you're in a bind." Lord knows I have enough of it.

Mia shakes her head. "Nothing. I don't want to owe anyone anything."

"It could be a gift."

My new friend just looks at me with sad, proud eyes. "Thank you, Georgia. It's fine. It's not as bad as it could be. I'll manage this month, but I might have to talk to Bailey's after-school basketball program about putting me on a payment plan. And I can trim some fat off the grocery budget, cancel a subscription or two. It'll be fine." She sips her coffee and scowls at the door leading to the apartment. "One thing I will *not* be doing is going to the Thomas family Thanksgiving. They're probably all awful."

"Maude and Arthur aren't," I point out.

Mia huffs, relenting. "True."

"Are you free tonight?" I ask. "We could do a girls' night."

"No," Mia tells me. "After my next client, I'm picking Bailey up from her sleepover. Tonight, I'm taking her to the museum. They have spooky night tours every Saturday in October. It doesn't cost anything, so…"

"Okay." I hug her tight, wanting to help but not knowing how. Mia squeezes me back, then walks me to the door just in time to open it for her next client. She greets the customer, then waves me away, and I head next door to see Sebastian's progress with the stair tread.

Worry gnaws at me for Mia, but all I can do is be there for support if she needs me. At least now, she has us to lean on. I just hope she realizes it.

FOURTEEN
MIA

LIFE IS FUNNY. Small moments—a failed date, for example—feel big and stressful and overwhelming. But then, routine takes over. As a single mother and owner of my own business, routine has been my mistress for a long, long time.

Sundays, Bailey and I do chores in the morning, grocery shopping around noon, and we have a home movie night in the evening. Once my kid is in bed, I usually have to prep myself for the week by checking my schedule at the barbershop to make sure everything is in order. From there, the whirlwind starts. School drop-offs, work, pick-ups, after-school activities, dinners, playdates, chores (and more chores), homework, dinner, clean-up, sleep, and on and on. Mondays and Wednesdays are basketball. Tuesdays, Bailey goes to a free after-school program at the local community center. Thursdays, we have an evening at home. Weekends seem to fill up with cleaning and cooking and errands and activities without any conscious input from me.

Then, through it all, there are phone calls to my parents and my sister, dentist appointments, doctor's appointments, school projects, PTA meetings, and a million other little things to keep on top of.

I blink, and a week has gone by. If I stop paying attention for a while, suddenly it's been two years. Or ten. Time has no meaning anymore.

So, when three weeks pass after my disastrous date with Desmond without me even noticing, it's not very surprising. Maybe it's a sign that I wasn't meant to date in the first place. When would I have the time? Shouldn't I focus on my life with my daughter, on my business?

With extra hours at the shop over the past few weeks, I've scraped enough to get by this month, which is a small miracle. If I'd been busy flirting with a mystery man or getting kissed in parking lots, I might not have been able to make ends meet. It requires all my focus and energy just to keep my head above water.

In a way, the date was a good reminder that my priority has to be my daughter and my business. Nothing else matters. And having Bailey as a priority means making sure my daughter is fed, clothed, healthy—and happy.

One thing that Bailey loves is Halloween, and our decorations have gotten progressively more elaborate over the years. I can't help it; seeing the joy on her face is worth the effort.

I place a plastic skeleton in one of the chairs in the barbershop, positioning him just so, then tangle fake spiderwebs over his body to hold it in place. Stepping back, I plant my hands on my hips. "There. Sir Bones is nice and comfy."

Bailey giggles, then tugs me over to the front of the chest-high reception desk. "Look what I did!"

My daughter used cottony spiderwebs, plastic spiders, and orange lights to create a spooky front to the desk, on full display to anyone who walks in.

I grin, kissing my daughter's head. "It looks amazing, Bailey."

"Yeah," she agrees.

In one of those strange moments of awareness, it hits me that it's the middle of October. Before I know it, another month will be over, and what will I have done? My best claim to fame is that I've succeeded in avoiding my landlord almost entirely. Sometimes I hear noises coming from the apartment behind the barbershop, but I mostly manage to ignore them. Once, when I heard footsteps approaching the dividing door, I ran out of the barbershop and hid around the corner like a lunatic. I was huddled behind a pile of garbage when Dorothy, one of the older ladies that runs the hotel, spotted me. I had to pretend I'd accidentally thrown my phone in the trash and was out looking for it.

Not my proudest moment.

I just don't want to see Desmond's face. I don't want to hear his voice. If I spend any more time one-on-one with him, I'll end up assaulting him. Either that or I'll kiss him again, which is even worse.

So, I've been focusing on my daughter and on my work and trying to put the idea of male companionship out of my mind completely. I don't have time for it, anyway.

"Hey, Mom?"

"Yeah, honey?"

"Can I go trick-or-treating with Toby and Katie this year?

They live in the neighborhood with the big houses, and Toby told me he got full-sized chocolate bars at six different houses last year."

I snort. "No problem. Have you figured out your costume? It's two weeks to Halloween." I dump the mints in my reception desk's candy bowl into an empty drawer and replace them with suitably spooky-themed goodies instead.

"Yeah. I want to be an electrical outlet," my daughter answers.

I pause, hands on the candy bowl, and glance at my daughter. She's busy tugging at one end of the desk's spiderweb that won't stay put. "Excuse me? An electrical outlet?"

"Uh-huh."

"Do you mean a plug?" Not that I know how you'd make a plug costume, but somehow it makes more sense than an outlet.

"No, I mean an electrical outlet." She points at one of the outlets near my barber's chairs for emphasis. "I can get a big box and cut out the holes. Then my face will be right here." She crawls over to the outlet and puts her finger on the screw in the middle of it, turning to meet my gaze. "Can you help me make it?"

"Um. Sure."

My kid is such a weirdo. I love her so much.

So, that evening, my daughter and I go on the hunt for a cardboard box big enough to use as her electrical outlet costume. We find a treasure trove of cardboard behind a furniture store, and I grab a few extras for good measure. Dinner will be late tonight, but Bailey is laughing and bouncing on the balls of her feet, which is worth it.

That's how I end up carrying a large purse, a few groceries I stopped to get on the way home, and three massive boxes as I'm heading back to my temporary condo on Seventh Avenue.

Bailey is carrying a box of her own, explaining to me exactly how she wants to craft the outlet while I try to picture the finished product in my mind. Neither of us have any visibility down the hallway. My left side is slightly overloaded with bags while my right is carrying the bulky boxes, so I'm hobbling, awkwardly lopsided.

Then my daughter, in her excitement, spins around at light speed to tell me that she wants me to paint her face metallic silver so she looks like a screw—but the box she's carrying knocks the cardboard I have under my right arm. Because I'm unbalanced, I try to recover by spinning, but the heavy bags over my left shoulder carry me too far.

I spin a hundred and eighty degrees, wobbling, then yelp as my shoe catches on a wrinkle in the carpet. My legs twist around each other, my left side tilting over so far I must look like a sailboat about to capsize. I flail and flap like a moron, screeching, and crash against the wall on my way to the floor.

Groceries tumble out of my bags, an orange rolling all the way to the fire exit at the far end of the hall. My cardboard boxes splay around me like an angel's broken wings. Bailey's eyes grow wide as she checks me over, and once she sees that I'm not hurt, she bursts out laughing, folding over at the waist as she wheezes. She drops to her knees and starts chasing after the oranges, still giggling.

"Stop laughing, Bailey," I groan. "That's not nice."

"Sorry, Mom," she says, not sounding sorry at all.

Heavy footsteps approach at a rapid pace. Great. My

daughter wasn't the only witness. Then, of course (because...who else?) Desmond Thomas pops into my field of view, dark brows furrowed. "Mia. Are you okay?"

Oh, God. No. I'm not okay. I was okay, until my stupid landlord watched me attempting to do a ballet pirouette while carrying enough cardboard to open a moving company.

"I'm fine," I croak.

His hands touch my arms, curling around my back to help me sit up. I scowl at his bicep, inexplicably angry that it flexes against the fabric of his sweater the way it does. The fabric is a deep green color, and it looks great with his skin tone. It even makes his eyes appear slightly brown, instead of their usual black-as-the-bowels-of-hell color. Ugh.

Heat rises to the surface of my skin. My gaze darts to his lips, which is ridiculous. They're full and firm, which I know because I kissed him three weeks ago.

Concern shimmers in those black-brown eyes. "Are you sure you're okay?"

I haven't had a man hold me or look at me like he cared in a long, *long* time. If I allowed myself to enjoy it, I might not want to go without. And that's unacceptable.

"Please let go of me," I answer icily.

He drops his hold on me, and cold rushes in. Damn him for being so nice and warm. Damn him for caring—or pretending to.

Gathering my dignity, my cardboard, and my groceries, I lift my chin and give him a curt nod. "Goodnight, Mr. Thomas."

"Let me help you carry something," he says.

Just as I'm about to spit some scathing remark about him pretending to be nice when he's in fact a huge, arrogant jerk,

Bailey thrusts two cardboard boxes at him. "Here," she says brightly. "I'm going to be an electrical outlet. We're going to make a practice one so Mom doesn't mess up the holes. We might need to use a utility knife instead of scissors, so I'm not going to cut them because it's dangerous. I'll go grab the last orange." Then she takes off at a sprint toward the lone orange by the fire exit.

Des looks at the cardboard, then at me. I decide I don't feel like explaining anything to him, so I say nothing.

I hobble toward my condo door. My cheeks are smarting and my whole body feels flushed and prickly. Once I've got my door unlocked, I stand in the opening and shove my things inside, then turn to grab the boxes from him. There's no way I'm letting him past the threshold.

When I meet his gaze, I see kindness there, which renders me speechless for a moment. I've spent the past few weeks vilifying this man, reminding myself that he lied to me and tricked me, that seeing this look on his face doesn't fit with the image I've created.

If I were honest with myself, I might admit that it was nice to have someone show concern for me. It was nice to have someone else to carry the bulky items while I walked to my door. It would be nice to have someone else to rely on for all the little things that I've been doing on my own. Would he take out the trash without being asked? Would he make sure my coffee was brewed in the morning by the time I woke up?

No. This is Desmond, the man who raised my rent, the man who lied to me and concealed his identity.

The man who kissed me like he'd pictured it a thousand times. The man who moved to town to take care of his grandparents' affairs. The man who put me up in a nice condo without a second thought. The man who's been working in my apartment every day for weeks.

I shake my head to clear my thoughts. Men like Desmond Thomas—most men, really—can't be relied on. I learned that with Colin. Unless I want to open myself up to be let down and abandoned again, I'm better off on my own.

"Thank you for the assistance," I tell him archly, letting Bailey duck in under my arm. Then I give my landlord a curt nod, and I close the door.

THE NEXT TIME I see Desmond is even more embarrassing than the last. It's a little over a week later, and I've been working myself to the bone taking extra clients, offering discounts and running promotions to drum up more business at the barbershop. Trina has been a huge help with Bailey, babysitting after school and helping with pick-ups and drop-offs. She says she's going to the school to pick up her own kids, but I know she's doing it to give me more time to work. I gave Georgia the green light to tell the rest of the ladies about my date, but I haven't had time to sit down with anyone myself. They've all managed to drop by the barbershop, though, bringing me coffees and goodies and gossip.

It's nice having friends. A part of me wonders how long they'll stick around, though, when I have so little time to give. People always leave, after all. It's easier to deal with the aftermath when you know it's coming.

Today, with only a couple of days until Halloween and two hours free in my schedule, I finally managed to spend some time attaching the straps to the back of the prototype cardboard electrical outlet the way Bailey wanted. I can already see some improvements to make with her version, which we've sketched out on another large panel of cardboard.

Not only that, I went to the dollar store to find metallic paint and also snagged a bright-red curly wig. Wanting to surprise my daughter with my finds, I end up painting my face with silver paint and shoving the wig on my head. Dressed like a cross between the Tin Man and Ronald McDonald, I wait until Trina buzzes the front door to strap the cardboard electrical outlet on my front, giggling the whole while.

Bailey is going to *love* this. It's so good. I can't wait to see the look on her face.

I'm giddy, laughing, and practically jumping up and down when I finally hear a knock on the door. Pulling it open, I spread my arms and say, "Ta-da!"

Desmond stares back, blinking. Shock flits across his face, followed by amusement.

The metallic paint hides my blush, which is a small mercy. Microscopic, really. I clear my throat. "Um."

"I was just letting you know that I've finished the work on your apartment. You can move back anytime." His lips tremble as his gaze coasts over the costume. "I love the outfit. You got another bite on Blind Date?"

Now he's mocking me. Wonderful. I put my hand on my hip behind the big cardboard rectangle strapped to the front of my body. "So what if I did?"

Des's eyes narrow, laughter disappearing from his gaze. "Do you? Have another date?"

"If I did, it would be none of your business." It's hard to be prim when you're dressed like an electrical outlet, but I just about manage.

"MOM!" Bailey comes running, crashes into Desmond's side, then touches the front of the cardboard box strapped to my body with reverent hands. "YOU DID IT!"

I laugh, awkwardly hugging my kid around the cardboard. "I did. You like it?"

"IT'S AWESOME! I want to go see the face paint. Is it in the bathroom? Where's mine? Can we finish it tonight? THE HAIR!" Bailey starts cackling, clutching her stomach. "Des, do you like it?"

"Very much. Is this your costume?"

"Yeah. My friend Vicky is dressing up like a skateboard, but mine is better. Right?"

"Uh-huh." Des grins, gaze coasting over me, amusement lighting his eyes. I stand there, with my silver face and my cardboard clothes, feeling like a buffoon. Des turns his smiling face to Bailey. "One year, I dressed up like a bunch of grapes."

My daughter's face brightens. "Really? How?"

"Purple balloons taped to my body and a green top hat for the stem."

"Oh, man," Bailey says. "I wish I thought of that."

"I'll show you a picture if I can find it. You could be grapes next year."

"Can I?" Bailey spins toward me.

"Sure." I shimmy out of the cardboard and tear the wig off, so now I'm just a Tin Man wearing athleisure. Des's gaze lingers on my body, and I try to ignore the way everything inside me tightens in response.

"It's a pretty awesome costume," Trina admits, grinning. Then her smile drops as she looks at the man standing across from me. "Desmond," she greets him, frost crackling in her words.

"Katrina," he answers neutrally. His gaze slides back to mine. "Let me know when you're moving back into the apartment. I'll get cleaners organized for this place once you're out."

"Of course." I give him a curt nod, then watch him disappear behind his door.

Trina gives me a wide-eyed stare. "You told us things were done and dusted between you and Des," she whispers so Bailey can't hear.

"They are," I insist.

"Mm-hmm," she says, arching a brow. "Is that why you're avoiding us?"

I purse my lips, the metallic paint feeling oddly stiff on my skin. "I'm not avoiding you."

She grins, winking. "Good. You can't hide from us, Mia. We like you too much. I'll see you tomorrow."

THAT WEEKEND, the day after a late evening trick-or-treating with Bailey (during which her costume was a huge hit and she got eight full-sized candy bars), I manage to get us packed and moved back to our apartment. It's dark out by the time we make it home, and I'm bone-tired—until I walk through the door.

"Whoa!" Bailey cries, dropping her bags just inside the back door. She rushes into the new space, spinning in a circle. "It's huge!"

It's far from huge, but it's definitely bigger. The sink and appliances are in the same locations, but a partition wall has been knocked down to make the kitchen, living, and dining spaces an open-plan L-shape. There's extra counter space where a useless nook used to be, and when I poke my head inside the bathroom, I audibly gasp.

There's a huge walk-in shower with a rain showerhead and clear glass partitioning it from the rest of the bathroom. New toilet, new vanity, new faucet, new sink...this looks incredible.

He did this in a month.

"Is this all for us?" Bailey whispers near my elbow, wrapping an arm around my hips. "We get to stay here?"

The hushed wonder in her voice makes my heart squeeze and expand. I wrap my hand around her shoulder and pull her close. "It's all ours," I answer.

Bailey beams at me. "I'm going to go unpack my things."

"Okay," I answer, throat tight. If I could put that smile on her face every day, I'd know I was doing something right.

Desmond put that smile on her face.

The realization hits me, and I grip the wall for balance. Huh—new tiles, too.

For the next hour, Bailey and I inspect our new space. The floor has been replaced with good-quality, hard-wearing, wood-look vinyl instead of old laminate. The hallway carpet is the same, but it looks like it's been steam cleaned. The kitchen counters are some sort of engineered stone and are way nicer than any rental I've ever had. The cabinet doors have been replaced, but the cabinets themselves are the same. Even the appliances are new. Bailey spends time making faces in the distorted reflection of the stainless-steel fridge while I laugh at her antics.

Desmond did this. Day after day after day, he came into this apartment and renovated it—for me. For us.

I could have guests here. Sure, it's small, and it's tucked at the back of my barbershop...but it's *nice*. I could invite the girls for a dinner party or just drinks and nibbles at my place, and I wouldn't be ashamed. Desmond gave that to me.

Or maybe, he's just fixing it up to sell it? He wants to gouge more rent out of me? This is all an effort to push me out of my home?

My phone dings.

Desmond: Did you make it to your apartment? Is everything okay?

I'd texted him earlier to let him know we were gone from the Seventh Avenue condo, so he was free to schedule the cleaners. I stare at his message, heart thumping. That's not what he'd write if he were planning on raising my rent again... Is it? It almost sounds like he's nervous about my reaction to the renovations. Or am I reading too much into this?

I should call him. Thank him properly. My finger hovers over the call button, trembling—and my phone rings.

Colin's name blazes across the screen, making me flinch. I'd emailed him back when he first contacted me, telling him I was willing to let him meet Bailey if she was open to it. The only problem is, I haven't brought it up to Bailey yet. With the move, and the extra work, and Halloween, and basketball practices, and dentist appointments, and, and, and...

Okay, yes, I'm making excuses. I swipe to answer.

"Colin?"

"Mia," he says, sounding relieved. "I didn't think you'd answer."

"You're not that scary."

He laughs, and I'm transported back in time. We laughed a lot together. I remember many nights cuddling on the couch, making plans for our future together. It was always full of travel and adventures, spontaneous weekend getaways. We'd laugh and plan and dream together.

Then I got pregnant, and he left me.

My ex-husband takes a deep breath. "I haven't heard back from you after your last email. I wanted to follow up and tell you that I went ahead and scheduled time away from work. I've booked a room in Heart's Cove for Thanksgiving weekend and the week following."

He—wait, *what?*

Panic jolts through me. "Um. I...uh. Thanksgiving isn't ideal."

"Are you visiting your parents? I could go to Eureka. I haven't seen Earl and Irene since the divorce."

No shit. Why would he see my parents after we divorced?

"No, my parents live in an RV now. They're touring around the States."

"Oh, good for them!" He laughs. "Earl finally got his dream. How's Irene handling it? She was worried about the bathroom situation, wasn't she?"

The past knocks against my bones again. Colin knew my

parents, *liked* my parents. And they loved him. The room tilts and expands around me, like I'm viewing the world through a carnival mirror.

I clear my throat. "Look, Colin, I have plans over Thanksgiving weekend." *Lie.* "I'm going to be out of town." *Double lie.* "We'll have to do this some other time."

There's a pause, then: "Are you seeing someone?"

My spine straightens. The world around me sharpens into focus again. I turn to frown at my new stone countertop. "That's none of your business, Colin." Why do I have to keep reminding the men in my life that they have no claim over me?

My ex-husband sighs. "You're right. I'm sorry. I just... Please, Mia. I really want to meet Bailey. When I didn't hear from you after your other email, I figured I should clear my schedule. Prove to you that I was serious."

I close my eyes. It was never in doubt that Colin was serious. He's always, *always* followed through on what he says. When he told me he didn't want kids, he was serious enough to leave when I got pregnant.

The phone buzzes while I'm trying to think of a way to answer. It's Desmond, and his message says, "*I can change things around if you don't like what I did. You can paint the walls any color you like. I know white is boring, but I figured Bailey might like to choose.*"

He did this for us. My gaze travels around the new layout, the renovations.

Frazzled, I put the phone back to my ear. "Look, Colin, let's aim for the week after Thanksgiving, okay?" That gives me three weeks or so to get myself together and tell my daughter her father wants to meet her. "We can meet up when I'm back in town."

He lets out a breath. "Okay. Great. Thanks, Mia. I mean it. And—if you have pictures of Bailey, my parents have been asking... And I'm asking too. I'd love to know what she looks like."

"Yeah. Okay. Bye." I hang up and collapse on the couch. I grip my phone in a tight fist, trembling as tears prickle my eyelids.

Colin is coming here. To my sanctuary, my home. Will he judge how I've been living and find me lacking? Will he try to take her away from me?

And where the heck am I going to go over Thanksgiving weekend? I can't stay with my parents. I can't afford a plane ticket out to see my sister. I can't afford a hotel or an impromptu trip during one of the more expensive weekends of the year.

Heart's Cove is small enough that if he's here during Thanksgiving, we could conceivably run into each other even if I'm trying to keep a low profile. Plus, the main hotel in town is practically right across the street from my barbershop. I can't exactly take Bailey to Georgia's house and hide out there. I'd never live it down.

No, I need to leave. I need a little bit more time. I need the holiday with my daughter; I'm not ready to give that to Colin. Selfish, maybe, but it's the truth. I don't appreciate him elbowing his way into my town on a holiday weekend, bullying me into meeting my daughter on his terms.

"Mom, look!" Bailey comes tearing down the hallway, waving something in her hands—socks. They're white, with the Golden State Warriors logo on the front.

Oh, my word. Des bought her a present. I'm going to have a nervous breakdown.

"Mom? Are you okay?" Bailey skids to a stop in the middle of the room, then creeps over to the couch, blond brows drawn together. She's wearing her favorite slippers, the ones shaped like green dinosaurs with floppy tails that trail behind her. The socks dangle from her fingertips.

I blink my tears away and smile. "Of course, honey. I'm a little overwhelmed at how cool our house looks now."

"I know." Bailey smiles wide. "There's a new window in my room. It doesn't stick when it slides now, and the screen doesn't have any wrinkles like it did when you fixed it. And look!" She brandishes the socks in front of me, then drops them in my lap. "They're so cool."

My lip wobbles. "Wow," I whisper.

Bailey hops up onto the couch and snuggles into my side. She hugs me around the belly, burying her head in my chest.

Time to put my big girl pants on. I kiss my daughter's blond head, stroking the fine strands, then take a deep breath. "Hey, Bailey, can I talk to you about something?"

She nods. "Uh-huh."

"You know how I told you that when you were born, your dad went away and that's why it was just the two of us?"

"Yeah. He didn't want me."

My heart turns to a small, hard ball. I squeeze my daughter close. "That's not true, honey. I never said that, did I?"

"No, but why else would he go away?" Her head pops up, and light hazel eyes meet mine. "I know he didn't want me. It's okay, Mom. I was sad about it for a while, but I'm okay now."

Who knew nine-year-olds could deliver such hard gut punches? It takes all my self-control not to burst into tears. I can't believe my daughter's been through this kind of pain at such a young age. That's my fault too.

With my arm around her shoulders, I lean my cheek against the top of her head. "If you could, would you want to meet him?"

Bailey is silent for long enough that I pull away to meet her gaze. Her brows are furrowed, and she's chewing on her bottom lip. "I don't know," she finally says.

"That's okay," I whisper. "You don't have to decide right now."

"Is he mean?"

I shake my head. "No. He's nice."

That seems to surprise her. "Oh. What's he like?"

"His name is Colin. He has brown hair and green-brown eyes, and he works with computers."

She's silent for a while. "Would I have to call him Dad?"

"No. You could call him whatever you want."

"So I could call him Colin?"

"Yeah," I answer. "And if you decide you don't want to meet him, you just let me know and you don't have to."

Pursing her lips, Bailey kicks her dinosaur-clad feet up and down. She grabs the socks from my lap and starts running them through her fingers, tracing the logo, touching the seams. She drums her fingers on her thighs, then finally lets out a loud huff. "Okay, I'll do it," she decides. "I want to meet him."

My throat gets so tight, it's hard to breathe. Finally, I manage to croak, "All right." I hug her once more, then pull away. "What do you want for dinner?"

A mischievous gleam enters her eyes. "Pizza?" she asks hopefully.

With my tight budget, ordering pizza has always been a special treat. And my little emotional blackmailer knows I can't say no after a conversation like the one we just had. Laughing, I nod. "Fine."

When Bailey has disappeared back to her room, I finally pull up Desmond's messages to answer.

Mia: The apartment looks amazing. Thank you. And Bailey loves the socks, by the way.

FIFTEEN

DES

I CAN'T HELP WALKING into Blade Barbershop the next morning. My feet carry me to the doorstep without me being able to stop them. My hand pushes the door open before I can change my mind.

Mia stands on a footstool, tearing down Halloween decorations in the front corner of the room. She glances over her shoulder at me, wobbles, and lets out a little squeak. I'm beside her in an instant, hands on her waist, steadying her. The heat of her body soaks into my palms like sunlight warming my skin.

I drop my hands and take a step back.

"Thank you," she says, stepping off the stool and onto the ground.

The top of her head reaches my chest. She tilts her face up to meet my gaze, her blond hair glinting in the sunlight streaming through the big windows at the front of her barbershop.

"Hi," I say, like a lump.

"Hi," she replies. Red sweeps over her cheeks, and she clears her throat. "Thank you for what you did in the apartment, Des. It's more than I ever expected."

"Everything I did needed to be done." I shrug.

Mia gives me a wry smile. We both know I'm lying. I spent twelve hours a day nearly every day in that apartment, fixing up everything that I could see. I spent my own money on the renovations, not wanting to dip into my grandparents' property management funds for something that wasn't precisely necessary.

It was necessary for Mia, though. For her to have a home—and for me to make amends.

"Can I help you with anything?" Mia finally says, wrapping up old fake cobwebs into a ball and ducking past me to shove them into a box full of other decorations.

"I was hoping for a shave," I say.

Mia pauses, straightens, and finally gives me a bland, professional smile. "Sure. Take a seat."

The dance begins. A cape is swept over my shoulders, each snap clicked into place at the nape of my neck. Her hands flick the black fabric to straighten it out, and she meets my gaze in the mirror. Hot towel, shaving cream, razor. Mia works with practiced efficiency, skillful and quick.

When she's got the skin of my cheek pulled taut and is shaving down with the grain, she speaks. "I wanted to ask you something, actually."

"Mm?" My eyes are closed, but I crack them open a slit to watch Mia's face in the mirror.

She's focused on my face, her movements sharp, but there's a tension in her shoulders I don't like. I open my eyes fully.

She pulls away to clean the razor, then meets my gaze. "Do you still need a date for Thanksgiving?"

My heart bangs against my ribs so hard I think she might hear it. I nod. "Yeah."

Her chin lifts. "I'm prepared to consider it," she says. "But half off my rent for one month isn't good enough."

My eyebrow lifts. "Oh? What do you propose?"

Mia's jaw clenches. She looks determined, defiant. With me sitting and her standing, she's still only slightly taller than I am, but she meets my gaze with a steady, steely expression on her face.

I can't live without this woman. As long as I'm in the same town as her, in the same state, the same country, I'll find my way back to her. How could I possibly resist coming into her barbershop every week?

"I need more information," she finally says. "Why do you need a date? What's the big deal? Do I need to pretend to be in a relationship with you? Pretend to like you?"

That makes me laugh. "I mean...yeah. You'd have to at least *try* to hide your hatred of me."

The corner of her lips twitch, and I almost want to do a victory dance. This is the most relaxed she's been with me since the date. Finally, Mia lifts her chin. "Unfortunately, how much I like you—or don't—is outside my control."

I chuckle again, unable to keep my eyes off her. I want to kiss her again. Desperately. To feel her soften against me the way she did in the Dolce Vita parking lot.

"So?" she asks. "Why do you need a date so badly?"

I click my tongue, tilting my head to the side. "It's going to sound ridiculous."

"Try me."

I gulp, suddenly nervous. It's one thing to ask for a date, but to admit that I need one because I want to beat my adoptive brother at a stupid race?

"We have this family tradition," I say. "It's been going for a few generations."

Mia shifts all her weight to one leg, causing her hip to round. She tilts her head, listening.

"Every Thanksgiving, before we eat, we have a race."

Mia straightens. "I need to pretend to like you *and* I need to run? I don't know, Des..."

"It's a three-legged race," I clarify. "All the couples participate. I haven't had a date, so I've been paired up with my grandmother for the past few years, and my brother has won three years in a row."

Still holding her razor, Mia leans against the wall, frowning. "You need a date on Thanksgiving because you want to beat your brother in a three-legged race?"

I snort, looking up at the ceiling. "Basically, yeah." When I look back down, Mia is staring at me strangely. "What?"

"I can't figure you out," she says.

I spread my hands. "I'm not sure there's that much to figure out."

"Is your family really dysfunctional, or something? What am I walking into? Is this really just about a stupid race?"

"Well...there's a trophy involved."

She rolls her eyes, but her lips twitch. Almost there. I've

almost made her laugh. She huffs. "This is ridiculous. No way. Forget I even mentioned it."

I chuckle, gripping the armrests of the chair to stop myself from reaching for her. Then I quiet down and realize I need to tell her some truths—things I don't usually talk about with anyone. "My family is average-level messed up," I admit. "My parents died when I was eleven, and my aunt and uncle adopted me. They gave me a home and all the basic necessities to raise me, but..." I shrug. "It wasn't the same. My brother, Vince—cousin by blood—took a real disliking to me. It never really went away."

"He's the one who's won the trophy three years in a row?"

I nod.

Mia hums, watching me. "You think winning the trophy will change any of that history?"

"No, but it might wipe that smug smile off his face, and that's got to be worth it."

To my surprise, Mia laughs. It's as gorgeous as I imagined it would be. I freeze, watching her, my heart beating a mile a minute, my breath heavy in my lungs.

She steps up beside me and tilts my head to the side to start shaving me again. "I can't believe I'm actually considering it."

When I find my voice again, I say, "A free weekend away. I'll pay for everything. Plus, Lovers' Peak is a popular tourist destination. You might like it."

She pauses, razor suspended above my skin. "Lovers' Peak, Colorado? Where Georgia's sister just moved?"

I meet her gaze in the mirror and shrug. "Not sure."

She bites her lip, and I can almost hear the gears turning in her head. I could have her beside me at Thanksgiving. I could walk into my aunt's chalet in Lovers' Peak with Mia and Bailey by my side and silence all their jokes about me being alone, me never belonging.

But beyond that, the idea of having the two of them by my side feels *right*. I would be so damn proud to be anywhere with Mia and Bailey beside me.

Suddenly, I need it. I can't bear the thought of spending that weekend without Mia. I *need* her to agree. "What's it going to take for you to say yes?"

"Six months' free rent," she answers, voice hard. "And I want a guarantee that you won't raise the rent again for at least two years."

I whistle. "That's asking a lot."

"You're the one who needs a date to a family reunion, big guy." She brings the razor to my face again, working on my jaw. "For six months' rent, I'll even pretend to like you."

My throat grows tight.

The silence stretches as she works for another minute or two, then she pulls away and meets my gaze. "So?"

"The guarantee, I can do," I say. "But the most I can give you is one month rent-free."

"No deal." She moves to the other side of me, her breast pressing into my arm as she leans over to position my head. Then she backs away slightly, so all I can feel is the heat of her body beside me. She shaves my face, my jaw, my neck, then cleans me up and moisturizes.

When she steps back and puts the razor away, I watch her chest rise and fall as she takes a deep breath. She spins to face me, eyes determined. "Three months," she counters. "Final offer."

"Three months' free rent and a two-year guarantee of no more rent raises in exchange for Thanksgiving with my family, including participating in the three-legged race," I summarize.

"That's right."

"I think I might be getting the better deal," I admit, grinning.

"So, you agree?"

I nod. "It's a deal." I extend a hand.

She hesitates, leaving my palm hanging in the air between us. "Bailey is coming too," she informs me. "I'm not spending Thanksgiving without my daughter."

"I wouldn't ask you to."

Mia's shoulders drop, and a small, victorious smile steals over her lips. She slides her palm into mine and seals the deal, shaking once. "Pleasure doing business with you, Mr. Thomas."

"The pleasure is all mine," I answer. "Believe me."

That beautiful flush returns to her cheeks, and Mia gives me a full-fledged smile. She takes her hand back, inhaling deeply. Then her eyes narrow. "This is a professional arrangement," she says. "Nothing more."

"Of course."

"I'm not going to sleep with you." For some reason, her voice lifts slightly at the end of the sentence, making it almost sound like a question.

I can't help the grin that lifts the corners of my lips.

She points an index finger at me. "I'm serious."

"No sex." I nod, my body screaming at me to grab her around the waist, lift her onto my lap, and make her forget that stupid rule.

"No sex," she repeats, voice trembling the slightest bit. "No kissing. No touching."

"I might have to hold your hand," I hedge, "if you're going to be my date."

She inhales deeply and dips her chin. "Fine. You can put your arm around my shoulders. But no PDA. I don't want to confuse Bailey."

"That's fair."

"Do we need to come up with a backstory? Some funny anecdote about how we met?" she asks.

"We could tell everyone I took over the management of your building and raised your rent so much that you hated my guts."

Mia laughs again, and the sound of it sends all my blood rushing south. God, she's beautiful. I can't stop looking at her. Everything fascinates me: the way her nose scrunches, the lines around her eyes, the shape of her teeth.

Her face settles into a fading smile, and she shakes her head. "I have a feeling this is a terrible idea."

"Maybe. Just think of the trophy. That's what I'm doing." *Sort of.*

She giggles again, sending another wave of desire rushing through me. I need to get out of here before I break her rules. The need to kiss her is mounting inside me with alarming speed. I stand, but Mia doesn't step back. Her chest is inches from mine, that sweet face tilted up to hold my gaze.

Her lips—beautiful lips—are begging for a kiss. Her eyes are more vulnerable than I've ever seen them, desire sparking.

This woman needs to be reminded that she's allowed to want.

I bet she doesn't even remember what it's like to be treated like she deserves, to be worshipped and cherished.

But I already messed up by not telling her I was the one talking to her on the app. I've only just regained a bit of ground with her and gotten her to agree to come to Thanksgiving with me. I can't screw that up by acting like a horny idiot.

"Des..." Her voice is so soft, it makes me ache all over.

Needing to leave before I break the no-kissing rule before we even make it to Colorado, I take a step back. "I should get going."

She snaps her body back, rocking onto her heels, and glances away. "Of course."

I pay and leave. Once outside, I glance through the window and meet Mia's eyes.

She watches me from behind the reception desk, a million unsaid words in her eyes. I wonder what she sees in mine.

SIXTEEN

MIA

EXACTLY ONE WEEK LATER, when I'm about to close up the shop, Des walks in again. He has a week's worth of scruff on that hard jaw of his, and he arches his brow in question.

I spin the nearest chair toward him and pat the headrest.

If I were honest with myself, I might admit that my heart starts thumping a little bit harder at the sight of him in my barbershop. Or that my face feels a little bit more flushed than usual.

I might even admit that I don't hate his presence quite nearly as much as I used to.

He stalks into my space, and instead of despising the feeling of being so small next to him, I find myself yearning for him to wrap his arms around me and tug me close. Feeling small in Des's arms is a lot like feeling safe, protected, cherished. My pulse pounds in my ears, between my legs.

In the past week, I've had time to think things over. Desmond has layers I hadn't seen before—or hadn't wanted to see. I find myself wondering about his childhood. How was it to move to his aunt and uncle's house at such a young age, wrestling with so much grief? How did his parents die? How did he cope? How did his aunt and uncle treat him?

Does that explain why he seems to keep himself apart from other people? I thought it was arrogance. When he walked into my barbershop and watched me with his dark, unreadable eyes, I interpreted his gaze as haughty. Judgmental. But what if that's just guardedness? What if I've been hating him simply because he doesn't allow strangers to see through to the real him?

He's not the brute I thought he was. He's thoughtful and caring. He bought my daughter socks that she wears proudly to every basketball practice. He fixed up my apartment way beyond what was necessary. He agreed to a ridiculous rent freeze just to win a stupid race.

I like that about him. I like the absurdity of it. I like that he wanted me there with him.

I also like his body, his face, and his voice. I've dreamed about our kiss—while sleeping and while awake—and as the days pass, it's getting harder and harder to ignore the need building inside me.

I've tried to remind myself that he lied to me, tricked me to get a dinner date with me. But didn't he also back off anytime our conversations turned sexual on the app? He was always respectful, even when I was rude and hateful to his face.

When he told me he did it because he was attracted to me and he didn't want me to turn him down, I didn't believe him. Then he kissed me, and I tried to deny it.

Now, when we've struck this silly bargain and agreed to go on a fake date together...I'm not sure where we stand.

But I do know I want him. I know that's asking for trouble.

"Clean shave?" I ask, voice sounding a little thin.

"Please."

As he takes a seat in the chair, I find myself studying the scruff on his cheeks. Dark, coarse hair gives him a slightly intimidating appearance, but now I know it's not quite the truth. He's funny and sarcastic and cares about winning silly family trophies. He's good with my kid. He cares about giving us a nice place to live. He loves his grandparents enough to uproot his life to make sure they're okay.

Desmond Thomas isn't a bad man at all. In a lot of ways, we're very similar. We're both wary of opening up to people. We're used to being on our own. We spend our time taking care of other people.

Is it possible that I've misjudged him completely?

Heart thumping, I get to work. This isn't the first time that I've shaved Des, but it's the first time I've done it while not actively hating him. My body feels warm, jittery. I'm keenly aware of the bulk of him, sitting in my chair, the power hidden in those relaxed muscles. I feel the roughness of his skin when I pull it taut, smell that heady scent on his skin.

And when I'm nearly done, I get distracted studying the curve of his lips—lips that were on mine not too long ago—and I accidentally cut him with the razor.

"Shit," I whisper, grabbing a towel to dab at the blood. "I'm so sorry. I haven't done that in years." I press the towel to his face, wiping stray bits of shaving cream with the free end of it, frowning.

"It's fine," he says in that deep voice of his. "Don't worry about it, Mia."

I shake my head, not meeting his eyes. "So unprofessional of me." I click my tongue. "It's still bleeding. I should have been paying attention instead of—"

Stop. Talking.

"Instead of what?" His lips curve beneath the corner of the towel. "Why were you distracted?"

My heart is thumping uncomfortably. His leg presses against my thighs. I dab the towel and check his skin, brows drawing together at the sight of the little nick on his cheek. After everything he's done for me, all I've managed to give him in return is a bleeding cut.

"I wasn't thinking about anything," I lie. "I'm sorry, Des. Is it sore?" I put the towel back on his cheek, finally meeting his gaze.

Those inky eyes suck me in, turning me to stone where I stand. He reaches up but instead of holding the towel to his cheek, he grasps my wrist in his warm hand and gently tugs it away. Then he spins the chair to face me, long legs framing mine, and uses his grip on my wrist to pull me closer.

In a daze, I follow his lead. I'm staring at his lips again, remembering how it felt to have them on mine. His body is so big and warm, so relaxed in this chair beside me. I find myself leaning over him, draping my chest against his, seeking his warmth, his strength.

What am I doing? Do I care?

Memories rush in from that evening in the parking lot. I

remember how it felt to be wrapped up in his arms, and how easy it was to let go of all my worries and lose myself in him. Would it be so bad to give in to that urge once more?

If he isn't the villain I thought he was, why am I resisting this attraction between us?

As if Des can sense me losing the fight against my own inhibitions, he grips my hair and angles my head, his other hand banded across my back—and kisses me.

Oh, I've missed this. I let out a moan as my hand slides up to touch his freshly shaved cheek, smooth and damp from my ministrations. I feel his jaw working as he deepens the kiss, sliding his tongue against mine. The noise he makes—a groan of pure male need—sends electric shivers buzzing through my veins.

I arch my body, pressing my breasts into his chest, needing more contact, more warmth, more of him. The arm clamped across my back shifts, his hand dipping down to the curve of my ass. He slides his fingers down the center seam of my jeans, until I feel the pressure of his hand against the very core of me, holding me tight to him.

I moan, kissing him harder, lost to this—to him. To the sensation of this complicated, infuriating man who told me he was addicted to me. The hardness behind his zipper tells me he was speaking the truth.

He's hard—for me.

The thought turns everything liquid inside me. I melt in his arms, suddenly delirious. This man *wants* me. Craves me. He touches me like he can't help himself, like I'm the most desirable woman in the universe.

"Mia," he growls. "You taste so fucking good."

"You taste like shaving cream." I sound dazed, dreamy.

He smiles against my mouth, nipping at my bottom lip. His hand is still between my legs, squeezing in slow, rhythmic pulses that are quickly driving me mad. "You have no idea how many times I've wanted to do this," he says, running his lips down my neck, biting gently. "No idea what I've imagined doing to this beautiful body of yours."

"Oh?"

It's official—I've lost my mind. We haven't even left Heart's Cove, and I'm breaking my own rules. No kissing, I told him. No touching. No sex.

Ha! What an idiot I've been. Right now, all I want is to slide his zipper down and climb on top of him. It's like a switch flipped inside me, and I'm desperate for it. Ten years of sexless routine calcified into a hard shell around me, but hairline fractures begin to appear. I'm allowed to want sex. I'm allowed to give in to baser needs. I'm allowed to be wanted.

Des untangles his hand from my hair and slides it down to my breast. He kneads it gently, pressing his mouth to my neck. His breath is hot against my skin, and when he speaks, his voice sends tremors racing through me. "When I saw you in your pajamas, I got so hard so fast, I thought I was going to pass out." He pinches my nipple through the fabric of my shirt, groaning. "I could see the outline of your perfect tits, Mia. These beautiful breasts just begging for my mouth."

He got hard at the sight of me in a hole-ridden, stained T-shirt. This man is as delusional as I am.

"Maybe we shouldn't..." I trail off when he squeezes between my legs again, sending sparks shooting through my thighs. I gasp.

Oh, my. It's been ten years since a man touched me there. I'd forgotten how good it felt. There are layers of fabric between us, and he's already making me lose my mind.

"We should," he growls. "We definitely should. I have a feeling you need this as badly as I do."

If only he knew. The chair creaks beneath us as I shift my weight, lifting my knee to hook around his hip. He grabs me around the waist and lifts me like I weigh nothing, bringing me up so I'm straddling his hips. I can feel him, hot and hard beneath me, right where I need him most.

All I need to do is just—

"Keep doing that, baby," he grates, hands on my hips, helping me grind myself against him. The chair squeaks as I move over him, panting, my hands twisted into his shirt. There's a little bead of dry blood on his cheek where I nicked him, speckles of shaving cream I missed wiping off. I fall forward onto his chest, hips bucking.

"Oh, fuck," Des says, helping my movements with his hands clamped over my hips. "That's it, girl. Ride my dick like you've always wanted to. Grind yourself on that cock until you come in those nice, lacy panties I know you like to wear."

My eyes roll back in my head. I'm so close—so close. Just a little bit more friction. A little bit more of his hands gripped on my hips, the feel of his chest beneath mine, his breath coasting over my cheek—

The chair collapses with a mighty groan, and we both tumble through the air. Des manages to shield my head and the side of my body, taking the brunt of the fall on his shoulder. I crash on his arm and side, then roll away from him onto the black-and-white checkered floor.

Reality slams into me. I freeze, gripping the floor with my fingertips, sucking in a hard breath.

What. Did. I. Just. Do.

Des groans, hauling himself up to all fours. He glances at me. "You okay?"

"Yes. No." I gulp. "You—you need to leave."

Hurt splashes across his features, quickly hidden behind that familiar shuttered, arrogant expression. He licks his lips, clears his throat, and stands. "Right. Okay. That was obviously a mistake."

"Obviously." I stand and follow him to the door.

Des hesitates in the doorway, meeting my gaze.

I nod. "Have a good day!" I use my work voice, but it rings false in the heavy air between us.

His shoulders drop, and he walks away.

I END up locking the shop and making my way to Bailey's school with my whole body shaking. I manage to hide my frazzled state of mind all the way to her basketball practice, where I drop her off and head home. I really shouldn't be driving in this condition. As soon as I'm safely inside, I spin around in a circle and try to figure out what the heck I'm supposed to do.

I need to calm down—but how? A cold shower? Meditation?

The imprint of Des's fingers still burns on my hips. I close my eyes for a beat—and...oh, screw it. I know exactly what I need, and it isn't freaking meditation.

Rushing to my bedroom, I strip off my jeans and my panties

(yes, they were lacy. I've started wearing nice undergarments again, and I don't want to think about why) and lie back on my bed. In the bottom drawer of my nightstand are a few toys that have kept me company for the past decade. I pull out my favorite vibrator and go to town.

It takes about six seconds for me to explode. When I'm limp on the bed, vibrator silent in my hand, the lower half of my body completely bare, I start to laugh.

I'm such a colossal idiot. Wasn't I supposed to be done making mistakes by now? I'm meant to be a full-fledged adult, not some hormonal mess who makes out with her landlord where anyone could walk by and see.

I need my head examined.

Then there's a knock on the door, and I'm scrambling to pull myself together once more.

SEVENTEEN
MIA

WHILE I PULL my pants on, I make a decision: I'm canceling Thanksgiving. I'll find some discount hotel somewhere and take Bailey out of town. Maybe I'll buy a tent and meet up with my parents wherever they are. Or I'll suck it up and meet with Colin.

Hurrying through my newly renovated home, I button my jeans just as I make it to the back door. The frosted glass tells me there are two people outside, but I don't immediately recognize them.

"Mia," Maude Thomas says when I open the door. "We're so sorry to come by unannounced, but we were in town and wanted to come say hello. Didn't we, Arthur?"

"I hope you don't mind us coming by unannounced!" Arthur says a little more loudly than necessary.

Covering my shock with a smile, I ask the elderly couple to come in.

"Oh, wow! Des told us he was doing some repairs in here,

but…" Maude does a slow circle, then clicks her tongue with a fond smile. "That grandson of mine is such a gem."

"He sure is," I answer, grimacing. "Coffee? Tea? Water? Please, have a seat." I put my arm around Arthur's to help him into a chair.

"Oh no, honey, we won't stay long." Maude pats my arm and smooths Arthur's hair on her way to her own seat.

The hard rock in my chest softens. I love the Thomases. They're such kind people. I would have been on the street if they hadn't offered me the shopfront with this apartment attached at such a low rent. They did me a favor and never even asked for more money in the decade I've lived here.

Really, I have no right to be angry at Des about a rent hike. They've been more than generous with me.

"What can I do for you?" I ask, getting a jug of cold water from the fridge and a few glasses, just to give myself time to calm my thumping heart.

Maude smiles when I pour her a glass. "Well, we heard you were going to spend the holiday with us! We had to come by and see you, of course!"

I freeze, the water in the jug sloshing slightly. "Oh. Right. Um…"

"Desmond is a good man," Arthur shouts at me, using his liver-spotted hand to pat mine. "We're happy he found you."

"He doesn't open up very easily, our grandson," Maude says fondly. "He's like his late father that way. Al was always on his own, keeping to himself. But out of the three kids, he was the one who felt the most deeply." She smiles sadly and touches her chest.

"We're so, so happy to know that Desmond has found someone who understands him."

Sliding into a chair, I try to hide the trembling in my hands by clasping them together. "Look, about Thanksgiving..." I hesitate.

These two are absolute sweethearts. They've been ripped off by their property manager for years. They're old and Arthur is in failing health. They basically gave me my life back when Bailey was born, allowing me to get on my feet and start a business.

It'll break their hearts if I cancel Thanksgiving.

"Don't worry about a thing," Maude says decisively, sipping her water. "Desmond told you about the race, I gather?"

I let out a surprised chuckle. A part of me still didn't believe about the three-legged race until this very moment. "He did," I say, "but—"

"It's just a bit of fun. I know he wants to beat Vince this year, but honestly, who wouldn't? With the way Vince struts around like a peacock with his feathers out, it's a wonder he hasn't been put in his place yet."

Another surprised laugh falls from my lips. "Right. Desmond mentioned that Vince and he had some sort of rivalry."

"Vince has been spoiled since the day he was born," Maude states, rolling her eyes. "I love my daughter Wendy, but she did that boy a disservice. Coddled him far too much, and now look."

"Does she know about the race?" Arthur shouts, leaning toward his wife.

Maude smiles at her husband, nodding. "Yes, darling."

"Good," Arthur says. He meets my gaze, his eyes clear and surprisingly fierce. "You win that race with Des this year, Mia. I'd like to see my grandson smile again."

"Hush," Maude says quietly. "You'll scare her away." She squeezes her husband's arm, then makes to get up. We both help Arthur out of his chair, and I walk them back to their car, which is parked outside the back door. Maude can still drive, but I know she doesn't drive at night.

I glance at the purple sky as I help Arthur into the passenger seat. "Would you like me to drive, Maude? It's getting dark out."

Maude straightens, then wraps me up in her arms with surprising force. "You're such a dear, Mia. I'm so, so pleased that you and Desmond are together. Yes, I'll let you drive us back. And Desmond will drive you home."

"No, that won't be necessary—"

Her phone is already at her ear. "Des, honey, it's me. Yes, yes, everything's fine. Mia is driving us home, so can you come by to pick her up and bring her back? Great. Yes, ten minutes is fine. Okay. You too, honey." She hangs up and beams at me. "Let's go!"

TEN MINUTES LATER, I'm lingering in their foyer when Maude returns from getting her husband settled in his armchair. She finds me looking at family pictures in the hallway. Hobbling over, Maude smiles at the photo I'm staring at and points to a young Des, probably twelve or thirteen years old and as brooding as ever. "You recognized him, of course."

"I'd know that solemn expression anywhere."

Maude laughs and pats my arm. "He's been smiling a lot more now that he's with you. Arthur and I have been wondering what's put him in such a good mood."

I frown. I've been experiencing Desmond in a *good* mood? And why does Maude think this has anything to do with me?

She tugs me over to an older photo. Two parents hold a child. They have huge, backcombed hair and sweaters that scream the early 1980s. The man is wearing humongous glasses to frame his dark eyes.

"Is that Des with his parents?"

Maude smiles sadly. "They loved him so much. Al and Lorelai loved each other more than any couple I've met before or since. Completely devoted to each other, and when Des came into the world, you could just sense the happiness pouring off of them." She touches the frame, letting out a soft huff. "My eldest grandson was such a happy baby. So giggly and always curious—and he turned into such a serious man." She drops her hand from the frame, shaking her head. "I wanted to take him in after Al and Lorelai left us, but we'd just moved to Heart's Cove, and Wendy—my daughter—had just married her husband Eric. He came from a family that claimed to be 'comfortable,' which really just means 'wealthy.' They had that big house on the mountain, and we thought it would be best if Des could stay at his same school with all his friends. We wanted to keep things as steady as possible for him, but sometimes I think…" She snorts and shakes her head. "Oh well. That's all in the past, now."

"How did they die?"

"Car accident. They hit a patch of black ice and ran into a tree. Killed instantly, which was supposed to be comforting, somehow, based on how everyone kept repeating it. Desmond was at school. I'll never forget the look on his face when I finally made it back to Lovers' Peak. He was just sitting on the sofa in Wendy's living room, staring at the rug, not moving. The grandson I knew was gone." She clicks her tongue and wipes her eyes. "No sense going over sad, old memories right now. You're here, and he obviously adores you."

My throat grows tight. This is too much. She's reading into our relationship and seeing things that aren't there.

But what if...

I think of his words in the parking lot. *Mia, I'm insanely, unbelievably attracted to you. I've wanted you since I first laid eyes on you. When you walk into a room, I can't fucking think straight.*

That sounds like lust to me. He doesn't actually *care* about me, does he?

I mean, besides the fact that he gave me a brand-new apartment. And that he cared about my daughter enough to buy her a small gift. They were only socks, but I have a feeling he would know how much they meant to her. Apart from not telling me that he was TallDarkandHandy, Des has been considerate, thoughtful, and caring.

I can even forgive him for raising the rent. As loath as I am to admit it, it was in line with the market. It was fair—and he was still willing to negotiate with me to make sure I wasn't out on the street. Maude and Arthur obviously have no idea about our deal— so he must be paying three months of my rent out of his own pocket.

My heart feels three sizes too big for my chest. I don't want to rely on him. I *can't*. I can't trust that a man will sweep into my life and make it better. What if he leaves? What if this is some passing fancy? What if this really is just about some stupid family tradition? He wants to win that three-legged race, and I happen to be a convenient woman in his new town.

But what if it's real? What if he cares? What if I could rely on him for support, for love?

Maude touches my cheek. "You've brought my grandson back to life, Mia, and I'll always be grateful."

Before I have time to think of a response, a car pulls up outside the house. Desmond is here to take me home.

"There he is," Maude says, smiling wide as she hurries to the door. She pulls it open and waves at her grandson with vigor, gripping my arm with her other hand. "There, there, Mia. You go with Des. Bye-bye now."

She shoves me off her porch and smiles from the doorway, urging me toward the car with little shooing motions. My mind is reeling. I don't know what to think.

Desmond exits the vehicle and walks around to the passenger side, opening the door for me. I risk a glance behind me to see Maude with her hands clutched at her breast, a dreamy expression on her face, and I know I can't possibly disappoint this sweet, old woman by refusing to go to Thanksgiving dinner with Des.

Even worse, I think I actually *want* to go.

EIGHTEEN
DES

THE ATMOSPHERE in the car is tense. I knead the steering wheel, glancing over at Mia while I scrounge around my empty brain for something to say.

She sits in the seat, eyes forward, hands clasped on her lap. I can barely tell if she's breathing.

"Mia..." Not knowing where my sentence is going, I let it trail off.

"You told your grandparents about me," she says, voice flat.

"Have you ever tried dodging my grandmother's questions?" I protest.

To my horror, Mia buries her face in her hands.

"Hey." I drive down Cove Boulevard and turn off on her block, heading for the back door. "Mia. You okay?"

"No."

I pull up outside her home and cut the engine. "You don't have to come to Thanksgiving with me. We can talk about your rent, find something that works for both of us. Hey..." I gently pull one of her hands away from her face, needing to see her expression.

It's bleak. She looks at me with wide, worried eyes, shaking her head. "I can't cancel Thanksgiving. It would kill them. Maude looked so *hopeful*. I can't do that to her."

It would kill me too.

She takes a deep breath. "Your grandmother thinks we're seriously dating, Des."

"I never told her that. I just said you'd agreed to come to Thanksgiving with me."

Her head falls back onto the headrest with a soft thump. "I can't believe I agreed to this."

"You don't have to come."

Her laugh is bitter. "I do, though."

"What do you mean?"

Those awful, desolate eyes stare at me, as if from a vast distance. "My ex-husband is coming to town. I told him I'd be away for Thanksgiving, because I'm the biggest coward that ever existed. So I actually need to go with you, because I can't afford to book a trip out of town for me and Bailey otherwise."

Her words send tension stealing through my body. She has so much on her plate. So much that she carries without even showing it. Her snark, her temper—that's just a defense mechanism. I've seen past it, and I want more. I want her to turn to me when she's worried, when she needs help.

The only place I've ever felt like I belong is beside Mia.

Unable to resist, I let my fingers coast along her hairline, tracing the shell over her ear. Whenever my skin is in contact with Mia's, it's like some incessant noise ringing in my ears goes quiet.

She shudders when my thumb coasts over her cheek. "I told you I'd do that silly race with you," she whispers. "So I will. But you have to stop touching me."

"Why?" I've leaned closer without noticing, my face just inches from hers.

"Because it muddles my mind too much," she whispers. "I can't think straight when you touch me."

"Maybe that's a good thing."

Her eyes open again, meeting my gaze. "What about after?"

My movements still. "After?"

"After Thanksgiving. After the race. After we come back. What then? What do we tell your grandparents?"

"Well..." There are rocks in my throat that make it hard to speak. I've been careful not to think about after. Mia's gaze is serious, and I think I know what she wants to hear. She wants assurances that this arrangement will end, that it won't come back to bite her. She wants to know that she and her daughter will be on solid footing, for once. So even though I don't want an after with Mia—because "after" sounds a lot like "ending"—I say what I think she wants to hear. "After, I can sell the two condos and find a decent property manager to take over your lease and Georgia's. My grandparents' finances will be in good shape. And I'll—I'll leave. I can tell them it didn't work out. Clean break."

"Clean break," she repeats. Mia's lips pinch, the corners turned down. She nods, pulling away from me. She looks at the screen on her phone. "I need to pick up Bailey from basketball."

"Okay. Can I see you again before we go? Maybe try that

dinner again? I can give you a run-down of what to expect with my family. We can get to know each other a bit…"

A deep inhale, and Mia shakes her head. "I don't think that's a good idea. I think we should go back to the rules and forget today ever happened. No kissing, no touching, no sex. This is a business arrangement."

I clear my throat and nod. "That's probably smart." Even though I hate it.

She puts her hand on the door latch, then pauses to look at me. "Are you really planning on leaving after you sell their properties?"

Her face is shadowed, her voice low. Every piece of me wants to haul her across the car and pick up right where we left off this afternoon. Make her mine. Make her realize that she doesn't have to carry the weight of the world on her own.

I tell her a partial truth: "I don't know. I hadn't thought that far."

She nods once. "Let's forget today ever happened," she repeats, then slips out of the car and disappears into her home.

NINETEEN
MIA

I'VE NEVER SEEN anyone laugh as hard as Simone when I finally tell the girls what's been going on in my life. Simone actually falls off the sofa where she'd been sitting and continues cackling on the floor. She leans her head against the couch, wheezing, and finally shakes her head. "Amazing."

I give her a flat look, which nearly sets her off again.

It's midafternoon on a cool November day, with gray light streaming through the big windows at the front of the library. We're above Four Cups, in the sanctuary that Wes created for Simone.

"I want to hear the part where you broke the chair and then had to have an emergency masturbation session again," Simone says, wiping her eyes. "Priceless."

"We were humping like feral cats. What else is there to say? I wasn't thinking straight."

She giggles, glancing at Fiona, who has tears in her eyes.

Candice kicks her feet up on the coffee table, braiding her hands on her stomach as she chuckles.

Meeting Georgia's gaze across the space, I shake my head. "My life was normal a couple of months ago. Then I met all of you."

"Your life was boring," Simone corrects. "We made it better."

My smile betrays me. They all know it's the truth.

Simone gasps, her eyes suddenly going wide. She plants her hands on the floor on either side of her hips, then whips her head around to look at Georgia. "You're going to see Piper in Lovers' Peak for Thanksgiving, right?"

Georgia nods. "Yeah. I have to drive her car over to her, and I want to see how she's settling in to her new job."

"Let's all go." Simone clambers up to her feet and claps her hands. "*Let's all go!*"

Fiona sits up straighter. Candice gets an interested gleam in her eyes. Georgia bites her lip.

"Could we?" Candice asks quietly. "Allie wants to spend the holiday with her boyfriend's family. They live near her college, and she said she has to prep for exams and can't make it back."

"There are a ton of rentals," Fiona notes, tapping on her phone. "Oh! Look. We could even rent both sides of a duplex. 'Sleeps twenty,' it says."

"My mother's on a cruise this year, so I'm free. We could go with Trina and the kids. All the men..." Candice looks at Simone, who's still bursting with excitement.

"Book the duplex," Simone shouts. "I'll look at flights. We'll need cars. How long? Two nights? Three? We could do Wednesday, Thursday, and Friday nights, and be back here for the weekend."

"There's some fancy light show the day after Thanksgiving," Fiona says, still looking at her phone. "The town is famous for it. At least two nights. We could do a potluck dinner for Thanksgiving, or something. Keep it simple."

"Jen's making pie," Candice notes. "She and Fallon can probably coordinate the food."

"Amazing," Simone says. "Potluck. Mountains. A light show. Mia having hot monkey sex. I love it. We're doing it."

I finally give in and start laughing. "Really? You guys are going to come to Colorado?"

"Girl. You obviously need a bunch of forty-something-year-old cheerleaders. It's like those elderly women from that town—"

"The Sun City Poms."

"YES!" Simone fist-pumps the air. "Let's get pompoms and stand outside the Thomas residence chanting Mia's name."

It's my turn to fall out of my chair. I laugh until my cheeks hurt, then shake my head as the women get on a phone tree and plan an impromptu Thanksgiving getaway for the whole gang.

Fiona catches my gaze and sends me a wink. "Worst case, if it's a disaster, you and Bailey can always come sleep at our place."

"Is this whole trip an excuse to provide me with an exit plan?" I ask.

"Hell no," Simone cuts in. "I want to see the fireworks, girlie. Chairs are breaking. Vibrators are buzzing. Deals are being made. I'd pay a premium for front row seats." She walks over and throws an arm around my shoulders. "Mia, honey, you're the best show in town."

"We wouldn't miss it for the world," Candice adds with a giggle.

"I wonder if we could get an invite to watch the race," Fiona muses.

"If we do, we're definitely bringing pompoms," Simone says, deathly serious.

Georgia cackles. "Is it too late to get matching T-shirts made?"

I'm suddenly laughing again, the weight of the past few weeks melting off my shoulders like the first snowflakes of winter hitting asphalt. My trip doesn't seem so daunting anymore. The deal I struck with Des—a fake date to Thanksgiving dinner in exchange for free rent—doesn't seem so ludicrous. So what if I kissed him? So what if I had to have an emergency masturbation session? So what if I'm kind of freaking out about him leaving afterward?

These women make me feel normal for wanting more than what I have. They make me feel part of something bigger than myself.

"I'm going to call Maude and casually mention that we're all going to be in town," Georgia says, pulling out her phone, "see if I can score us some spectator seats to the race, at least."

"Wait, do you think participation is on the table?" Simone straightens, intrigued. "I haven't done a three-legged race since I was a kid."

"Guys," I say with a laugh. "This is getting out of control. Plus, Des wants to win! I don't want to be competing against all of you. We're supposed to be sticking it to his cousin-brother-douche guy. I can't do that if we lose to Georgia and her hot, Texan, muscle-bound husband." I bite my lip, and finally laughingly admit: "And *I* want to win, damn it!"

"Too much of a height difference," Simone says, looking at me with a critical eye. "Des is what, like a foot and a half taller than you? Ain't gonna win with those little stumps of yours. You'll trip all over each other."

"Agreed," says Georgia. "No chance at the trophy."

"Hey!" I laugh, kicking my stumps up toward them both.

Simone shrugs as if to say, *What are you gonna do? I only speak the truth.* "Best you can do is sabotage Vince so at least he doesn't win. Which isn't a bad idea…"

We all start laughing again. Soon, though, a phone rings, and real life intrudes. It's time for me to go pick Bailey up and bring her to whatever after-school activity is on for today. I don't even know anymore; I can't keep track. I say goodbye to my girlfriends and pick up my regular routine right where I left off—except now, I have a smile on my face.

WHEN I TELL Bailey about the trip, she lights up. "We get to fly on an airplane?"

I nod. "Desmond is organizing the tickets."

"Cool."

We're sitting on the couch after dinner. Now that I've told her about the trip, I definitely can't back out.

"I knew you didn't hate him," Bailey says, kicking her legs up and down off the edge of the sofa. "And he likes you a *lot*."

"We're just friends," I say softly. "He needs a partner for a race."

Bailey sits up, then climbs onto her knees beside me. "A RACE? Can I do it? What's the prize?"

Laughing, I shrug. "Bragging rights, I think. They say there's a trophy. I'll ask him if you can participate, but I think it's just adults."

She hums, then gives me an assessing look. "Are you dating Des?"

"What? No!"

"It's okay, you know. Vicky Flanders's parents are divorced, and she has a stepdad now. She says he's nice and she gets more birthday presents than before."

I huff, curling an arm around Bailey's shoulders. "Is that what you want? More presents?"

"Yeah. More Golden State Warriors stuff." She giggles, poking my side.

Before I can stop myself, I pull away from my daughter to study her face and ask, "Have you ever wanted to have a stepdad?"

"Sometimes," Bailey answers. She's so matter of fact about it, so honest, completely oblivious that her answer sends an ice pick through my heart. "All my friends have dads. But I like when it's just us two. I guess..." My daughter leans back and braids her fingers over her stomach. The look on her face reminds me so much of Colin, it makes my heart ache. Then she nods once, sharply. "If he was nice to you and me, a stepdad would be good. He could help with chores and fix stuff that's broken in our house, like Des did."

That makes me laugh. Clearly Bailey and I have the same priorities when it comes to the benefits of having a man around.

"Go brush your teeth," I tell her past the lump in my throat. "It's almost bedtime."

My nine-year-old grumbles but heads to the bathroom to start her evening routine. I stare after her, motionless, feeling raw.

I GET the news later that evening: Georgia secured an invite from Maude. They're coming to Thanksgiving at the Thomases' place—every single one of them. There's Georgia and Sebastian; Fiona and Grant (his daughter Clancy is away at college too, begging off to study for midterms); Simone and Wes; Candice and Blake; Trina, Mac, and her two kids, Toby and Katie; Jen and Fallon; Lily, Rudy, and baby Liam; and finally, Nora and Lee. Who in their right mind invites nineteen extra people to Thanksgiving on short notice? When I ask, Georgia informs me the dinner is catered, and the extra people are no problem for the Thomases.

That begs the question: What in the world am I walking into?

Whatever it is, it's happening. And a couple of weeks later, the gang heads off on various flights and cars, making their way to Colorado by any means necessary. After a one-hour flight from the nearest regional airport to San Francisco, I end up standing at our connecting gate with Des and Bailey, our little carry-on suitcases beside us. We're at our quick stopover on our way to Denver...watching the flight take off outside the big windows.

Crap.

Bailey watches the plane taxi away from us, then glances up at me. "What do we do now, Mom?"

I blow out a breath and glance at Des.

Since our conversation in the car, we haven't really spoken. He came in for two shaves since then, but all my barber's chairs remained intact and I've kept my hands to myself. It seems we'll be sticking to the original rules, with no more hanky-panky happening.

Fine by me. Absolutely, totally fine. I promise. That's not disappointment in my gut; it's just nerves.

Right now, Des smiles at my daughter. "Now, we go talk to the airline and see if we can get another flight."

"Won't that be expensive?" Bailey asks, a wrinkle appearing between her brows.

Not for the first time, I cringe. How much has my daughter picked up on about money? How many times has she been worried when she shouldn't be? I'm supposed to shield her from all this. She's just a child.

Des just smiles. "Maybe. But I always budget a little extra when I'm traveling, in case something goes wrong. And I got travel insurance, so you don't have to worry."

Bailey brightens. "Oh. Okay. That's good." She nods, and to my shock—and Des's, judging by the thunderstruck expression on his face—she slips her hand in his. "Who do we talk to?" she asks, glancing around the gate.

"Let's start with the lady at the counter," Des says, holding my daughter's hand very, very carefully. I let them walk ahead, heart banging at the sight of my daughter with this big, surprisingly gentle man.

I...I *like* the sight of them together. I like the way Bailey leans against his side when she pokes her head above the airport gate's counter. I like the way Des starts laughing and ruffles her hair. Bailey grins back at him, then glances over her shoulder at me. She waves me over, and I hurry to their side.

"The next flight is in three hours," the woman says, batting her long lashes at Des. Painted red lips tilt into a smile. "I can bump you up to business class for the inconvenience."

Jeez. Being a devastatingly attractive man has its perks, apparently.

"That would be great," Des's deep voice rumbles. He smiles back at the woman, and I feel the urge to hop on the desk and kick them both in the face.

That can't be healthy. I pretend to study my nails until the feeling passes.

We get our new boarding passes and find empty seats at an unused gate. Bailey pulls out a deck of cards and challenges Des to a game of Go Fish.

"What do you call a fish with no eyes?" she says, picking up a card and staring at her hand.

"I don't know," Des replies, frowning at his cards.

"A *fshhhh*," Bailey says, then giggles. Des's warm chuckle makes my heart expand until it crowds out my lungs and breathing becomes difficult.

"I'm going to get us some snacks," I say, needing some space. When I come back, having been extorted by a friendly old man running an airport kiosk, I find the two of them locked in the most intense game of Go Fish I've ever seen.

Bailey wins, and she throws her hands in the air with a loud cheer. Des tosses his cards onto the pile and clicks his tongue, shaking his head. "Unbelievable." He meets my gaze with sparkling, laughing eyes. His arm curls around the back of my chair as we settle in to wait a little longer, and Bailey comes to my other side to rest her head against my shoulder.

Contentment settles over me like a warm blanket. We hit a snag on our travel plans, and it didn't even seem to ruffle Des in the slightest. Things that would have been stressful and difficult with just me and Bailey are suddenly no problem at all. Des took care of it all.

I could get used to this...and that's dangerous.

TWENTY

DES

HAVING Mia and Bailey beside me on the way to Lovers' Peak has allowed me to avoid the big, messy feelings lurking under the surface of my skin at the thought of returning to my childhood home. It's only been a few months since I left the small mountain town, but it already feels like a lifetime has passed. I'm a different person now.

As our rental car crosses the stylized sign depicting the double-peaked mountain that gave the town its name, my heart starts to beat faster.

I never belonged here. From the time my parents passed until the time I decided to leave, I was an outsider. As we enter the town, dusk is darkening to night, and the streetlights illuminate the quaint shopfronts and bare trees. I tighten my hold on the steering wheel, letting out a long breath.

"Everything okay?" Mia asks quietly from the seat beside mine.

A quick glance in the rearview mirror tells me Bailey's asleep in the back seat. I nod. "I'm fine. It's just that I'm realizing this place never really felt like home, even though I spent my entire life here."

"We're staying at your aunt's place, right?"

I dip my chin. "Yeah. It's the only place big enough to host the whole family."

Taking a turn off the main road that leads up the side of the mountain slope feels surreal. I've driven on this road thousands of times. Every house is familiar; every crack in the pavement is etched into my memory. Small changes ping my eyes, like a new paint color on an old house, or a "For Sale" sign staked into a front yard.

The farther we drive through the winding streets, the more space appears between the houses. Pine trees shoot up from the ground between the estates, interspersed with the skeletons of their deciduous brothers. Soon, this place will be a winter wonderland. It'll be blanketed in perfect, flawless white, and the air will be crisp and pure.

But the memories remain beneath it all.

We turn onto the long, winding driveway leading to my adolescent home. Mia inhales sharply when we make the final turn and see the house nestled in amongst the trees. The black shingles on the roof and the planks of siding are weathered, letting the whole place melt into its surroundings as much as a mansion can. Cheerful yellow light spills from the many windows, with strings of fairy lights illuminating the massive second-story porch that opens out from the big kitchen and dining areas.

I park the car on the garage level below, off to the side beside one of the support posts for the porch. Bailey stirs in the back seat, and Mia climbs out of the car to help her daughter. It takes me a moment to gather myself, to gird my proverbial loins before entering the building that houses so many memories—not many of them good.

I still feel like an outsider. Always have.

Grabbing two bags out of the trunk, I lead Mia and Bailey up the steps to the front door. There's a stepped front garden that's been stripped bare for winter, mulch and bare trees waiting to be covered with snow. With every step I ascend, my heartbeat speeds up.

"This place is huge," Bailey whispers. "Is this just one house?"

"Yes," Mia answers back in the same hushed tone. "Look up there. You can just see the top of the mountain."

"There's snow on it!"

"The snow probably never melts, even in the middle of summer."

"Really?" Bailey's voice is louder now, more confident.

I smile and glance back at them. "Really," I confirm. "Sometimes, in the summer, the sunset hits the snow and turns it all kinds of colors like pink and purple. Most years there'd be snow on the ground everywhere by now, but it's been a warm fall."

"Whoa." Bailey glances at the shadow of the mountain, eyes wide.

We make it to the front door, and I deposit our small suitcases beside me so I can ring the doorbell. It's one of those grandiose, multi-tonal chimes that seems to come from different areas of the house at once. I've always hated it.

The tall, oversized timber door has a window of cut glass in the center. A distorted image of a dark-haired woman approaches, and tension seizes me until a hand appears on my forearm—Mia's. She smiles at me and sends me a sly wink, then turns to the opening door.

My sister-in-law Caitlyn appears in the opening, giving us a broad, false smile. "Des!" She steps onto the welcome mat to hug me while I stand stiff as a board. She turns to Mia and gives her an assessing stare. "And you're his date. You know, Des has never brought a date to Thanksgiving. Well, not since high school." She smiles, but it's a little cold. "Everyone is *very* curious about you."

Mia gulps.

"Caitlyn, this is Mia. Mia, Caitlyn. And the scruffy little munchkin is Bailey."

"Hey!" Bailey protests, planting her hands on her hips in the exact same way Mia does.

I laugh, the tension in my muscles dissolving. Caitlyn gives me a strange, startled look, then ushers us inside. My aunt Wendy comes gliding down the wide hallway, arms spread. She greets us in a flutter of blue silk, diamond earrings dangling from her ears. Next is her husband, my uncle Eric. His white hair is combed back, his belly protruding slightly past his belt buckle. He's wearing his usual golf shirt and tan slacks.

My other aunt and uncle, Henrietta and Reggie, come next, followed by second cousins (or is it first cousins once removed?), family friends, and strays that have found their way to this place for the holiday. Hugs, kisses, and greetings are exchanged. I hear my grandmother's voice from the living room as she yells at my grandfather that we've arrived. Mia looks beautiful and flushed and overwhelmed. Bailey is quieter than usual, clinging to her mother's side.

Then the children come to investigate. A veritable stampede of nieces and nephews come tearing down the hallway, staring at Bailey curiously.

My nephew, Mav (short for Maverick, because my cousin Lyle is a big *Top Gun* fan and his wife Olivia apparently gave him naming), approaches Bailey. "You don't dress like a girl," he accuses.

Bailey frowns. "I'm a girl, and I dress like me. So that means I dress like a girl."

Everyone—adults and children alike—seems to pause and consider her words. Mav is the first one to react. He nods. "That's true. You want to play video games?"

Bailey glances at her mother, who smiles. "Go ahead, Bailey."

"Let me show you to your room," Wendy says with a smile. "Lyle, help with the bags!"

"I've got it," Caitlyn says, grabbing the carry-on suitcase from Mia's hand. She smiles. "We put you two in the craft room." She means my old bedroom, but Wendy didn't waste any time converting it to her craft room after I moved out.

Mia starts, and glances at me with a panicked expression on her face.

That's when I realized we never discussed sleeping arrangements. After our interlude on the barber's chair—and the conversation that followed in the car—the two of us have mostly avoided each other.

"I was planning on sleeping with Bailey," Mia says lightly. "She gets nervous when we're away from home."

"We put Bailey with the rest of the kids," Wendy says, sweeping down the hallway. We turn toward the big rec room at the back left corner of the house, which has been filled with bunk beds like some kind of kid-themed army barracks. Bailey's laughter echoes from the next room, and Wendy arches an eyebrow. "See? I'm sure she'll be fine."

While Mia glances at the room and I try to figure out how to salvage this sleeping situation, Bailey, Mav, General, and Hunt (Lyle and Olivia had three boys, which Lyle named) come tearing into the room.

"This is your bed!" Mav cries, jumping onto a Ninja Turtles bedspread. "We thought you would hate it because you're a girl, but all the pink beds were already taken."

"I have a Ninja Turtles shirt at home!" Bailey says, hopping onto the bed and bouncing. Her smile is bright and undeniable. She meets her mother's worried gaze and spreads her hand on the comforter. "Can I get one of these for my bed at home, Mom?"

"We'll see," Mia replies, her smile tight and tense.

"There." Wendy claps her hands. "Bailey is all settled. Let's show you to your room."

My childhood bedroom was in the basement, accessible through the garage. It was always dank and dark, but as we enter the space, I see Wendy and Eric finally got around to those improvements they'd always promised me. The walls are no longer bare concrete but insulated and covered with smooth drywall painted a soft gray color. There's a double bed pushed against the corner, and piles of craft supplies and Tupperware boxes all along one wall.

"This is my craft room, but we set the bed up especially for you," Wendy explains. "Des used to sleep here when he stayed with us."

Not when I lived here, from the time I was eleven till I was eighteen. When I "stayed with" them.

"Des always loved his own personal cave," Caitlyn says, laughing. "I snuck in here once or twice. Do you remember, Des?"

Mia frowns, eyes flicking between the two of us.

I blink. "I remember. Thanks, Wendy. We'll get settled and meet you upstairs."

"Okay," Wendy singsongs. "Holler if you need anything."

The two women sweep out of the room. Caitlyn grabs the doorknob and gives Mia a long glance before softly closing the door behind her.

We stand in silence for a few seconds while their footsteps fade, then Mia rounds on me. "You are delusional if you think we're going to be sharing a bed, Desmond."

I SHOULD HAVE STOOD my ground and asked for six months' free rent.

I have three nights of this. Three nights in this tiny room, where Des seems to suck out all the air. We haven't been alone since I got out of his car a couple of weeks ago. I don't like it. Not one bit.

"I'll sleep on the floor," Des says, placating.

"You're damn right you will," I spit, my temper whipping up a storm inside me. "If this is some ploy to get me to have sex with you, Des, you're out of your mind."

"It's not," he says, and I want to believe him. I do. But I'm also overwhelmed, I don't remember anyone's name, and the look on Caitlyn's face when she left the room keeps popping up in my mind. I plant my hands on my hips, which seems to amuse Des for some reason. And that makes me angrier. "What's up with your sister-in-law? What was with that comment about sneaking into your room? Why is she giving me all those weird looks?"

Des rubs the back of his neck, not meeting my gaze. "We kind of...dated...in high school."

I rock back on my hips, stumbling until my butt connects with a tower of plastic Tupperware containers. "You *what*? Is *that* why you wanted a date? It's not about the stupid race at all, is it?"

"No," Des says, stepping toward me. He pauses, putting his hands up. "No, it has nothing to do with her. I promise. Other than the fact that she and Vince keep winning the trophy."

Oh. My. God. Vince married Des's high school sweetheart. No wonder Des is so bitter—and no wonder he didn't want to show up here alone.

I *definitely* should have asked for six months. This is messed up. And this room! I peeked into some of the other bedrooms, and it looks like Wendy kept her sons' rooms just as they were growing up but evidently wasted no time converting Des's to her own craft room. Is that a subtle dig to let him know he never really belonged here? There are way too many undercurrents for me to understand. I feel like Indiana Jones being dropped in a pit of snakes.

"Hey." Des approaches, his hands coasting down my arms. "Do you want to leave? I'll book the next flight. I'll get us a hotel."

All the fight in me disappears. The dragon didn't even get to make an appearance. Awareness of Des enters my body, making every skin cell extra sensitive as his hands tangle with mine. This man would drop everything to make me feel better. I don't know if I've ever experienced that before. I don't know that anyone has ever put me first. It's overwhelming.

"No touching," I whisper.

He drops my hands but doesn't move back. The warmth of his body soaks into my front, comforting, safe. I could lose myself in him, allow myself to love this man the way I loved Colin. I'd give myself to him completely, open every door and window to the vulnerable inner core of me, and it would break me into a million pieces when he inevitably walked away.

Des has already told me he'll leave when this is over. I'd be a fool not to believe him.

WHEN WE RE-EMERGE UPSTAIRS, I finally get to meet Vince. On first sight, he reminds me of Sebastian Finch, Georgia's husband. He has the same golden-brown hair and blue eyes, tanned skin, and a perfect, white smile. But as soon as he opens his mouth, I can already tell he's nothing like our Texan implant.

"Look who finally found someone who could put up with him!" Vince calls out, slapping Des's back a little too hard. Then he turns his icy-blue eyes to me, and I realize on closer inspection that they're not like Sebastian's eyes at all. There's something cold in Vince's gaze. "And you're the lucky lady," he grins. "How much is he paying you to be here, and are you free for Christmas? I might need a date." He leers, dropping his gaze to my breasts.

I stiffen. Des curls his arm around my shoulders and pulls me back, facing Vince with murder in his eyes.

"Boys! Dinner!" Wendy calls out, then frowns. "Desmond, why are you looking at your brother like that? Honestly, you haven't changed a bit. Be *nice*, for once. Vince has been looking forward to seeing you for weeks."

Vince gives us a victorious smile. "Yeah. Be nice, Des." Then he turns, gives his mother a kiss on the cheeks, and saunters toward the kitchen.

Des, with his arm still around my shoulders, meets my gaze. "Are you okay? I'm sorry about that."

I narrow my gaze and turn to watch Vince disappear around the corner. "We're winning that fucking trophy, Des. I don't care if we have to cheat our way to a victory."

A surprised laugh tumbles from his lips. He squeezes me close, and for a moment, I think he's going to kiss me. But he drops his arm and jerks his head to the kitchen, where food and company await.

Tonight, dinner is buffet-style and fairly light in preparation for the massive amounts of food we'll eat tomorrow. I find myself sitting between Des's aunt Henrietta and his adoptive brother David, who both end up being lovely dinner companions. David is recently single and tells me he's looking forward to finally getting his chance as Maude's race partner.

"Des has had the privilege too long, hasn't he, Grandma?"

Maude, sitting diagonally across from us, smiles at her grandson. "I was supposed to retire from the race this year." She winks at me. "But once more won't hurt."

I find myself almost enjoying the evening, so long as I stay on the opposite side of the room from Vince and Caitlyn. Tomorrow, I'm going to wipe that smug grin off his face. I came here to hold up my end of the bargain, but after the way Vince spoke to me, the subtle jabs I've seen everyone level at Des...

This is personal. Now, I want to win for my own pride.

Later, when Des is constructing his makeshift bed on the floor and I'm fluffing my pillows, I tell him as much. He plops down on the floor and curls his thick arms behind his head, studying me. "I knew you'd be a good race partner. You're too stubborn and competitive to let me down."

"We're winning," I state, flopping back on the bed. "End of story. Goodnight."

His warm chuckle curls around me, warming me from the inside out.

MY LEGS ARE STUCK in sticky black tar. My voice is hoarse. My baby is gone, and I can't get to her. The terror that grips me is like no other, chilling me down to the marrow of my bones, making panic grip my throat with icy fingers. I fall, my hands sinking into the inky muck, and I'm trapped—

"Mia." Des shakes me awake, his body a looming shadow against the darkness of our room. "Mia, wake up. It's a dream. It's not real."

I sit up, panting, unable to speak. I close my lids and rub the heels of my hands into my eye sockets, trying to get enough oxygen. "I have to check on Bailey," I say. "I have to make sure she's okay."

Expecting Des to try to dissuade me and tell me I'm being ridiculous, I brace myself—but he just says, "I'll come with you."

With my top (a new, matching set of button-down navy jammies with white piping, *thankyouverymuch*) clinging to my damp back, I finger-comb my hair away from my face and follow Des through the garage, up the stairs, and down the long hallway to the back of the house.

I crack the kids' door open and see Bailey in bed, her eyes closed. Creeping in, I kneel next to her bunk and put my hand on her shoulder, only calming down when I feel her breathing steadily. I rest my head on the edge of the bed, throat tight, exhausted.

A large hand coasts down my back. Des rubs gently, lending me his strength, until I can stand on shaking legs and head back to our room. Shadows climb up the walls and fall across our path. Strange noises echo in the house. I'm jittery and unbalanced, and the only thing tethering me to sanity is Desmond's warm hand wrapped around mine.

When we're back in our room, I sit on the edge of the bed and let out a long breath. "You must think I'm ridiculous."

The bed dips as he sits next to me. "Not even a little bit."

I curl my fingers into the edge of the mattress, squeezing my eyes shut. The last tendrils of fear still tease through my body, remnants of a recurring nightmare I thought I'd left behind years ago. Warmth soaks my side as Des shifts closer, his arm curling around my waist. Gently, he urges me to lie back on the bed, flicking the covers over us both. I lie on my side with my back to him, lulled by the movement of his hands up and down my spine, down my arms, over my sides, and up into my hairline. He strokes my body until I have no choice but to relax. It isn't sexual, but it's intimate in a way I didn't realize I needed.

"I used to have that dream all the time," I admit when my heartbeat is back down to normal.

"When Bailey was little?"

"Mm. I felt like I was losing my mind. I loved her so much,

but I was terrified that I'd mess up, that I wouldn't be able to care for her the way she deserves."

His hand pauses on my back, then keeps stroking. "Well, you've done a fantastic job."

I glance over my shoulder, meeting his gaze. "You really think so?"

A soft smile tugs at his lips. "I really do."

I turn back to stare at the wall, the movement of his hand on my back lulling me closer to sleep. "She likes you, you know," I tell him. "She'll be sad when you leave. I probably shouldn't have done this, brought her here. She'll be confused."

"She's a great kid," Des replies. His strokes are soft, soothing, until I let out a long breath and finally relax. The bed shifts, and I feel him sit up behind me.

Before I can stop myself, I say, "Stay."

He freezes.

I glance over my shoulder, seeing nothing but the shape of him in the dark. "The floor can't be comfortable. You won't get a wink of sleep, and you need your energy for the race."

Yes—the race. That's why I want him to lie in bed beside me.

His shadowy form watches me for a long moment, then he slowly, tentatively, lies back on the pillows beside me. There are a few inches of space between us. I keep facing away from him, and I can tell he's on his back with his hands curled behind his head, staring at the ceiling.

I want him to touch me the way he did before, soothing and tender. And in the darkness of our bedroom, I can admit that I'd like him to touch me in other ways too.

But neither of us move, and after a while, I drift to sleep.

TWENTY-TWO
SIMONE

I. LOVE. This. Town.

It's the cutest thing I've ever seen. Georgia was right when she compared it to Seuss's Whoville. Lots of houses are painted bright colors, there are cute little shops selling all manner of unique and handmade goods, and the locals make sure to always say hello when they pass you on the street.

All nineteen of us arrived and checked into the duplex we rented last night. The hosts left us a case of wine and a list of things to do in town, highlighting the light show happening on Friday evening.

Now, we're out for breakfast at one of the diners with stellar reviews tucked just off the main drag on Thanksgiving morning.

I order eggs, bacon, and hash browns, and because I love my husband, I let him steal a piece of bacon from my plate. Truly, I don't recognize myself anymore, because it doesn't even bother me. Glancing out the windows at the cute, curlicued lamp-posts and the bare trees, I lean into Wes's side and sigh. "I bet this place is amazing in the winter. We should come skiing."

"You hate the cold," he reminds me.

"You could come skiing," I amend, "and I'll stay in the lodge drinking hot cocoa and mulled wine. Hey, Georgia, how's Piper's job going? When can we see the ski resort she's designing?"

Georgia sets her coffee cup down and smiles. "You can ask her yourself."

"Hello, hello!" Piper comes blowing through the door, two boys in tow. Nate and Alec hop around her like jumping beans, calling out what they want for breakfast.

When the three of them are settled at a nearby table, I lean over. "How are you doing, Piper? How's work?"

Her gaze darkens. "I don't want to talk about it."

I arch a brow. "That bad, huh?"

"Worse."

"You going to quit?"

Her brows tug together so close, there's nary a millimeter between them. "Hell. No. My boss can fire me himself if he wants to get rid of me."

"Atta girl," I laugh. Grinning, I turn back to my plate and see the rest of my bacon gone. "Hey!"

Wes chomps on the crispy goodness, not even a little bit sorry. He's lucky I love him so much.

LATER, when we've fueled up for the race with a big breakfast and lots of coffee, we make our way to the address Maude gave us.

What appears around the last bend of pine trees is a mansion of epic proportions. It gives my own forest fairy tale castle in Heart's Cove a run for its money.

"Welcome!" Maude says from the porch above. "Come around the back. We're setting up the race!"

We follow her directions, mounting steps at the side of the house, and make it to a vast backyard ringed with trees on two sides and a pond (it might qualify as a lake?) on the third. The porch wraps around the whole house, level with the ground behind the house. Maude hobbles over to us and greets us with shining eyes and a bright smile.

A table, decorated with an autumnal cloth runner, carries snacks and countless glasses of wine, juice, water, and coffee. Through the windows, I can see caterers hard at work prepping Thanksgiving dinner.

"Darling Georgia! Sebastian!" Maude kisses the two of them, gripping their arms to drag them into the mess of people on the lawn. "Everyone! Meet the woman with the art gallery! This is the one I was telling you about. She rented the old antiques store space and made it something special."

I smile and am soon accosted by another woman—Wendy— who greets me with polite courtesy and gets us all settled with drinks and more food. Gentle music plays from speakers, and I spy Mia across the lawn, kneeling in front of Bailey.

There are heat lamps dotted over the patio to keep the place warm, and waiters milling around offer drinks and nibbles to all the guests. Tables and chairs line either side of the grass, where the racetrack is currently being set up. To the right of the lawn, the pond/lake is still as glass. A naked woman made of marble rises up in the middle of it, her arms stretched above her head where water would probably spray if the fountain were turned on.

"Can we get a lake and a fountain for our place?" I ask Wes.

He arches a brow.

I jerk my head at the nude statue in the middle of the body of water. "I want one."

Wes's face cracks into a grin. "We'll see."

"This is intense," Fiona says as she stops beside me, a glass of water in her hands. "My family's Thanksgivings were nothing like this."

"Look at Des." I point across the lawn, to where the man is staring at Mia like she hung the moon and all the stars.

"Oh, my word. He's got it bad."

"A BOUNCY CASTLE!" Nate comes tearing over the lawn, sprinting toward the turkey-shaped inflatable bouncy castle. (Is it still called a castle if it's shaped like a fowl?) Alec isn't far behind his brother. Piper hobbles after them, purse hanging off her elbow, calling out at her sons to make sure to take off their shoes.

At the far end of the lawn, a group of men are animatedly painting a white line on the lawn. Stakes are set on either side, and a ribbon is strung between them. That must be the finish line. On the far banister of the wraparound porch, strips of fabric flutter in the slight breeze. Maybe what we'll use to tie our legs together?

The racetrack is being paced, measured, and triple-checked by a lot of serious-looking adults while kids rush around and more adults chatter, anticipation thick in the air.

Our own group infiltrates the gathering, making small talk, discussing race strategies, admiring the crisp, not-too-cold weather.

It's chaos. I love it.

When someone rings a gong—a literal gong—the whole crowd of people quiets down in an instant.

A man who looks a little like Seb walks out carrying a trophy. It's gold, gleaming in the weak fall sunlight, with a multi-tiered platform base, tiny etched writing on each level. Past winners, I assume. The top of the trophy is...a golden egg?

"What in the world?" Candice whispers.

"Is that an egg?" Fallon asks, and Jen replies, "Yup."

"This is nuttier than I expected," Nora says, "and that's saying a lot."

"It's amazing," I correct her.

"This race started as an egg-and-spoon race about fifty years ago," a woman tells me, smiling. "My great-grandmother was *very* competitive." She sticks out her hand. "Olivia."

"Simone." I grin. "I think she succeeded in passing down that particular gene to the rest of the clan. I can smell the fight in the air."

Olivia laughs, nodding.

"Will the children please step up to the starting line," the Seb look-alike calls out. "It's time for the junior race."

Bailey sprints toward the starting line near the porch, a little boy beside her. She's giggling, sticking her leg out to line it up with her partner's. Nate and Alec pair up together. Toby gets paired with a fierce-looking girl, while Katie decides to sit the race out, sitting down on a chair with her pretty dress perfectly arranged. Her mother's daughter, evidently.

The ribbons on the porch banister are ceremoniously removed and tied around each team's ankles.

Mia comes jogging beside us, smiling, and gives me a hug. "Thank you for coming. Seeing you all arrive...you have no idea how comforting it is to see a familiar face."

"Girl, you couldn't pay me to leave," I say. Then, louder, I yell, "Go Bailey!"

Wes sticks his fingers in his mouth and whistles.

"Toby! Woohoo!" Trina calls out. Mac makes her screech as he hauls her up onto his shoulders so she can see more clearly, the two of them laughing.

I lean against the banister, Wes pressed behind me with his arms on either side of mine, gripping the railing, and I hold my breath. Movement near the porch stairs to my left draws my eye. It's Maude, being presented a laptop. A man—her grandson, maybe—points to the spacebar and holds the laptop in front of her.

"Ready!" the Seb look-alike calls out.

Silence descends. The kids arrange themselves on the starting line, serious expressions on their faces. For some reason, I start to hold my breath. The tension mounts—

And Maude presses the spacebar. The sound of a gunshot echoes from the speakers, and the kids take off.

Nate and Alec immediately fall down, screaming. Two other kids, a boy and a girl I don't know, are the next to go, crying out in despair as they hit the grass. I shift my gaze to the frontrunners.

Two little boys are neck-and-neck with Bailey and her partner. As Toby falls behind, all of us start cheering for our last horse in the race. Bailey looks determined, her blond hair streaming behind her like a golden mane. We scream, and stomp, and cheer, urging her on faster and faster and faster. Mia stands on the bottom rung of the banister, screeching her daughter's name as her voice cracks. Des's booming voice echoes around the mountains.

Birds flap and cry as they fly from the surrounding trees in a mad panic to get away from the crazy humans.

I start hysterically laughing. I can't help it. Tears and snot run down my face as Wes's arms close around me, his whole body shaking behind me.

"Bailey! Bailey! Bailey!" I scream between laughs.

The Thomas clan is rushing on either side of the racetrack, following the race. At the finish line, one of the grandsons is holding a stopwatch in front of him, every bit of his attention on the finish line. There's a tripod with a camera on the other side for an official instant replay. Ridiculous. Amazing.

From my angle, it's hard to tell who's in the lead between the two teams—until the finish line's ribbon comes away around Bailey's chest. She screams, arms up, and turns to hug her race partner as they jump up and down in jubilation, ankles still bound together.

Our crew on the porch is about to break through the planks of wood below us. It's pandemonium. I've never heard a group of soon-to-be fifty-year-olds cheer so loudly before. Bailey turns toward us and meets her mother's gaze.

Mia is there, sticking her hands out with thumbs-up toward her daughter, pride shining in her eyes. She glances at Des, who curls an arm around her shoulders. Cute.

Wes holds me close, his dimples in full view as he grins at me. "You think we can win that trophy, Simone?"

"I'll die trying," I vow, giggling.

TWENTY-THREE
MIA

MY ANKLE IS SECURED to Des's. Our sides are pressed together, and he loops his arm over my shoulders. I glance down, noticing that my knee hits him somewhere just above mid-shin, well below the level of his own joint.

Georgia was right. We're going to trip over each other. The height difference is too much.

"Ready to lose?" Vince says from the other side of me, his gaze crossing above my head to meet Des's. Ever since he asked me to be his escort to Christmas, he's ignored me entirely.

I hate this guy.

My temper rises up, a silent volcano erupting under the surface of my skin. Des evidently senses it, because his hold on my shoulders tightens. Gritting my teeth, I hook my arm around his hips and grab onto the waistband of his pants. He's stripped his jacket off and is only wearing a white tee. He should have goosebumps, but the man's body temperature must run a few degrees warmer than normal.

"Let's just see what happens, shall we?" Des grates.

"You're on," Vince replies, eyes hard.

We're standing on the far-right side of the starting line, the grassy racetrack stretching in front of us. It's been cleared of stray leaves and shorn to an inch in height, with a gentle upward incline on the way to the finish line. To our right, the ground falls away slightly into the huge pond.

"Four in a row, eh, babe?" Vince croons to his wife.

Caitlyn smiles, then glances at the two of us. "Good luck, you two." She meets my gaze. "I was nervous my first time, standing right there where you are. But don't worry, Des will take care of you."

Another not-so-subtle reminder that she had Des before I did. Too bad for her, I graduated high school twenty-two years ago, and I'm done reliving those particular glory days. She picked the wrong brother. I set my jaw and turn my head forward. There's only one thing I can do to wipe that smug smile off of Vince and Caitlyn's faces, and that's win this stupid race.

Listen to me. I've lost my mind.

I think I burned away the last remnants of my reason overnight. I woke up snuggled against Des's side, my head on his chest, my arm curled over his opposite shoulder. I had one leg hooked over both of his, and he had his arm holding me close to him.

I can't even blame him for it. All the evidence points to *me* snuggling up to *him* in my sleep—and since then, I feel like I've been living in a dream world. It's like I've given myself permission to let go of my fears and inhibitions, if only for this holiday. We'll be home by Saturday night, and who knows what state my mind will be in by then. It's better not to think about it.

This three-legged race is all that matters right now. I want Des to smile. I want him to feel good. I want to show him that he can win with me at his side. We're a team, no matter what happens.

But we're not going to lose. No freaking way.

I narrow my gaze, staring at the fluttering ribbon at the finish line. I've always looked like a wiener dog when I run, with my little legs pumping like crazy, but I'm going to be the fasted freaking wiener dog this town has ever seen.

"Ready!" Arthur calls from his throne on the back porch. "Maude, are you ready?" He glances at the far left of the starting line, where Maude and David are strapped together. David looks completely relaxed, his arm around his grandma like he's going for a stroll. Maude looks like she actually wants to win.

I steal a glance at all my friends, lined up between the Thomases, in various stages of giddiness and competitiveness. A deep breath fills my lungs. This is it. This is how I show Des that he's worth a thousand Vinces. This is how I earn my three months of free rent. This is what this weekend is all about.

The sound of a gunshot echoes, more birds go flying from the trees, and we take off.

Des's steps are huge. He hauls me along beside him with an arm around the waist while I try to keep up as best I can. Vince lets out a long shout beside me. He and Caitlyn have obviously practiced. Their arms are linked around their backs and their steps are in sync.

They're good. The jerks.

Needing a burst of adrenaline, I let out a scream and redouble my efforts. Des tightens his hold on my waist, and we stay level with Vince and Caitlyn. We're in with a chance.

Hobble, hop, run. We make our way up the lawn in a cacophony of shouts and cheers. I hear Simone's cackling laughter somewhere behind us. Sebastian yells, "C'mon, Sweet Peach! Hurry up, girl!"

"I'm not a fucking horse, Seb," Georgia screams back. "Stop slapping my ass!"

A team falls to the ground in my peripheral vision in a heap of limbs and laughter. I can't think about who it is right now. All I see is that white ribbon swaying in the gentle breeze. The finish line, calling to us.

"That's it, Mia," Des pants beside me. "We're nearly there. We can beat them."

"Yeah," I huff, trying to match his stride. Why does he have to have such long legs?

Then, like magic, we sync up. He shortens his stride; I lengthen mine. Suddenly, running is easy. Our three legs move like they're part of the same body. Our arms clamp around each other, and the air flows sweetly in and out of my lungs.

We can do this. *We're going to win.*

We gain half a step on Vince and Caitlyn. They speed up, gain half a step on us. I grit my teeth, grunting, and get my little Dachshund legs to go faster. We gain our lead back.

"To the left," Des says between breaths. "Move left."

I see what he means. We're being edged to the right, but we need to angle left if we're going to finish between the stakes and win the race. Otherwise, we'll be off the course entirely. With my muscles screaming and my lungs burning, I follow his lead and angle left—which takes us directly into Vince and Caitlyn's path.

They say when you have a near-death experience, your whole life flashes before your eyes. When Vince shoves my shoulder with surprising strength, the only thing that flashes before my eyes is a pond and a tacky nude marble statue with cantaloupe-sized breasts.

I fall across Des's front when Vince hits me. Des, surprised, pitches forward to catch me. That sends our momentum even farther forward and to the right, and our tied legs get tangled together. There's no stopping it. We're going to hit the ground.

Unfortunately, we hit the ground at the exact location where it slopes more steeply down into the pond. Des wraps his arms around me, and we tumble around and around and around, down the slope, straight into the ice-cold depths of Wendy's water feature.

Okay, "depths" is an exaggeration. I land with my butt in about eight inches of water. I sit up, drenched, only to see Des checking me over with frantic hands. "You okay?" He touches my face, my shoulders, runs his hands down my legs. "Any injuries?"

My teeth chatter from cold and adrenaline, and I shake my head. "I'm fine."

Cheers occur behind us. I glance over my shoulder to see Vince and Caitlyn hugging and spinning, celebrating their fourth victory in a row. Despair hits me like a rocket. I feel it right in the middle of my chest, almost strong enough to knock me back into the water.

"We lost," I say as I watch Des struggle to unknot the wet fabric around our ankles.

Eventually, he gets frustrated and just rips the thing apart with his bare hands. What's it like to be that strong? He stands, completely soaked, his white tee clinging to every inch of his perfect chest, and turns back to help me up.

I sit on the muddy bottom of the pond, water lapping at my hips, and give him a disconsolate look. "Des. Did you hear me? We lost."

Des blinks, then glances at the finish line. When his gaze returns to me, he just shakes his head. "Who cares? Let's get you warmed up, Mia. You're soaked."

"Wait!" a voice screams from the lawn.

I turn to see Simone sprinting toward us, red hair wild around her head. She skids to a stop at the top of the incline. "Des. Don't move."

Then she lifts her phone and snaps a picture. She spins the phone toward me, and even from a distance, I can see Des's shape, wet T-shirt clinging to his body in all its transparent glory. "Got it," she says, turning the phone back around to tap on its screen. "Sending it now."

Desmond looks at her like she just sprouted scales. Then he stares at me, utterly confused.

Laughter bubbles up from my chest, causing my whole upper body to shake as it explodes out of me. I nearly fall down onto my back, but Des scoops me out of the water and carries me toward the house.

"I can explain," I tell him in between giggles.

"You're hypothermic," he says. "That explains it all. I'm taking you to the downstairs shower."

"We'll watch Bailey!" Trina calls out. "Take your time!"

I wave at her over his shoulder, still laughing. Des pauses, then shifts his hold on me to touch my forehead, checking for a temperature.

I try to glare at him, but more giggles come out. "No, you don't understand. It's your T-shirt. You look really hot in a wet T-shirt. We were objectifying you. We do it all the time, because you're really handsome and sexy."

He stops halfway around the side of the house, staring at me. "Mia. You're scaring me. Say something mean to me, otherwise I'm taking you to the hospital to make sure you don't have a concussion."

"Hey," I protest, letting my fingers climb up his neck to tangle in his hair. "I'm only mean when you're being a jerk."

He huffs. "Good enough."

"You're not actually supposed to put hypothermic people in hot water, you know," I tell him when we enter the garage, my hands still stroking his hair. He hasn't put me down yet, even though I can definitely walk. I decide I don't want to mention it right away. "It shocks the system. You're supposed to strip them naked and use your body heat."

Des grunts. "We can do that too."

He kicks the door to the downstairs bathroom open. It bangs against the washing machine and closes again behind us. Des finally sets me on my feet, his hands immediately moving to strip off my shirt. I lift my hands to make it easier. The saturated fabric falls on the floor with a wet slap.

Next is my bra. Des unclips it and strips it off my chest with almost vicious movements. Without his body heat against me, goosebumps sprout all over my skin, my nipples tightening into hard points. My fingers feel like sausages as I try to unbutton my jeans. Des pushes my hands away and tugs at the button, causing me to step forward to catch my balance.

I let my hands fall onto his shoulders to steady me as he shoves the wet denim down my thighs along with my underwear, then I step out of the whole wet mess.

Completely naked, with the man of my dreams kneeling before me, I finally allow myself to think about what I'm doing.

This isn't like what happened in my barbershop. I'm not in a daze. I'm not out of control.

I'm choosing this. I want him.

As Desmond lets out a shuddering breath and lifts his dark gaze all along the length of my body, I keep my hands on his shoulders and then slide them to his neck, stroking my thumbs along his jaw. His stubble rasps against my fingertips, already long enough to need a shave.

Des's hands are on the backs of my thighs, warm and strong. He slides them up to the globes of my ass, kneading gently, sending fresh heat spilling through my core. Black eyes meet mine, a desperate question hanging in them.

I only have to lean back a couple of inches before my butt hits the side of the washing machine. Des watches me, hungry, not taking his hands off my body. I widen my stance, then, leaning on the washing machine to keep my balance, I lift my leg and slowly hook it over his shoulder. The fabric of his wet tee is cold against my calf, but the body beneath is warm. I already feel like I'm burning up.

This is more brazen than I've ever been. It's me asking for what I want.

Des's breaths grow faster. His grip on my behind tightens, spreading my cheeks. Then he runs his nose and mouth along my inner thigh until he gets to the wet seams of my core. There's something intensely erotic about seeing this big, strong man coming undone at the sight of me. He closes his eyes, his whole body trembling as he inhales deeply, as if he's addicted to the scent of me.

I didn't know it was possible to be this wanted. I grip the edge of the washing machine as Des uses the flat of his tongue to take one long lick from my core.

We both moan.

His hands move to my thighs, thumbs near my entrance, spreading me wider. He probes his tongue into me, groaning, then moves to the little bundle of nerves where I need him most. My hand flies to the top of his head, tangling into his wet locks.

"Grind on my tongue," he says. "Be as rough as you want, Mia."

I twist my fingers into his hair and buck my hips. His lips and tongue work magic between my legs, soon joined by a finger sliding inside me. This man knows what he's doing. He curls his finger just so, then adds another. All the while, his tongue laps at my clitoris while my hips grind.

Pleasure twists and curls inside me, spreading through my stomach and thighs. I start to tremble, whimpering. Des uses his fingers to plunge inside me, teasing, stretching. The noises he makes stoke the fire of my lust, every grunt and moan winding me tighter. I like that he makes those sounds for me—because of me.

"You taste so good, Mia," he says, kissing my inner thigh while his fingers work inside me. "Better than I imagined. I don't ever want to stop."

"So don't," I whine.

A dark chuckle, and Des returns his mouth to where I need it most. I feel the edge approaching, that tall cliff that I'll hurtle over in a blaze of ecstasy. My hands twist in Des's hair, my knee falling out to rest in the crook of his elbow. I'm spread wide for him, and I love it.

I'm sick of fighting this attraction. Even though it might burn me in the end, I care about this man. I want him to feel loved and happy and cared for—the same way he makes me feel when he does a thousand little and big things to make my life easier. Ever since he arrived in Heart's Cove, I've tried pushing him away, and all it's done is hurt us both.

I don't know what will happen after this weekend is over, but I know that being here, with him...it feels right.

And when Des's fingers slide out of me to reach farther behind, teasing the rim of my rear, my control slips even more. While his tongue flicks over my clit, he sinks one knuckle into my hole—

I fly over the edge with a cry. Gritting my teeth to muffle the noise, I writhe and whimper while he holds me against the washing machine, delivering the most intense orgasm I've ever felt in my life. When I'm afraid I'll collapse, I find myself wrapped up in his arms, pulled tight against Des's body like he's the only support I'll ever need.

He kisses me then, and it feels like coming home. I taste myself on his tongue, loving the way his stubble rasps against my lips and chin, adoring how desperately he seems to need my kiss. It matches how I feel about him.

When the coolness of his wet clothes finally gets to me, I shiver. I'm promptly scooped up in his arms and carried to the shower.

Still wearing all his clothes, Des flicks on the water and checks the temperature, then sets me down inside. He strips off his top and shucks his wet pants, erection dangling heavily between his muscular thighs, and joins me inside.

I can hardly stand on my own. I find myself gripping the tiled wall with one hand, my back leaning against his chest for balance. Skin to skin, we stand under the hot spray while I come back to myself. I tilt my head to the water and take a shuddering breath, Des's arms around me like solid supports, his cock hard against the small of my back.

Body wash squirts out of the bottle into his palm, and I find myself thinking I could fall in love with this man. Maybe I already have. All the times I've convinced myself he's an arrogant jerk, maybe I've been trying to deny what's been happening in my own heart. I lean my head against his shoulder and let out a sigh, happy to be limp and sated against him.

He lathers up the body wash between his hands and starts running it over my body. Between the adrenaline of the race, the shock of cold in the pond, and the intensity of my orgasm, my body is completely overwhelmed. But slowly, with smooth strokes of his calloused palms, Des brings me back to life.

Suds spread over my breasts as he washes them, cupping and kneading as his head dips toward my neck. I moan as he kisses below my ear, his hands tweaking the hard tips of my breasts at the same time.

"You have such a beautiful body, Mia," he says softly, his hands coasting down to my stomach.

Normally, I'd feel self-conscious if someone touched me there. I have stretch marks, a bit of loose skin below my navel, and I'm softer than I used to be. But the reverence with which Des touches my stomach, my sides, and my hips convinces me that he's telling the truth.

Then his palms sweep to my inner thighs and move up, cupping between my legs. I buck, my behind hitting his upper thighs.

"I'm sensitive," I complain, panting.

"I'll be gentle." His voice is a dark rasp just beside my ear. His palm slides between my thighs, cupping me in a possessive move that sends more heat splashing through me. "Give me one more."

"We need to get back," I protest, not really meaning it. "Someone's going to come looking for us."

"So you better be quick," he tells me, nipping at my earlobe, his fingers spreading my folds.

With his warm chest at my back, his arms around me, and the water pelting us with more heat, I give myself to this man, to pleasure. I let it consume me whole, from head to toe, not caring about the consequences. We grind our bodies against each other, my back to his front, his hand stroking between my legs like he knows exactly what I like.

"Come for me, beautiful," he growls, pressing his hips into

me, grinding the palm of his hand against my bud. "Come for me and scream my name."

"Des..." My fingers grip his iron-hard thighs.

"Do you know how many times I've thought of this?" Des asks, nipping at my ear. His cock throbs against the small of my back. "I've wanted you since I laid eyes on you. I've jerked myself off thinking of my head between your thighs, picturing you just like this, imagining how good it would feel to sink my cock inside you."

I moan, a trembling starting in my thighs. Des must feel it, because his movements grow more frantic, his hips punching forward. Whatever he's doing to my clit with his fingers feels like heaven. Heat builds and overflows in the pit of my stomach, and my second orgasm of the afternoon detonates in my core.

From a distance, I hear Des urging me on, telling me I'm beautiful, saying he can't wait to feel me do this around his cock. I let myself sink into his words, knowing that sex with him will happen, finally admitting to myself that I want it. I let myself go completely, crying his name as hot water and steam wrap around us like a cocoon.

Des's arms are like steel bars. His hips grind against me in punchy, jerky movements, and when he grunts, I feel warmth spread over my lower back. I close my eyes and lean my palms against the tile wall, allowing myself to love the feeling of his orgasm against my skin. I'll think about what it means later. Right now, I'm pleasure-drunk and finally admitting to myself that I have feelings for this man that aren't hatred and annoyance.

He loosens his hold on me, spinning me so my back is to the

spray of the shower, and cups his hands around my face. His gaze flicks between my eyes, looking for something—

Then he relaxes. Whatever he sees in my eyes makes him smile, and he dips his head down to take my lips in his.

Far from the frenzy of our previous kiss, this one is soft, tender. He finishes it by brushing his lips against mine, then kissing my forehead, his hands still stroking my cheeks.

"We should get back out there before they come looking for us," he says.

I pull back, frowning. "That's what I said. You can't just pass it off as your bright idea."

His answering smile sends a thunderbolt searing through my chest. It's official: I'm in so much trouble.

TWENTY-FOUR

DES

WHAT I WANT to do is throw Mia over my shoulder, carry her to our bedroom, and make love to her until the next century. Unfortunately, there are about fifty people in the house, and one of them is bound to come knocking.

After finishing our shower and finding clean, dry clothes, we head back outside in time to see the whole crowd of people laughing and drinking on the porch. The trophy is gleaming on its own end table, ready to be presented to the victors.

"We made sure to wait for you," Vince says, smirking.

With one hand on Mia's lower back, it feels like I'm wearing impenetrable armor. Nothing Vince says or does can land. I feel too good. I'm walking on air.

"Congrats, Vince," I tell him. "Four in a row. New family record."

A wrinkle appears between my brother's brows as my sincerity sinks in. "Thank you?"

Mia finds Bailey in the pack of feral children near the bouncy castle and spreads her arms wide. "You did it, Bailey!"

Her daughter comes running, crashing into her arms. I watch them, unable to stop the smile from curling my lips. Bailey drops out of her mother's arms and comes sprinting toward me. Before I know what's happening, Bailey is nearly tackling me, so I have no choice but to catch her and spin her around.

She squeals and laughs, legs flying in the air until I set her down again.

"Mav and I won," she informs me. "We're going to get medals."

"I know. I watched you." I grin. "You did better than me and your mom."

"Have you ever won the race?"

"Not once," I admit.

Bailey looks shocked. Then she pats my arm and says, "Maybe next year. I can be your partner; I'm faster than Mom. I gotta go," and takes off toward Mav, who's shouting for her to come and play.

There's a strange pain in my chest. I clear my throat and turn to my brother David, who walks up beside me and hands me a beer.

"Cute kid," he says.

I nod. "She's great."

We're silent for a moment. David's only a year younger than me—just turned forty this year—but we were never close. Vince was obviously Wendy's favorite; he could get away with murder. David and I mostly just stayed out of everyone's way.

Finally, he says, "It's good to see you happy, man," then claps me on the shoulder and walks away.

That's as much connection as I've ever had to my adoptive brother. I've spent decades feeling like an outsider, wondering if I'd ever find my place in the world. Maybe it's time for me to accept that a clap on the back and a few polite words are as good as it gets—and maybe I don't need anything more from these people.

I turn and see Mia with her girlfriends, doubled over with laughter. Simone is gesturing madly, obviously retelling a story, and Mia starts wiping her eyes.

This twisting in my chest—it's more than lust. It's more than attraction and desire. I'm in love with Mia. Every part of her, from her temper to her smile. I was a goner from the moment I walked into her barbershop, and I'm only realizing it now.

Before I can absorb this realization, Mia is sidling up to me and tugging me toward the far end of the patio. Her hand feels perfect in mine. She's flushed and gorgeous, her hair twisted into a hat to keep her from freezing. Bailey comes running and slips her hand into my other one, and the three of us find seats to watch the trophy presentation.

If someone asked me to speak right now, I wouldn't be able to. I feel elated to be so close to Mia and terrified that I'll lose her before I even get to call her mine. It's like my ribs have been peeled back, and my heart is beating out in the open, exposed, vulnerable.

"...Bailey and Mav!" Grandma Maude calls out, a wide smile on her face. I snap back to the present and watch Bailey jump up from her chair and run forward.

She nudges Maverick with her shoulder, grinning, a hank of hair falling out of her ponytail onto her face. While my grandfather hands the medals to Grandma Maude, I steal a glance at Mia.

She's teary-eyed and smiling. Catching me glancing at her, she shakes her head, abashed. "It's silly to be this emotional about a three-legged race. But whenever Bailey's this happy, it just hits me extra hard."

Unable to resist, I sling an arm around the back of her chair and tug her closer. "You're allowed to be as emotional as you want, Mia."

She sniffles, laughing at herself, and finally rests her head on my shoulder. That simple movement causes painful tightness behind my ribcage. I let my fingers coast over her shoulder, leaning my cheek against the top of her head, afraid that if I make any sudden movements, the moment will be over.

"Now, it's time for the adult's trophy," my grandmother calls out. She nods at David, who brings the egg trophy closer and sets it on a small table. There's a hushed excitement in the gathered crowd, a sort of reverence that seems almost silly now.

I can't believe I cared about winning that thing. Who cares if Vince wins it four times in a row? Who cares if he wins a hundred times in a row?

Mia is in my arms, and that's worth more than any trophy. I don't need to prove to anyone that I belong in this family; I can make my own way, find my own family.

If she'll have me.

Vince and Caitlyn's names are called, and Mia straightens to clap for them. Reluctantly, I bring my arm back around and join the applause, feeling not even a tremor of annoyance when Vince lifts the Thomas Trophy over his head.

I truly don't care.

Instead, my eyes are drawn to Mia, who's whispering congratulations to Bailey as she shows off her medal. Mia kisses her daughter's forehead and hugs her close, looking radiant and beautiful.

No, I don't care about Vince and Caitlyn, about Wendy, about this big house and this town—but I do care about Mia and Bailey.

When Bailey wiggles out of her mom's hug and comes to show me her medal, warmth spreads through my chest, diffusing through my veins like ink through water. I like being the person Bailey shows off to. I like that she wants to share her victory with me.

With Mia and Bailey, I finally have a place in the world where I'm accepted just as I am.

LATER, when the kids are in bed, the turkey is eaten, and the pies are demolished (Jen's apple pie being a raving hit), Mia and I head to our room. With the warm yellow light of the bedside lamp illuminating the room, Mia steals a glance at me and flushes.

"So..." she starts, then trails off.

I can't help myself from wrapping my arms around her. When she tilts her head up, I take the opportunity to kiss her long and deep, until my heart settles and I feel like I can pull away without falling apart at the seams.

"So," I repeat.

She smiles. "I had fun today."

"Surprisingly, I did too."

Her hand comes up to stroke my cheek, the tender touch settling some old discomfort that had lived in the depth of my heart for decades. "I don't know what to make of you," she says quietly.

"What do you mean?"

"I thought after meeting your family, I'd have you all figured out. But apart from Maude and Arthur, you don't seem to fit in here at all."

A bitter smile touches my lips. "That's because I don't." I sit on the edge of the bed and pull her down on top of me, nuzzling into her neck. Her fingernails feel like heaven on my scalp, her body small and warm in my arms. I want to tell her I love her. I want to pour my heart out to her and tell her that I don't think I can live without her, but I'm not an idiot. I know that will scare her away.

A woman like Mia, who's independent, who hasn't had anyone to rely on but herself for so long—she doesn't want professions of love. She doesn't want promises. Maybe if I tell her who I am, if I explain why I'm so closed off all the time...maybe she'll understand me. Maybe, of all people, Mia is the one who will accept me for who I am.

But maybe she won't—and I can't take the risk of losing her so soon.

So, instead of telling her I'm falling in love with her, I give her another truth. "Even after my aunt and uncle adopted me, I never felt like I was part of the family. I didn't get a college fund like Vince and David. This room didn't even have drywall when I lived here. I always felt like an afterthought. After my parents died, everything was confusing and it made sense that they would treat me differently. I wasn't Wendy and Eric's son, after all."

"That's awful, Des," Mia says, her fingers making slow sweeps through my hair.

"I couldn't afford college, so I started working for a general contractor as a laborer. I worked my way up, helped him expand the company, got a certificate in project management and grew the business like it was my own. Finally, I'd found someone who treated me like a son. He told me he'd give me the company when he retired. He walked me through exactly how it would work, how much all my help had meant to him, how much *I* meant to him." My fingers dip under the hem of her sweater, finding the soft, warm skin of her waist. I pull back and give Mia a sad smile. "I bought a house on his street. It was my first real home, the first place that felt like my own since I'd been eleven years old."

"He was your family," she says softly.

Bitterness coats the back of my throat. "Yes, until his real son returned from college with an MBA and zero work experience under his belt. They'd had a fraught relationship, but they were finally getting along. The old man retired—and gave the company to his son. His real son."

That betrayal cut deeper than Wendy's indifference. It hurt more than Vince's bullying. My old boss going back on his word... that was true pain.

Mia says nothing, but her eyes speak volumes. They tell me she understands, she empathizes, but she doesn't pity. She presses her lips against mine and kisses me softly, then cups my face with her palms and stares into my eyes.

"When I moved to Heart's Cove," I continue, voice raspy, "the only goal I had was to take care of my grandparents. They were the only ones who still talked about my mom and dad. The only ones who made me feel like I belonged in the family."

"No wonder you acted like such a jerk," she whispers.

A laugh falls out of me, and I lean my forehead against hers. I inhale the sweet scent of her shampoo—shampoo I helped lather into her hair a few short hours earlier. "I'm sorry for how I treated you, Mia. I'm sorry I didn't tell you it was me on the app. I'm sorry I raised your rent so much."

Her fingers tangle at the nape of my neck, reminding me of how it feels when she snaps the cape on in her barbershop. Her touch is soft, feathery, like her body is made of nothing more than air and light. "You had every right to raise the rent," she says. "I was the one who was being unreasonable. For the past ten years, I feel like I've been constantly on the verge of panic. I'm one piece of bad news away from disaster all the time, with no safety net except what I can create for myself. I took that out on you. I'm sorry."

I love you. I want to be with you. I want to be your safety net, your strength, your lover. I want to be your everything.

Instead of saying any of those words, I tilt my head and kiss her. She tastes sweet, melting into my embrace like she was dying to kiss me too. For now, that's enough—because that's all I'm going to get from her.

TWENTY-FIVE

MIA

IT'S BEEN a long time since I felt a connection to another person like the one I feel for Des. I'm close with my daughter, of course. I've made new friends in town that have injected my life with laughter. But that's different.

Hearing Des talk about his childhood and the betrayal of his boss gives me context for every interaction we've had since he first walked into my barbershop.

He's just like me. He was abandoned, shoved aside, told to take care of himself. Just like I was.

Now I understand why he was rude when he put up the rent; it was the protective shell that he'd grown over his heart. It's the same reason my temper is on a hair trigger, and why I'm so quick to toss people aside. It's the same reason I ignore my attraction to him and put him in a box marked, "*Arrogant Jerk. Do Not Open.*"

If you push someone away, they can't reject you. They can't

tell you you're not good enough, or funny enough, or pretty enough—or simply *enough*.

When Colin divorced me, it stripped me of my confidence. It made me feel like less of a person, because I wasn't *me* anymore. Not the carefree, happy woman, anyway; I was divorced, and I was Bailey's mother. A new identity was shoved over me like ill-fitting clothing that I patched and altered to eventually make it fit. But it never truly felt like me—not the me I used to be.

Now, in Des's arms, I finally feel like myself again. Worthy of love. Worthy of affection. Worthy of sex and physical intimacy.

His hands stroke up my spine and tangle into the hair at my nape. I wrap my arms around his neck and kiss him deeply, trembling, wanting him to feel how much his presence affects me.

"I'll never get sick of kissing you," he says against my lips, a shuddering breath slipping through them after his words.

"That's good," I reply, "because I want you to keep doing it."

A yelp escapes me as I'm flipped onto my back. I giggle, grateful that we've been relegated to the basement craft room instead of a bedroom near the others. The extra privacy comes in handy at times like this.

A thought comes buzzing through my head like an angry mosquito: *Maybe I should stop this. It's going too fast. I'm letting myself become too vulnerable to him. It'll kill me when he leaves.*

But Des kisses me again, the weight of his body pressing me into the mattress. I wrap my arms around him and spread my knees until he's notched between them, and the mosquitoes buzz right out of my head again.

I'm wearing a thick, cable knit sweater and jeans (Outfit Number Two of the Queer Eye: Heart's Cove lineup, sans earrings now). Des lifts himself off me with a reluctant groan and starts at my feet, peeling off my socks before letting his hands coast up my legs to my hips. His warm fingertips brush against the skin above the waistband of my jeans, sliding to the front to unhook the button.

My heart is pounding so hard, it's hard to think. I lift my hips to allow Des to slide my jeans off, leaving my underwear clinging to my hips. He pauses, hands wrapped around my jeans at mid-thigh on my legs, and stares at the lacy black fabric covering my core.

My pants come off an instant later. I claw at my sweater and in my haste, I get stuck with my arms above my head. "Help," I squeak, and the sweater is yanked off and tossed aside.

Falling back onto the mattress, I watch Des reach behind his neck to pull his shirt off one-handed. Hot. Why is that so hot?

Des's body is thick, and it looks just as good shirtless as it does in a see-through white tee, which is saying something. His middle is packed with big slabs of muscle. His chest is huge. I reach up to run my fingers through the coarse hair dotted over it, letting out a happy sigh.

"You're so hot," I say before I can stop myself.

A wicked grin, and Des is falling over me, pinning me to the bed. He kisses me hard, his hand coasting down to tease my breast. While his mouth wreaks havoc on mine, his fingers move delicately over the edge of the lace, teasing, torturing.

When his head moves over my breast and he sucks my hardened nipple through the fabric of my bra, I let out a long moan, arch my back, and claw at the clasp to take the garment off. Chuckling darkly, Des tears it off my body and returns his mouth to my breast, this time on my bare skin. His big hands—how did I ever insult those hands? They're amazing—plump up my breasts so he can feast on them. I writhe beneath him, gripping his hips with my thighs, wanting friction, contact, everything.

Des reaches between my legs and gives me a hand to grind on. He watches my face while the heel of his palm works my clit through the fabric of my panties, studying me like he wants to record every reaction.

Frantic, I reach for Des's belt buckle. I can't do this again—let him wreck me without even touching him. My walls have crumbled, my defenses are breached, and I can't stop myself from wanting him. I manage to unclasp the buckle, unzip his pants, and reach inside to feel him.

A long, low moan rumbles out of his throat when I wrap my fingers around his girth. My heart jackrabbits in my chest, movements jerky and frantic as my body spirals out of control. I need more. Letting go of him, I reach for the waistband of his pants and shove them down. He rolls onto his back and shucks them off in one movement, letting the garment fall off the side of the bed after grabbing a foil condom packet from his pocket.

The sight of it is enough for me. I pounce.

Straddling his hips, I lean over and kiss him. My hair falls down like two curtains on either side of us, a little cocoon of intimacy while I taste him, kiss him, enjoy him. His hands slide down my sides and rest on either side of my ass, squeezing gently as I start to rock.

If the Kool-Aid Man burst through the concrete wall beside me, I wouldn't be able to stop. If the ceiling came crashing down on top of us, I wouldn't even blink. The only thing that exists in the world is Des's body beneath mine, his hands, his mouth, his cock.

The hard bar of his arousal is pinned between us, pressing against my soft flesh in erotic demand. I rock against it, whimpering, needing.

"Mia," Des grates. "Mia, if you keep doing that—" He squeezes his eyes shut, his neck turning red as the muscles in it grow stark. He squeezes my hips, holding me down on top of him to stop my movements. "Stop it, Mia. Fuck, I want you. I need to be inside you."

Finding the condom on the bed beside us, I rip the packet open with trembling fingers. Then I lift myself off his hips, roll it over his length, and shimmy forward. Holding the base of Des's cock in one hand, I glance up at his face, and pause.

No one has ever looked at me like that—as if they're watching something so beautiful, they can hardly stand it. My breath catches as Des's hand slides from my hip down to my thigh, his throat bobbing as he swallows.

He opens his mouth, but I know—I just *know*—that whatever comes out will be more than I can bear. There's emotion in his eyes that I'm not ready to face. There's an intensity between us that I might be able to ignore if I try very hard. I know, looking at Des's face, that the connection I feel for him goes both ways.

So, before he can speak, I pull the gusset of my panties to the side and sink down onto his cock.

We moan in unison. My head falls back, the ends of my hair dancing against my back. My hands drop to Des's chest, gripping his skin for support.

I wiggle, taking him deeper, feeling the beautiful stretch of his intrusion. Nothing has ever felt this good. Opening my eyes, I meet his gaze—and I start to move. Des's hips rock up to meet mine, and the friction—

I gasp, his hands holding my hips tight, helping me rock and buck and writhe—

Pleasure rocks through me, detonating without warning. I moan, fingers sinking into Des's chest, unable to control the movement of my hips. Everything from my navel down is numb.

Then I'm flipped onto my back, and Des has my calves hooked onto his shoulders.

"I love watching you come," he says, voice rough, "and feeling you milk my cock like that drives me fucking crazy."

He plunges deeper inside me. I moan, hands scrabbling at the wrinkled blankets beneath me. When Des drops my legs and curls his body over mine, it's almost too much. His head drops to mine, lips touching, and he destroys every last inch of the walls I'd erected to keep him out.

If I were honest with myself, I'd admit that this was more than sex. It's too intense for that. There's too much emotion buzzing between us, too many truths hovering just beneath the surface. But then another orgasm starts to wash over me, and honesty is too difficult a proposition.

While I fall into the ocean of pleasure Des delivers at my feet, he groans and stiffens above me. I hold onto him like he's my only lifeline, legs around his hips, arms around his shoulders, and we both give in to our bodies' demands.

When the only sound in the room is our staggered panting, I let my arms and legs fall out and do my best imitation of a starfish.

Des chuckles, his breaths tickling my ear. "Happy Thanksgiving, Mia," he finally manages to say in a voice so full of gravel it's a wonder I can make out the words. "I know what I'm grateful for."

Giggling, I let him roll off me and move my arm and leg out of his way, watching as he removes the condom and disposes of it. We clean up, I go pee, and I'm surprised to find there's no awkwardness in me when I pull on a nightie (yes, a light-blue silk one with a bow at the front. It actually is my favorite one, I just hadn't worn it in a decade when I mentioned it to him over text) and slip between the sheets beside him.

Des's arms curl around me, I'm tucked into his body, and—feeling safer than I ever have—I promptly fall asleep.

TWENTY-SIX
LILY

WHEN SIMONE first proposed coming to Lovers' Peak for Thanksgiving, I almost refused. I have a rambunctious toddler and a busy husband, and traveling across the country on short notice seemed like more effort than it was worth.

But now, with Liam in his stroller and Rudy walking beside me, I can't help but feel warmth flood my chest. All of us are down in the center of town, where we're meeting Mia, Des, and Bailey before the Lovers' Peak light display begins.

"You want me to push him for a while?" Rudy asks, his hand sliding over my lower back.

Smiling, I shake my head. "I'm good."

Coming here for Thanksgiving was impulsive, but in a way, it made me realize all the things I have to be grateful for. I have my health (still in remission!), my child—and I have Rudy. He smiles at me, hair perfectly tousled in the cool autumn breeze, and I feel a rush of affection for him.

"Oh, look!" My eldest sister Candice comes rushing toward me, tugging me toward the nearest street corner. At the far end of the street, in front of town hall, a gigantic Christmas tree rises up to brush the sky. "Isn't it amazing?"

Blake, her partner, walks with us and slides his arm around Candice's shoulders. She leans into him, smiling slightly.

"What time do they turn the lights on?" Trina, my other sister, asks as she hops the curb and comes to stand beside Candice. Mac has his hand wrapped around hers, their two kids looking into the window displays of a nearby store.

"An hour after sundown," Candice replies. "It's a famous event, apparently. The day after Thanksgiving, the town turns on the Christmas lights."

"Up!" Liam coos from the stroller. "Up!" He lifts his arms and Rudy dutifully picks him up, placing him on his hip as he turns to point at the Christmas tree. It's not quite sundown, so the lights are still off, but people in high-vis uniforms are on ladders, putting the finishing touches on the display.

I smile at the two of them, feeling luckier than ever.

"Is that Blake Harding?" a voice calls out from the other side of the street.

"Here we go," Trina says, rolling her eyes.

Laughing, I turn to see Blake's raving fans come to mob him and ask for photos. He's an actor and usually keeps a low profile, especially in Heart's Cove, but whenever I've seen him interact with fans, he's always gracious with photos and autographs.

It takes forever though, so the rest of us move partly down the street and wait for him to catch up.

At the next street corner, we find Simone and Jen deep in

discussion about a Danish pastry they're sharing. It's from the bakery just beside us, and Jen is busy admiring how skillfully the pastry is crafted. Simone is just eating it and nodding along. Fiona and Grant walk arm in arm out of the bakery with a pastry of their own, lips covered in powdered sugar.

"Where are we meeting Mia and Des?" I ask.

"At the Christmas tree," Georgia replies, joining us outside the bakery. Her dainty diamond ring glitters as she pushes a strand of hair behind her ear. "Sebastian's picking Piper and the boys up. They should be here right in time for the lights to come on."

"It's supposed to be amazing," Simone says, wiping her lips. She gives the rest of her pastry to Wes, who gobbles it up and winks at her. "The lights, I mean." She tears her gaze away from her husband's lips and glances around at our growing group. Then she frowns. "Where's Nora?"

"She and Lee said to go on ahead when we left the duplex," Fiona replies, eyes twinkling. "They wanted to stay behind for some private time."

"Gross," Fallon, Nora's brother, says.

Laughter echoes around the group, happiness thick in the air. If you'd asked me how my forties were going to go, I could never have guessed they'd end up this good. They started with two surprises—good and bad ones—that changed the course of my life forever.

Now, surrounded by friends and family, I feel luckier than ever. I turn to see Rudy giving Liam a kiss on the cheek before tossing him up in the air, and I know that right here—with all these people—is exactly where I've always been meant to be.

"Oh," Simone says, a wide smile spreading over her face, "look at the two of *them*. I can't *wait* to hear what put that look on their faces."

All of us turn to see Mia and Des strolling down the street with Bailey beside them, looking completely and utterly besotted with each other.

"Someone got lucky last night," Fiona says quietly, grinning.

"And I expect to hear every detail," Simone adds before turning to the three new arrivals. "Over here!"

Mia and Des glance over, see the group, and change their course to come meet us by the tree. No one misses the way Des puts his hand on Mia's lower back, or how Bailey slips her palm into his free hand.

TWENTY-SEVEN
DES

BAILEY DROPS my hand and runs toward the boy and girl hovering at the edge of the group from Heart's Cove. Trina's kids, I think. Mia watches her go, calling for her to slow down, then lets out a sigh and gives up.

"She's fine," I tell her, giving her hand a squeeze.

"I know," Mia huffs, glancing up at me. The sun has already dipped behind the peak of a mountain, but its fading rays still illuminate her beautiful face. She's small and fierce, this woman. I don't know what I'll do if I can't have her forever.

"Come on. The best view of the lights is from the far end of Main Street." I tug her arm, stopping beside Bailey to collect her on our way. Behind us, our ragtag bunch of friends and acquaintances follow, chattering, eating, sipping hot cocoa, and generally being merry.

Would it be possible for me to belong to this group too? For me to find a place in Heart's Cove that I could truly call home?

"Desmond!" My grandmother swings her legs out of a car and waves at me, then hauls herself up to her feet. I hurry beside her and help her out. Mia and Bailey are already on the other side of the vehicle, helping my grandfather.

"Aren't you nice?" he says, chucking Bailey's chin. Bailey smiles and ducks behind her mom, who takes my grandfather's arm and helps him up the curb.

"We're going to sit outside Rita's," Grandma says, motioning to the nearby bar. Rita's is famous in Lovers' Peak, and it has a great patio that extends all the way into the street to take up a couple of parking spots. We help them to find their seats, and when Mia and Bailey say goodbye and step back onto the sidewalk on the other side of the restaurant, my grandmother grabs my wrist.

"Hold onto her, my boy," she says, more solemnly than I've ever heard before. "She looks at you the way your mother used to look at your father."

Throat tight, I just nod. Maude turns to Arthur and starts fussing, so I slip away.

"All good?" Mia asks, rubbing her arms over her shoulders.

I take my scarf off and drape it around her neck. "Everything's great. Let's find a spot to stand; they're about to turn on the lights."

We find a spot at the top of a small incline, near the middle of the road. People crowd all around us, some with camping chairs, some standing, some sitting on the curb or the various benches on the side of the road. Main Street is closed today—if not officially, then because this has become a yearly tradition in town. Excited chatter bounces around the crowd, and Mia stays close enough for her arm to brush mine.

I like having her there, where I can smell her shampoo and her perfume, feel the heat of her body, see the light playing in the strands of her hair.

Darkness falls fast as the sun slips deeper behind the mountains, and then all at once, the town blazes with light. Gasps and cheers go up, and I find myself putting one hand on Bailey's shoulder, and the other around Mia's waist. The two of them glance at me and smile, eyes shining, as the magic of the moment permeates the air.

Lights are strung up in every bare tree along the street. They dangle from curlicued lampposts. They line shop windows and eaves. They dangle in zig-zagging lines across the street like a glimmering ceiling. And at the end of the road, a massive Christmas tree blazes like a beacon.

The whole crowd of people applauds the start of the holiday season.

We wander for an hour or so, heading down small side streets to find clever light displays in windows, or intricate ones strung up on roofs or projected onto building fronts. All different colors, big and small, the whole town explodes with beautiful light. Our friends follow, pointing out various displays, laughing and chattering. I feel airy, weightless. I've never had a group of friends this big. I've never felt part of anything, never felt like I had a place in the world that felt like home.

"You *bastard!*"

We all spin around to see Piper, Georgia's sister, going toe-to-toe with a dark-haired guy about my size. He looks like he wants to simultaneously rip her head off and throw her over his shoulder to cart her away.

Then he does just that. He grabs Piper, tosses her over a shoulder, and starts stomping away from us.

"Put me down! Hey! You overbearing pig!" She beats her fists on his back. "Put me down, Rhett! *Rhett!*"

Georgia has Piper's sons' hands in hers, and she's watching her sister being carried off with a slightly bemused expression on her face. "Call me in the morning!"

"I'm not—PUT ME DOWN!"

The man—Rhett—sets her on her feet, then opens the back door of a dark SUV and gestures for her to enter. Piper, fuming, huffs...and enters the car.

Nate looks up at his aunt Georgia. "Where's Mom going? Why is Mr. Baldwin carrying her?"

"Um...she has work to do," Georgia answers. "Remember?"

"Is that why we're having a sleepover at your house?" Alec asks, frowning at the leaving car.

"Yes, honey," Georgia answers. "Come on. Let's get donuts from that kiosk."

I glance at Mia, who's watching the scene, blinking rapidly. "Any idea what that's about?" I ask.

She snorts. "No, but I'm sure I'll find out."

"Crazy women," I mumble, and Mia punches my arm.

I'M NOT sure why I take Mia and Bailey to my old house. But as the air turns colder and Bailey starts shivering, I bring them both across town to a neighborhood that used to be quite rough but is now in high demand. My little three-bed, one-bath brick house sits on a large lot, cheerful lights strung on its eaves.

"What are we doing here?" Bailey asks, pressing her nose to the car window.

"I wanted to show you the first house I ever bought." The car's still running, and I don't intend to stay long. It's strange being here now.

Buying that place was the first time I ever felt like I had a home. I scrimped and saved through my early twenties to get a deposit together, borrowing money from my old boss when the bank turned around and told me I needed an extra five grand to get approved for the loan. Then I lived like a pauper to pay this place off as quickly as humanly possible.

It was all mine—the only thing in my life that felt like my own. I could be myself inside those walls.

I moved out only a few months ago, after living in that place for fifteen years. A nice family with two young kids moved in and have been renting it ever since.

"It's nice!" Bailey exclaims. She beams at me through the gap between the two front seats. "Maybe one day, Mom and I will live in a house with a big yard. Right, Mom?"

"Right," Mia answers, avoiding my gaze.

"But I like our apartment too," Bailey says, staring at my old house. "Especially after the renovations."

I put the car in gear, intending to drive off, when the front door opens. Bob Webber steps out and lifts a hand in greeting. I blow out a breath, exchange a glance with Mia, and step out of the car.

"Hi, Bob!" I call out.

He lets out a booming laugh. "I thought that was you! Come on in! Who have you got there with you?"

"Hello!" Mia says, exiting her side of the car. Bailey scrabbles out and takes her mother's hand.

We're ushered inside, where Bob introduces the girls to his wife Laurie and two young children, Beth and Will. Then we're plied with tea and coffee and cocoa and the best of Laurie's baking, and we sit in my old kitchen like one big family.

It feels strange. This used to be my sanctuary, and now it belongs to someone else.

"We were fortunate that Desmond offered this house to us," Laurie says, looking at her husband with shining eyes. "We're still so grateful."

"The kids love it," Bob agrees. "They've almost worn me down enough to get a dog."

Laurie laughs, arranging brownies on a platter before moving it to the center of the kitchen table. Her kind gaze shifts to me. "Any chance you'd want to part with this house permanently?"

Bob puts a hand on his wife's shoulder. "We'd love to take it off your hands. The bank is more than happy to give us a mortgage..."

I freeze. My immediate reaction is a flash of anger that burns through my chest like a gas explosion. Then I regain control over myself and manage to tilt my head from side to side. "Not sure. I'll have to think about it."

"The market is cooling down, you know. Now would be a great time to sell," Bob starts, but Laurie hushes him. "He's not interested, Bob," she says in a low voice.

Mia glances at me curiously, and I feel like she sees everything. Somehow, she can tell what this house means to me. She knows that it's more than four walls and a roof: it's a symbol of my emancipation. My independence. It's my *home*. The first one I had after my parents died.

We stay for twenty minutes, catching up on all the gossip in Lovers' Peak, then head back home.

"Do you ever miss living here?" Mia asks when we're back on the road.

In my peripheral vision, I see Bailey glance at me to catch my response. I shrug. "Not really."

It's the truth. So why is it so hard to consider selling that house?

"He likes Heart's Cove better," Bailey says with a satisfied nod.

I smile. "I do."

Mia watches me for a moment, then looks out her window.

Back at aunt's mountain mansion, Mia disappears to help Bailey get ready for bed. I find myself in the kitchen pouring a glass of water when Vince appears in the doorway. He watches me for a moment, then moves closer.

"You didn't tell anyone you were in a relationship." It sounds like an accusation.

I take a sip of water and shrug. "Yeah. So?"

"Afraid I'd steal her away from you again?" Vince gives me a cruel smile, his eyes hard.

Suddenly, I feel sorry for him. He was given everything: wealthy parents, a doting mother, a devoted wife, a great career launched from his father's business contacts. Anything Vince could ask for was handed to him over the course of his life. But he still feels the need to be petty, to needle me at every opportunity.

It's not worth the effort to engage. I'm not desperate for his family's acceptance anymore. I'm not orphaned, living on the scraps of attention and affection his parents could spare. I've moved on.

Mia enters the kitchen then, rubbing her eyes as she yawns like a cute, sleepy kitten. I want to wrap my arms around her and never let go.

She looks at the two of us, reads our body language, and gives me a quick once-over as if to make sure I'm okay. Then her shoulders drop and she says, "I'm going to hit the hay. 'Night, Vince."

He straightens, as if surprised by her courtesy. "Goodnight, Mia."

I drink the rest of the water, put the glass in the dishwasher, and nod to my brother. Then I follow Mia to the basement bedroom that used to be a reminder of how little I belonged here. Now it's just a room with a bed where I get to be alone with the woman I adore.

I take my time making love to Mia, because despite everything, despite how close we've been over the course of the trip, despite all the truths I've spilled and the intimacy we've shared, I'm not sure if it's real. It's like our first kiss; I think this could be my only chance to have her to myself, and I intend to make the most of it.

. . .

THE NEXT DAY, Saturday, goodbyes are said, bags are packed, and we head off on our trip back to Northern California. This time, we make our connection. I'd parked my car in the long-term parking lot, so I load the girls up and drive us back to Heart's Cove. Back home.

Crossing into the town limits, I feel a strange kind of pressure sitting on my chest. It was only a couple of days in Colorado, but it feels like it changed everything—everything with me, anyway. Now that we're back, will Mia pull away? Will we pretend Thanksgiving never happened?

"You can drop us off in front of the barbershop," Mia says. "Saves you going all the way around the back. We'll just walk through the shop." She glances over her shoulder, a soft smile on her face as she sees her daughter sleeping, mouth wide open. "She looks like such a little angel when she's asleep."

I grin. "I think Mav is going to miss her."

Mia chuckles, glancing at me before turning forward to look through the windshield.

I take the turn onto Cove Boulevard and slow down. My heart starts to thump, as if my body knows that the end is nearing. When Mia gets out of the car, will she shut the door on our relationship too? Was this weekend an aberration in our otherwise contentious relationship? Is this the end?

I slow as I approach the barbershop, then frown. There's a man there, peering through the darkened windows with one hand curled around his face. Mia stiffens beside me, her hands clenching into fists.

"I'll go run him off," I tell her. Whoever this guy is, he's not going to make Mia feel unsafe.

"No." Mia clears her throat. "No, it's okay. Just…" She looks at Bailey again, who's still asleep. "Just let me talk to him."

I frown. "You know this guy?" I pull into a parking spot just in front of the barbershop, and the man straightens, turning to face us. He squints at my headlights, but I don't turn the car off.

He's shorter than I am, with a slight build. He's wearing a dark button-down and black trousers with an open pea coat on top.

Mia's breath catches. I watch her force herself to relax, unclenching her fists as she exhales slowly. Then she nods and meets my gaze. "Yes, I know him. That's my ex-husband."

COLIN LOOKS GOOD. I, on the other hand, look like I just spent all day on an airplane.

Bailey's still asleep in the back, so I exit the car and gently close the door. Des cuts the engine, but he doesn't turn the lights off. They shine over us, illuminating everything, giving me nowhere to hide.

"Colin."

"Mia," he says, sounding relieved. "Hi."

"What are you doing?" I frown at him, then glance at my barbershop.

He rakes a hand through his hair, getting that sheepish look on his face I used to adore. He was so good at making my anger melt away, always reminding me why I cared about him so much. "I was curious. I just checked in to my hotel, and I noticed the sign for your shop..."

I clasp my hands at my stomach and pray he doesn't see them

shaking. I shouldn't be this nervous. I shouldn't care. I knew he was coming.

The air is cool, but not as cold as it was in Colorado. It smells like salty ocean and cut grass, the familiar, fresh scent of Heart's Cove. A breeze ruffles at the end of my ponytail, flicking it over the front of my shoulder.

"You look great," Colin finally says to break the stretching silence. "I... It's good to see you." He glances at the car, squinting into the headlights. "Is Bailey in the car?"

"She's asleep." My voice is frosty. It's hard to relax when the man who abandoned me with my unborn child is acting like I'm a long-lost friend he just happened to run into.

"Oh," he says, a sad smile touching his lips. "Are you still free for us to meet tomorrow? You said brunch at the café was good."

I'm as hollow as an empty drum. My heart echoes loudly as it thumps inside me, shaking loose all the feelings I thought I'd gotten over. I shouldn't feel afraid of this man. I'm not even sure if fear is the right word for how I feel. It's similar to fear, but it's not exactly caused by him. It's more like I'm afraid of becoming the shell of myself I was when he left. I'm afraid of being as alone as I was then, as terrified, as abandoned.

The refusal dances on my tongue, but I really have no excuse. I give Colin a jerky nod. "Tomorrow, eleven o'clock."

For one horrifying moment, it looks like Colin is about to hug me. I freeze. Then the driver's side door opens, and Des's massive form emerges. Relief washes over me like the pitter-patter of a cool rain, loosening the locked muscles that had been holding me immobile. I turn to face him as he walks over to stand next to me, grateful for the palm he places on my lower back.

The headlights still shine on us, harsh and bright, concealing nothing.

Colin recovers quickly, deploying his best good-ol-boy smile as he extends a hand to Des. "I'm Colin. Mia's ex-husband. I don't believe Mia's mentioned you."

Real subtle. I narrow my eyes at my ex.

"Des," the man replies, giving Colin's hand a perfunctory shake. "It's late. You should go back to your hotel. Mia and Bailey need to rest."

Wow. Des is also lacking the subtlety bone. Clearly neither of these men feel like wasting any time being polite or pretending like they're not beating their chests like silverback gorillas. Still, I feel oddly relieved at Des's words, like he's tossed me a lifeline at the moment I needed it most.

"Goodnight, Colin. I'll see you tomorrow."

My ex-husband hesitates very briefly, then nods at the two of us, crossing the street and heading toward the nearby Heart's Cove Hotel. I deflate like an old balloon, shoulders rounding. Des's arms come around me, warm and inviting, but my brain feels like cold scrambled eggs. I don't know if I'm supposed to be comforted by another man. Have I moved too quickly with Des? Bailey must be confused. She's supposed to be my priority, but here I am getting comfort from a man I told myself I hated only a few short weeks ago.

I pull away, needing to find my feet again. The problem with leaning on other people is that when they leave, you risk falling over.

"Thanks," I say. "I'll go grab Bailey."

"Are you okay?"

No, I want to say. I hate the thought of Colin weaseling his way into Bailey's heart. I worry that he'll walk away from her the way he did me. I'm terrified of the feelings I have for you. I feel like a piece of driftwood tossed around by an angry ocean. I don't know what's right or wrong anymore.

Instead, I just lift my gaze and meet his eyes, unsure what he sees when he looks at me. "I'm fine, Des. Just tired."

He nods. "Call me if you need anything."

My throat is tight, and I'm not sure why. I wish Des were sleeping beside me tonight. I wish I had the warmth and weight of his arm around my waist to remind me that I don't have to do this on my own. I wish Bailey had refused to meet her father, so I could tell Colin to go to hell.

On stiff legs, I walk to Bailey's car door and open it up.

She blinks, rubbing her eyes, and lets out a sleepy noise of complaint. "Are we home?"

"Yes, honey." I help her out of the car while Des carries our bags to the door. The independent part of me wants to take the bags from his hands and send him on his way, but I was telling the truth when I said I was tired, so I let him follow us through the barbershop to the back door.

Bailey stumbles through, kicking her shoes off, and Des deposits the bags in the living room. We glance at the closing bathroom door, then at each other.

Before I can stop him, Des has my jaw in his hand and is kissing me. It's a soft kiss, tender, and it makes me feel wobbly inside. Then he pulls away and says, "You'll call me if you need anything." It sounds like an order, but it makes me feel warm.

I nod. "I will."

He hesitates, dark eyes flicking between mine. "I'll miss you tonight."

Despite my best defenses, my insides melt like warm candle wax. I nod, throat tight. "Me too."

One more kiss, and Des pulls away. I follow him down the hallway and through the barbershop, locking up behind him. When he disappears into his car, I scurry back to the safety of my apartment and lock myself inside.

Bailey's already in bed, asleep. I comb her hair off her face and kiss her temple, then tiptoe to the bathroom to get myself ready.

A few minutes later, I climb into my bed, shivering. The sheets are cold and my pillow is lumpy, and I miss Des.

TWENTY-NINE
CANDICE

THE FOUR CUPS Café breathed life back into me. I love coming into the café, seeing all our customers chatting and eating and drinking, knowing that this little hub is my own creation.

While I rearrange the pastries in our display fridge, I hear familiar footsteps approach the register. There's a pause, then, "What's a guy gotta do to get an everything bagel with cream cheese around here?"

Smiling, I stand to see my husband, Blake, leaning against the counter with that dashing smile on his face.

I laugh at his order and tap the computer to type it in. "Will that be all, sir?" I ask, voice angelic. We're both playing the part, remembering those weeks when I resisted his advances, when he groveled like only he can, coming in every day for his coffee and bagel to remind me he wasn't going anywhere.

His eyes sparkle. "I'll take a kiss on the side."

Laughing, I oblige. I lean across the counter and kiss him,

enduring the wolf-whistles and hoots from the few patrons dotted around the café. Blushing, I pull away while one of our employees hands him his bagel. Blake winks at me, then sits down at one of the two-seater tables tucked into the corner. Strange. Usually, he orders and leaves; it's rare that he sits in the café for an extended period of time. Not that I'm complaining.

When my first husband passed away, I never thought my life could be complete again. I was weighed down by grief and guilt, thinking the happy years in my life were long over.

I was wrong.

Then the bell above the café door rings, and my daughter walks in. I gasp, hands flying up to clutch my heart.

Allie looks radiant. Her curly blond hair is tied up in a messy top bun, her smile wide and brilliant. She spreads her arms just in time for me to rush around the counter and crash into her. "You're here!" I exclaim. "Why are you here? I thought you had exams!"

"Blake flew me out," she says, hugging me tight. "He said you were all sad on Thanksgiving without me." She pulls away, watching me with familiar blue eyes. "You look really good, Mom."

I click my tongue, too happy to make words.

Then, behind her, another blond head pokes through the door.

"Clancy!" I yell, and Fiona comes running in front the back.

With tears in her eyes, Fiona wraps her arms around her stepdaughter and ushers her inside. "What—how?"

"Blake has a private jet," Clancy explains. "We fly back tomorrow evening."

Fiona squeals, then gives Blake a big bear hug as he comes to stand next to me. "I have to call Grant."

Allie grins, and Blake slings an arm around my shoulders. "What are you having, Allie? Breakfast is on me."

"Is Fallon cooking?" she asks. When I nod, she says, "Definitely eggs Benedict, then."

Buzzing with happiness, I almost don't notice the stranger walk into the café behind the girls. Heart's Cove has a healthy churn of tourists, so it isn't rare that someone I don't recognize walks in, but something about this guy—and the way he scans the café like he's looking for someone—twigs recognition at the back of my mind.

I hustle Clancy, Blake, and Allie to a table and glance once more at the man as he sits down at one of the unoccupied tables, watching the door. A few minutes later, when I've joined the girls and husband at their table, the man orders a black drip coffee and returns to his table to wait.

And twenty minutes later, when Mia and Bailey walk in, I realize who he is.

THIRTY
MIA

MASKING my nerves as Bailey and I enter Four Cups is one of the hardest things I've ever had to do, but I know that Bailey will pick up on everything. She's been unnaturally quiet all morning, more subdued than I've ever seen her. She must be as nervous as I am.

As we enter the café, Colin stands.

Bailey glances at me and asks, "Is that him?"

I nod. "Yeah. You ready?"

My daughter—nine years old, and apparently more courageous than her mother—squares her shoulders and meets Colin's eyes from across the room. "Yeah," she says, "I'm ready."

Over the past couple of weeks, Colin and I have discussed boundaries. I've sent him a list of Bailey's interests (basketball, space, turtles and/or tortoises) along with a few photos of her. It's been a battle for me to even give him that much of her. The petty part of me wants to slam the door in his face and tell him to leave the two of us alone. He left, didn't he? Why should he have any right to Bailey's affection?

But he's her father, and Bailey wanted to meet him. I owe it to her to be mature, to do what's best for my daughter instead of what my petty, black heart prefers.

We stop on the other side of the table, and the two of them stare at each other. Colin's throat works, and he forces himself to smile.

Bailey's the first to speak. She sticks out her hand, businesslike. "I'm Bailey," she says. "Nice to meet you, Colin." Her chin is high, and despite the flush on her cheeks, she looks as confident as I've ever seen her.

Colin, slightly taken aback, manages to shake her offered hand.

I almost start laughing. I love my daughter.

"Would you like a drink, Bailey?" I ask.

"Hot chocolate?" she says hopefully. "And an apple muffin?"

"I'll grab them," Colin says. "Mia, anything?"

"I'll have a drip coffee with lots of cream."

Colin nods and darts away to order.

I lean toward my daughter. "How are you doing so far?"

"Mom, I'm fine," she says, rolling her eyes. "He just looks like any old guy. It's weird."

I laugh, vaguely insulted. "He's not old. He's my age!"

Bailey arches a brow at me, lips pursed. "Mom. You're old."

"Hey! I'll remember that. When you turn forty, I'll remind you of this exact moment and call *you* old."

"Yeah, and I'll be old, so I'll agree with you."

The laugh that bubbles out of me is half-outraged, half-amused. I click my tongue at her. Bailey grins, glancing up as Colin returns with our drinks. He places them down and smiles a bit woodenly at the two of us, then reaches for a bag on the chair next to him.

"I brought you something," he says, and pulls out a Barbie doll. She's dressed like a basketball player and has a little orange ball strapped next to her in the box. "Your mom said you liked basketball. This is a limited-edition doll. I had to special order it from a business contact." He hands the doll over, nodding encouragingly.

Bailey frowns, looking perplexed. "Yeah, *playing* basketball. Or watching it." She glances at me and whispers, "What am I supposed to do with *this*?"

I give her a speaking glance, and Bailey sighs dramatically. Then she looks at Colin and says, "Thank you, Colin. It's a nice gift."

It's a nice gift that probably cost him a small fortune, but it missed the mark. That shouldn't make me happy, but it does. Hey —I never claimed to be a good person. I can be as petty as I like.

Colin adjusts the collar of his shirt, then finally leans his forearms on the table and says, "You can call me Dad if you want."

My heart seizes so hard I jerk in my seat. I'm not ready for this. Not ready, not ready, *not ready*. I want to throw Bailey over my shoulder and run away.

But Bailey just says, "No, thank you. Colin is fine," and sips her hot chocolate. While Colin clears his throat and leans back in his chair, she tears the streusel-covered top of the muffin off and hands it to me, then starts unwrapping the bottom part of the muffin.

I tear off a piece and pop it in my mouth. At Colin's questioning glance, I say, "She thinks the streusel is too sweet."

"Mom says I'm weird, because the top is the best part."

Colin laughs. "Well, you must get your lack of sweet tooth from me. I get sick if I eat too much sugar."

Bailey stops munching her muffin and tilts her head. "Oh." She takes another bite, clearly mulling over his words. Then she asks, "What else did I get from you?"

NOTHING. I bite the inside of my cheek to stop myself from yelling the word. This is good for Bailey. She deserves this. If she wants to know her father, I have every responsibility to make it happen. I take a deep breath to steady myself.

"You got my eyes," Colin says, studying her. And he's right, damn him.

Bailey's feet curl around the legs of her chair as she takes another bite of muffin. "Do you like Halloween? I like Halloween."

Colin shrugs. "Sure."

"What did you dress up as this year?"

"Um." He frowns. "Nothing this year. I was at work."

"They don't let you dress up at work? Mom dresses up. She's Edward Scissorhands every year."

It's true. It always gets a chuckle from my clients. Although this year, I seriously considered wearing the spare electrical outlet costume, until I realized I wouldn't be able to do my job wearing a cardboard box strapped to my body.

"No, no one dresses up at my office." Colin shrugs and sips his coffee. "It's a more professional workplace than your mother's barbershop."

Well, fuck you too, Colin.

"That sucks," Bailey replies, taking another bite. "When's the last time you had a costume?"

Colin is obviously uncomfortable with this line of questioning. He looks utterly baffled. It's kind of funny. "Um...college, probably? I was Bob the Builder one year." He bought a hard hat and called himself Bob the Builder. It was lame. "You know, mostly, adults don't dress up for Halloween anymore."

"Oh." Bailey glances at me. "But you do, Mom. And Des said he dressed up like grapes. And my teachers all dress up. They're all adults."

"I think Colin means adults at his work, honey," I say, and Colin latches on to my statement with a vigorous nod.

"Exactly. My office is serious."

Somehow, I manage to keep from rolling my eyes.

"What do you do for work?" Bailey takes a sip of her cocoa, continuing the inquisition.

"I work in tech," he says.

"Computers?"

"Mm-hmm," he nods, then launches into an explanation of his job, clearly more comfortable on familiar ground. Bailey peppers him with questions and answers some of his own. I sit there, mostly quiet, feeling strung out. As the minutes pass I relax slightly, grateful that Bailey seems to be handling this well.

Still, when we take our leave and head back home, I let out a long, relieved breath. Bailey threads her fingers through mine, the Barbie doll dangling from her other hand. She studies me while I unlock the barbershop door.

"What's going on in that blond head of yours, Bailey?" I ask, mostly to divert her from saying something too perceptive about my own state of mind. "What did you think of him?"

"He's okay. The doll is stupid."

A chuckle falls from my lips. "It was nice of him to get you a present."

Bailey doesn't look convinced. She drops the doll on an end table in our living room as soon as we walk in, then walks to her room and closes the door. I want to follow her, but I resist the urge. She must need time to think, to process things however a nine-year-old processes. I know her well enough to realize she'll come out when she's ready to talk.

I end up walking through to the barbershop, leaving the connecting door open in case she needs me. I start cleaning, just to do something with my body. There's too much energy coiled in my muscles, too many jangled nerves ringing off-key inside me.

When I'm sweeping my pristine floor for the third time, a gentle knock taps the glass door. I look up to see Des outside the barbershop, a questioning look in his eyes.

Relief sweeps through me, so intense I nearly stagger. I hurry to the door and unlock it to let him in.

"I called," he says, hovering just outside the door. "You didn't answer, so I thought I'd stop by."

"My phone is in my purse," I explain, jabbing a thumb over my shoulder toward the apartment. "Come in."

He enters, his presence filling the space from wall to wall. Suddenly, I know everything will be okay. Before I can stop myself, my arms wrap around his waist and I bury my head in his broad chest, inhaling deeply.

He hesitates, then curls his arms around me and kisses the top of my head. I nearly start crying, it feels so good.

Part of me knows it's dangerous to feel this way about someone. My feelings for this man are growing so quickly that I can hardly identify them, let alone come to terms with them. And what if I'm using him for support just because Colin's here, making me feel off-balance? What if my feelings aren't even real?

What if he leaves like he said he would?

"How did it go?" Des's deep voice rumbles above me, sending little thrills through my body. His hand sweeps over my back, soothing.

"Pretty good, considering," I answer, soaking in the comfort for another second before pulling away. I touch his jaw. "You need a shave."

His eyes smile without any other part of his face moving. "You offering?"

"Sit down, big guy."

I'm on safer ground when Des sits in the barber's chair, and I go through the familiar motions of readying myself to give a clean shave. The cape slides over his shoulders. My tools are lined up. I prep his skin and get the shaving cream lathered.

The ritual centers me, and when I finish shaving him, I feel like myself again. I smile at Des after removing the cape from around his neck, loving the way his hand coasts down my side.

"Thank you," I whisper.

"For what?"

For being here. For caring. For letting me lean on you.

"For letting me shave your face."

He grins. "Not even a nick this time."

"I did that *once*," I protest, and he laughs—then tugs me in for a kiss.

Desmond's kisses have always destroyed me. They're heat-seeking missiles fired at the most vulnerable parts of me. It's like he knows exactly how to tear me apart, bit by bit, rendering me completely powerless to his advances.

I kind of like it.

I stand in the vee of his legs, wrapping my arms around his neck, and I kiss him back with all the intensity I feel. He grunts like he's been starved for me, like nothing in the world exists but him and me.

Pulling back, Des meets my gaze. "I wasn't sure if you'd still want to do this after we got back to Heart's Cove."

"Do what?"

"This." He kisses me, his arms tightening on my waist. "I thought it might only be for the weekend."

"It's still the weekend until tomorrow." Grinning, I touch my nose to his, then pull away and hurry to the front of the shop. I flick the lock on the barbershop door and pull the blinds. He watches me from the chair, eyes dark. When I approach him again and slide my hands over his chest, Des lets out a low huff.

He pulls away before we can kiss again to stare into my eyes. Whatever grew between us in Colorado expands to fill the space that separates us now. Des's hands cup my cheeks, his thumbs coasting over my skin. "I lo—I really like you, Mia. But you have a lot going on. Bailey has a lot going on. I don't want to be in the way while you try to figure things out with your ex-husband."

In the way? What does that even mean?

He must see my frown, because he continues by saying, "What do you need from me?"

"Des, just kiss me, please," I say, not caring that I'm begging. "Stop talking and kiss me."

A violent shudder courses through Des's body, then he tightens his hold on me and crushes his lips to mine. I moan against his mouth, curling my arms around his shoulders. His thighs tighten on either side of me, pinning my hips in place.

"Mom? Des?"

I fly off Des's chest, sending the barber's chair spinning. Des clears his throat, stopping the chair with a foot on the ground. We both turn to look at the door at the back of the barbershop. Bailey stands in the open doorway, looking vaguely disgusted.

"Why were you kissing?"

"Hi, honey," I squeak. "I was just giving Des a shave."

Bailey arches an eyebrow. "Right."

A noise comes out of Desmond that sounds suspiciously like a snort. He swallows thickly, then glances at me, hands spread helplessly.

"Is Des staying for dinner?" Bailey asks.

"Um." I blink at my daughter, then at Des. They both stare back at me, so I look at Bailey again. "Do you want him to stay for dinner?"

"Yeah," Bailey says. "There's a Lakers game on tonight. We could watch it even though I hate the Lakers." She frowns. "Unless you were going to watch it at home? You don't have to stay."

"No," Des blurts. "I'd love to stay for dinner."

Warmth tingles in my chest. It sounds like he really means it.

Des stands, sending me a questioning glance. When I nod, he heads toward Bailey and ruffles her hair. She peeks around his chest to smile at me, and then they both disappear into the hallway.

Following after them, I find Bailey showing Des the doll, saying how much more she likes the socks he gave her. Des looks like he's trying not to laugh, but if I'm reading his expression correctly, it also looks like he's inordinately pleased.

I wink at him, finding the remote to turn the TV on to the sports channel. Bailey hops onto the sofa and pats the seat next to her for Des to sit in. When I'm in the kitchen getting snacks for the three of us, I hear Des ask, "What did you think of your dad?"

"He's okay," Bailey responds. "It's kind of weird meeting him."

"Good weird or bad weird?"

There's a pause. "Just weird."

Des grunts.

I cut up some veggies and find some ranch dressing for dipping, arranging it all on a platter for the three of us.

Bailey says, "Do you like my mom? Like, *like* like her?" and I pause what I'm doing to listen to the answer.

"Yes," Desmond replies.

My heart does a weird jumpy thing, and my face goes hot. I have to rearrange the carrot sticks for a few seconds to pull myself together.

"Oh."

"Is that okay?"

"Um... Yeah. I think she likes you too. And I think you're cool. Except for being a Lakers fan."

"Thanks, kiddo." I can hear the smile in Desmond's voice. "I think you're cool too."

"Are you going to marry her?"

I freeze.

There's a pause, and I hear fabric rustling, like Desmond is shifting in his seat. He says, "I don't know, Bailey. That's something your mom and I would have to talk about."

"Oh."

I frown, staring at the little ramekin of ranch dressing. Something we'd have to talk about? What? Does that mean Des wants to marry me? Was he just giving Bailey a bland answer? Why is my heart thumping? Why do I feel partially giddy but also like I want to throw up?

Oh my God. *Do I want to marry Desmond?*

"But you were kissing her. And people kiss before they get married."

"Right," Des says, and I know I need to go out there and save him. The living room/kitchen is L-shaped now, so I don't have a direct view of them even though I'm technically in the same space. I put the ranch on the platter, letting the dishes clink against each other loudly to remind them both that I'm right here.

Bailey, oblivious, says, "If you married my mom, you'd be my stepdad."

"Look, Bailey, your mom and I are just friends right now." He clears his throat. "Marriage is a big deal."

I deflate like an old balloon. Holy crap. I *do* want to marry him. What is *wrong* with me? That's a really good way of getting your heart broken all over again.

"Right," Bailey says, sounding dejected. I grab the platter and freeze when she says, "I would be okay with you being my step-dad, you know."

Des's voice is gruff when he says, "Thanks, Bailey. I... I'd be happy to be your stepdad too."

When I finally step around the corner and into view, Des looks like he just survived a Category Five hurricane, and Bailey's swinging her legs off the edge of the sofa like she doesn't have a care in the world.

I roll my lips inward, trying not to laugh, then put the veggies down on the coffee table and take a seat next to Des.

Then the basketball game starts, and the inquisition is over.

AFTER DINNER, when Bailey is in bed, I sit on the sofa with my feet tucked under Des's thighs while we both sip the last of a bottle of wine we had with dinner. I glance down the hallway to make sure Bailey isn't lurking, then I say, "I heard what Bailey was saying earlier."

Des sips his wine and sets it down on the coffee table, grinning. "I never knew being questioned by a nine-year-old girl would be the most stressful experience of my life."

"You did well." I laugh, wiggling my toes against his leg.

His eyes meet mine, solemn as he says, "I was serious, you know. I'd be happy to be a part of her life—and yours."

Oh, my. The glass I'm holding is lifted out of my hands and set on the coffee table. Then Des picks me up and sits me on his lap, one arm across my thighs, the other hand tangled into my hair.

Kissing this man is like coming home. Having him here all

evening—watching him interact with my daughter—has made my heart overflow. I touch his jaw, deepening our kiss, trying to convey all the things I feel for him.

We could have a life together.

His hand sweeps over my cheek and down to my neck while his lips devastate me. I melt into his chest, clinging to his shoulders like he's the only thing tethering me to earth.

When we pull apart, my heart is tattooing a rapid beat against its cage. For the first time in a long, long time, I feel the desire to open up to someone else. I want to let him in.

"What?" he asks softly, touching his nose to mine. "You look like you want to say something."

"How do you do that?" I half-laugh, shaking my head.

"Do what?"

"Read my mind."

"It's written right there on your face, Mia." His hand coasts down to my hip, squeezing gently. The other is across my thighs, its thumb sweeping gently against my pants. I love the way he touches me. It's intimate and casual all at once. It feels like I belong here, like this.

"Funny how no one else seems to be able to read me so easily."

He grins, leaning his head back to watch me. "So? What's on your mind?"

"Do you think I'm making a mistake by letting Colin meet Bailey?" I blurt, not realizing that's what's going to come out.

Des watches me, tilting his head from side to side. "No," he finally answers.

"Sometimes I just want to tell him to take a hike. He lost his chance at being a father, he doesn't get another one."

"So, why don't you?"

I chew my lip. "Because of Bailey. I couldn't live with myself if she was angry with me later on after finding out that I refused to let her know her father. I want to keep her to myself—keep things how they've always been, just the two of us—but I know that's not what's best for her."

"All you can do is protect her, then," he answers, echoing my own thoughts. "You just make sure she has you in her corner all the time, and make sure Colin treats her right."

I nod. "Yeah. It's just hard, you know? It's been me and Bailey against the world for so long, it's strange to let anyone in." I give him a rueful smile. "It's strange to let you in."

"Am I in? I still feel like I'm banging against the door, waiting for a response."

I click my tongue. "I'm not that bad."

He chuckles, squeezing his hands on my hip again. "No. You aren't."

"I know I'm closed off," I admit. "Ever since Colin left, it's been hard for me to trust anyone."

"He left when you were pregnant?"

I nod, throat closing up. After those first few horrible weeks, when we decided to break up, I poured all my focus into my pregnancy, then into Bailey. I haven't even spoken to my parents or sister about all this—not beyond the basics. But it's been a decade; I should be able to make the words come out now, with Des's arms encircling me. "We didn't want kids," I admit. "He was very clear about that from the start. I thought I agreed, and we were happily married for a while. I ended up going off the birth control pill because it was messing with my mood too much, and I guess we weren't as careful as we should have been. It wasn't entirely surprising that I became pregnant, when I think about it."

"And he still left?"

"He wanted me to get rid of her." I huff. "I refused, and that was it."

Des's eyes are shadowed. His hands coast gently over my hip and thigh, his warmth surrounding me completely.

"The divorce was amicable. As amicable as it could be, I guess. I was devastated, but I had a kid to take care of. My priorities changed."

"I understand why you don't want him here," Des says, shaking his head. "I don't know if I'd be able to be the bigger person in your situation."

"You get used to putting your kid first," I answer, snorting. "Comes with the territory." I touch his jaw, then let my fingers drop to the collar of his shirt. I trace its outline, shaking my head. "I haven't dated anyone since Bailey was born because I couldn't stand the thought of my daughter feeling the way I did when Colin left." And I couldn't bear the thought of going through it again, but that's harder to say out loud. I don't want Des to think I'm trying to trap him with me.

"I'm not going anywhere," he says gently, reading my mind once more. He catches my gaze and holds it, dark eyes deathly serious. "I'm right here, Mia."

"I haven't scared you away?"

"You'll have to try a lot harder if you want me to leave," he answers, pulling me in for a kiss. Something shifts between us, clicks into place. I feel it in the way our lips move, in the way we cling to each other. I kiss him hard, letting myself fall down, down, down...

"Bedroom," I say between kisses.

He pulls back. "You sure?" He glances down the hallway.

"She's asleep," I reply, then climb off his lap to lead him to the master bedroom. I pause in front of Bailey's door to make sure she is, in fact, asleep, then continue on to my room. "We have to be quiet," I tell him.

"That's on you," he answers, eyes glittering in the low light. Then his arms are around me, and I'm carried to bed.

It's hard to describe how much this man affects me. It's like I've been stumbling around in the dark for a decade, and I finally found a pinprick of light in the distance to guide me out. He's a lifeline in a stormy sea that I never expected to grab onto. I never realized how cold I was until I felt his warmth.

He breathes life back into me with every kiss, every touch.

Bodies bare in the darkness, we cling to each other and whisper sweet, dirty secrets. He tells me I'm beautiful, I taste amazing, I'm perfect. He makes me feel like I'll never be alone again, like I've finally found somewhere that's safe and steady.

Then he shatters me into a million tiny pieces, until all I know is a kaleidoscope of pleasure.

Panting, skin to skin, I come back to myself and press my lips to the soft skin of his shoulder. Despite everything that happened today, my world is right again. But the seconds tick by, and reality comes knocking.

"Des," I start. "I want you to stay the night, but…"

"You don't want Bailey to be confused."

"There's just a lot going on with Colin in town," I explain, hating myself a little bit. The last thing I want to do is kick Des out, but what choice do I have? I have to put my daughter first. I won't have Des walking out of my bedroom, making Bailey ask him when he's going to propose.

"I get it," Des replies before pressing his lips to my forehead.

"Thank you. I'm sorry."

"Hey." He gathers me in his arms and kisses my lips. "Don't be sorry. I want to stay. But if I'm here when Bailey wakes up, I don't know if I'll survive the questioning."

I huff a laugh, then watch Des dress in the dark. Finding a robe to wrap around myself, I pad down the hallway behind him and follow him through the barbershop. The lock slides open with a soft snick, and I stand there shivering in the cold.

He wraps me in his warmth once more, then kisses me softly. "I'll call you tomorrow," he promises.

"Okay."

"Can you come to dinner at my grandparents' house? Maude was asking."

Reality comes slamming into me. I bite my lip. "I can't. We're meeting Colin again," I admit. "I'm sorry. Rain check?"

Des clears his throat and nods. He drops his arms from around me and takes half a step back. It feels like a chasm. "Yeah. Sure. Let me know when you're free."

"He'll be gone by next Saturday," I tell him. And thank goodness for that. As much as I'm pretending to be the bigger person, I really don't feel like dealing with my ex-husband for more than a week.

When Des leaves the barbershop, I feel emptier than I did before.

THIRTY-ONE
DES

"WHERE'S MIA, DEAR?" my grandmother asks as she heaps mashed potatoes onto my plate.

I hold out my hand to stop her, but she slops another heaping spoonful onto the mountain of mash. I guess I'll always be a "growing boy" to my grandmother. "She was busy tonight," I tell her, not sure why I don't want to admit that she was meeting her ex-husband for dinner.

I know, I know. She's not going on a date with him; she's trying to introduce him to his own daughter. I admire that about her. Witnessing her reaction to him on the evening we arrived, and then seeing how shaken up she was yesterday, I know it isn't easy for her to let him in. Mia is strong—stronger than she even admits to herself—but she's also fragile in unexpected ways. She's brittle when she thinks she's about to get hurt. She has vulnerabilities that she tries desperately to hide.

I love her vulnerabilities, her softness. I love everything about her.

In her position, I'm not sure I'd let my ex back into my life, even if I knew my kid had a right to know them. I wouldn't be able to get over the bitterness.

Still, the thought of her out to dinner with another man—a man who has such a long, complicated history with her—makes the back of my neck itch. I'd rather she be here beside me and Colin as far away as possible. Last night sealed it for me. Spending time with Mia and Bailey felt like I was part of a family. I didn't want to leave; I didn't want to let her go see her ex today.

I wanted to wake up next to Mia and pad to the kitchen to make her coffee. I wanted to help Bailey make breakfast and listen to whatever crazy shit comes out of that kid's mouth. I wanted to *be* there. I wanted to belong there.

But I don't—at least not yet.

"Where's Mia?" Grandpa Arthur shouts, comparing his pitiful pile of potatoes to my ginormous mound. He frowns at his wife.

Maude pats his arm. "She's busy." She says it only slightly louder than normal, but Arthur seems to hear her. The two of them must have a connection that goes beyond volume and hearing.

They're two humans so tightly twined around each other that it's obvious to anyone that they belong to each other. They've been married seventy years—a lifetime. I've never been that close to anyone. There's no frame of reference I can even use to imagine what it would be like to have a connection like that.

I wonder if my time in Lovers' Peak was a hallucination. That feeling that I might belong to Mia, and she might belong to me... What if that *was* just lust—or delusion? The relationship my grandparents have is so rare. What if it's unreasonable for me to imagine that I could have the same thing?

It's possible that last night wasn't as significant for her as it was for me. I haven't heard from her all day; maybe that's a message in itself. She doesn't think I belong by her side at all.

"What's Mia doing tonight, Des? Why's she so busy?" Grandma cuts a tiny piece off her single slice of roast beef and spears it with her fork.

I swallow my mouthful and take a sip of water. "She's actually meeting her ex-husband for dinner."

"Goodness!" Maude leans toward my grandfather. "Did you hear that?"

Arthur determinedly scoops mashed potatoes onto his fork and brings it to his mouth. "Hear what?"

A short translation later, and my grandmother turns back to me. "Why is she doing that?"

"He wants to spend time with Bailey," I explain, discomfort twisting in my gut. "Mia wants to supervise."

"Well, she is a mother," my grandmother concedes, slightly mollified. "Will you see her afterward?"

I keep my eyes on my plate. "Probably not, Grandma. It'll be late." Needing to redirect the conversation, I nod to the back door. "Might be good to prune the hedges now, before the winter hits."

The reaction is immediate: "Des, don't be ridiculous. It's best to wait until the end of the winter to cut back the hedges. I have high hopes for the garden next year, and I won't let you go hacking at my bushes willy-nilly."

"Any plans for roses? You said Agnes had beautiful ones last year, right?"

"That horrible woman!" Maude exclaims before launching into a rant about the local bookstore keeper, suitably distracted from the topic of my woman on a dinner date with another man.

Later, when I'm helping clean up the dishes, I get a phone call from the realtor, Samantha. She has offers on both of the condos on Seventh Avenue. The buyer wants to close on them as soon as possible.

My grandparents are delighted with the news—and more than a little relieved. Their money stress will soon be over—as will the reason for me to be in Heart's Cove.

But that's not quite true anymore. There's another reason for me to stay here—a bigger reason. Mia and Bailey are here, which means there's nowhere else that will be quite right for me.

The problem is, I don't think Mia understands what I feel for her. I messed up so badly at the start of our relationship by not telling her it was me on the app and by raising her rent without speaking to her first, and I know she's holding back from me.

Then I get an idea.

There's something I can do to prove to her how much I love her. One simple act will show that I want to be with her. I want to build a life where I *do* get to call Bailey my daughter. I'm serious about the two of them. No more dating apps, no fake dates, no dancing around my feelings and pretending anything about us is casual.

What we have is real, and I have the means to make Mia understand—but first, I'll have to go back to Lovers' Peak one last time.

THIRTY-TWO
MIA

COLIN, Bailey, and I eat at Taqueria for dinner. Bailey's legs swing below her chair as she eats a messy taco and tells Colin about her recent field trip to the fire station.

He listens, rapt, laughing when Bailey tells him about sliding down the fireman's pole.

"I met the old fire chief," she says. "Mr. Allen hurt his knee, so he doesn't fight fires anymore, but he still volunteers and does training. He said I could be a firefighter when I grow up, and then he let me meet the only woman firefighter in Heart's Cove. Her name was Sandy. She was kinda scary, but I liked her."

Grinning, I touch my daughter's hair, sliding her ponytail back over her shoulder. Colin meets my gaze and shakes his head. "It's good to be here." He looks at Bailey. "I'm glad we get to spend time together, kiddo."

Bailey eats the rest of her taco, chews, and swallows. She

meets Colin's eyes and says, "You're nicer than I thought you would be."

"Oh?"

"Yeah," she replies. "Mom never really told me about you, and I kind of figured you were mean, because you left. But you're pretty cool."

Colin's face goes through a complicated series of emotions, which he manages to get under control by sipping from his glass of sparkling water. My own insides feel like they're going through a meat grinder over and over again. Thank goodness he's leaving at the end of the week. I can't take too much more of this.

"Not as cool as Des, because he likes basketball," Bailey continues, oblivious to the punishing blows she's delivering to both of us, "but still pretty cool."

"Des," Colin says. "That's the guy who was driving you home? The guy who spent Thanksgiving with you?"

"Yeah," Bailey cuts in before I can respond. "Mom was kissing him. It was gross."

Colin frowns at me, which kind of pisses me off. I decide to ignore it altogether, because, really, it's none of his business who I kiss. Hasn't been his business for ten years.

By the time the meal is over and Colin is saying goodbye to Bailey, I'm about ready to collapse into bed. Then he touches my elbow and says, "Can I talk to you for a second?"

Here we go. What now?

I nod, opening the back door of my car for Bailey and closing it gently, then turning to face my ex-husband.

Colin adjusts the collar of his shirt and lets out a long sigh. He fusses with the buttons of his pea coat, then tugs at the cuffs. My patience wears thin as I watch him preen himself.

My ex is only a couple of inches taller than I am, and I used to like that he didn't tower over me. He has the body of a software engineer, by which I mean, he's kind of scrawny. He's not out of shape, but he looks like he'd run marathons instead of lift weights. I liked that about him too. His size never intimidated me—I used to think that was great. I didn't understand how nice it would be to be in the arms of a man of Des's stature. How safe and loved I could feel with someone as strong as my landlord.

I was so in love with Colin, but now, I feel nothing. No bitterness, no anger, no love...just a sort of exhaustion and emptiness. He's just another thing I need to add to my to-do list (Item One: Make Sure My Daughter Doesn't Resent Me for Keeping Her From Her Father. Item Two: Make Sure Father Doesn't Leave and Break Her Heart (Again)).

"She's great," Colin starts, nodding to the car. "You did a fantastic job with her."

Well, duh. Instead of sassing him like I'm a moody teenager, I just answer, "Thanks." Look at me, taking the high road. I should get an award.

"I've talked to my boss, and they're willing to let me work from home for the foreseeable future."

"Oh," I say, my heart starting to pick up speed. Why is he telling me this?

"I've decided to stay in Heart's Cove, try to get to know Bailey more." He glances at Bailey and gives her a little smile and a wave. I feel the need to punch his nose until it breaks and decide I don't deserve an award after all. He looks at me with those sad, soulful eyes. "I know it's not nearly enough to make up for leaving, but meeting her... My priorities have changed. I've put an offer in on a home here in town, and it's been accepted."

My whole body goes cold. The emotion that rushes through me is unfamiliar; it takes me a second to realize what exactly I'm feeling. Then I get it—it's pure, icy terror.

"You're not getting custody of her," I blurt. So much for being the bigger person. Saint Mia dies a quick and ugly death.

Colin blinks rapidly, then shakes his head. "I know. I just want to be in her life."

"You don't get to swoop in and be a hero, Colin. She's *my* daughter." Cold fear gets burned up by dragon's breath as my temper finally, *finally* comes out to play. I grip it with both hands, needing to cling onto something familiar to tow me out of this storm of emotions.

My ex-husband will *not* take my daughter away. He won't be the hero. He won't waltz into my life and mess everything up again. Never, ever, ever.

Colin rocks back on his heels and shoves a hand through his hair. "I know. Fuck, I know, Mia. I'm sorry. Look, I'm just trying to do the right thing, here. I'm trying to be a father."

"Well, good for you," I spit. "You're about ten years too late, though."

Then I stomp around to the driver's side and get in, slamming the door. I start the engine, and it's not until we turn down the back lane where our apartment door is that Bailey speaks.

"What happened?" Her voice is small, tentative—nothing like she usually is.

I park outside the door and let out a long sigh, hands sliding off the steering wheel. Then I wrestle my expression into something (hopefully) neutral and turn to meet my daughter's worried gaze.

"Don't worry about it, Bailey," I say, forcing a smile. "It's a grown-up issue."

She doesn't seem convinced, but my daughter nods and exits the car. We snuggle on the couch and watch a movie together, then go to bed early. Bailey has school tomorrow, and I learned a long time ago that routine is paramount, no matter what else is going on.

It's not until I'm lying on my bed that I look at my phone. There's a text from Des.

Des: How was dinner? My grandma missed you, btw.

I read the text over a few times, then let my arms fall down to my sides. I'm so *tired*. It was selfish of me to think that I could start a relationship with a man at a time like this. I need to be there for Bailey; I need to make sure she's my priority.

It's weak to want Des here beside me. It's selfish of me to wish Colin had never shown up. Life was so much easier when I was on my own—even if it was a lot bleaker.

I've made so, so many mistakes lately. But hey—what else is new. That's how I've operated my entire life.

Putting my phone on the bedside table, I curl up on my side and let sleep take me away.

· · ·

DES SHOWS up at the barbershop the next day and takes a seat in one of the chairs near the door while I finish up a haircut for Hamish, Margaret's beau. When he's paid and left, Des stands and walks toward me.

My heart speeds up. There's a war going on inside me, a push and pull that threatens to tear me apart. On the one hand, I want to run to Des and let him wrap me up in his arms. I want to bury myself in his embrace and never come up for air.

But on the other, I want to stand on my own and be strong. Nothing can stop me from doing what's right for Bailey. If (or when) this man walks away from me, I need to ensure it won't break me completely. Scrambling, I use anything I can to build my defenses back up, to protect myself from the assault this man wages on me.

"You never answered my text," he says, approaching slowly. "Is everything okay?"

I spin the barber's chair toward him and give him a grim smile. "Define 'okay.'"

He huffs and takes a seat. My hands find their way to his shoulders, smoothing the wrinkles in his button-down shirt. I watch him in the mirror, this big, burly man, and feel a strange, painful twist in the center of my chest. I take my hands away from him. I should know by now that touching Des is dangerous.

"How was dinner?" he finally asks.

My palms itch to smooth over his hair, to touch his shoulders, to feel the warmth of his skin against mine, but I curl them into fists to stop myself. I'm relying too much on Des's strength and support. "Dinner was okay." *Until Colin dropped a bomb on me.* "How was your evening?"

Maybe if I keep him at arm's length, it won't hurt so much when he leaves.

Des holds my gaze in the mirror, frowning for a moment. Then his expression clears and he shrugs. "My grandparents missed you."

"I would have much preferred to have dinner with them," I answer, smiling a little bit too wide for it to look real.

Des huffs. "I'll let them know. They might call you to keep them company for the next couple of weeks."

"What happens in the next couple of weeks?"

"I'm going back to Lovers' Peak. I've got a few things to sort out."

Keeping my eyes on the back of his head for a moment, I let the words sink in. Then I clear my throat and move to the little counter by the mirror, angling my head so he can't see my face. I don't want him to see whatever's written there. I'm sure he'd be able to see right through me to all the bitterness inside.

He told me he'd leave, didn't he? He warned me.

Still, my blood runs cold and my heart beats unsteadily. I didn't think it would hurt this much to hear that he decided to go through with it.

Finally confident my voice is under control, I face him and ask, "How long will you be there?"

Des leans back in the chair, letting out a long sigh, gaze sliding away from mine. There's something he's not telling me. "That depends on a few things."

Of course it does. I knew he was leaving, and I still managed to get myself tied up in knots over him, my heart jumping like a jackrabbit when my daughter asked about marriage. Marriage!

I'm a special kind of delusional.

Not able to bear the chance of eye contact, I turn back to my tools, touching the handle of my razor gently. I feel hot and cold and tense. I wish I knew what Des was thinking, what he wanted from me. I have feelings for this man—strong feelings—and they terrify me.

I begin, and Des closes his eyes. "How did Bailey feel after dinner?"

None of your business, I want to scream. If he's just going to walk out of our lives willy-nilly, why should he have the right to know anything about my daughter? Then I talk myself down and remind myself that he's coming back, he just doesn't know when.

But what isn't he telling me?

Maybe this is a sign. I'm not supposed to open up to Des—or anyone, for that matter—anytime soon. I need to focus on my daughter and my business.

"She's happy, I think."

Another silence, then: "She deserves to know her father."

"So I keep reminding myself," I answer grimly. I take my time with his shave, loving the sound of the razor against Des's skin, the warmth of him so close to me. Shaving him is different from shaving my regular customers. It's intimate, almost domestic.

I like it—maybe too much.

"What aren't you telling me about dinner last night?" Des finally asks when I'm putting my tools away.

With my back to him, I can frown without Des noticing. Shuttering my expression, I glance over my shoulder. "What?"

"You seem on edge."

Ya think? Maybe because the first man I've been attracted to has done nothing but confuse me for the past three months. And my ex-husband suddenly reappeared, acting like the father of the year. And both of them will probably be gone for good within a few weeks, and I'll have to pick up the pieces and make sure my daughter and I survive.

"I'm fine," I answer. "There's just a lot going on."

Des opens his mouth to answer, but the ringing of my phone interrupts him. We both look at the little counter below the mirror, where Colin's name is lit up on the phone's display. I grimace.

"Answer it," Des says, his eyes losing their softness. "Might be important."

I nod, then take a few steps away and answer. "Yeah?"

"Are you busy?" Colin asks.

"Um. Kind of." I glance at Des. "I'm with a customer right now."

Something strange happens to Des's face when I say that, but I have to look away to focus on what Colin says next.

"How do you feel about me taking Bailey out next weekend, just the two of us? I could take her to her basketball game and then out to lunch after."

I can almost feel Des's eyes on me, and discomfort twists in my gut. I bite my lip and say, "I'm not sure I'm comfortable with you being with her one-on-one yet, Colin. It's only been a couple of days."

"I understand. Can I take you both out to dinner, then?"

"Um, fine," I answer, catching Des standing behind me. He gestures toward the door, like he has to leave. He wasn't in such a hurry before my phone rang. What's that about? Is he upset I'm speaking to Colin? He's the one who's taking off without warning for who knows how long!

I realize I've missed what Colin is saying when he asks me a question, and I have no idea what he's talking about. "Sorry, Colin. Text me the details. I have to go." I hang up just as Des reaches the door. "Wait!"

He pauses, turning to face me. "You're busy," he says quietly. "I shouldn't take up so much of your time. I have to pack and get ready to go, anyway."

My stomach plummets. I blink once, twice, then nod and do my best to smile. "Oh. Of course."

There's a lengthy pause while Des stares at the door, and then he turns around and meets my gaze again. "Why did you tell your ex-husband you were with a customer, instead of saying you were with me?"

"What?"

"When you answered the phone. You said you were with a customer."

"Des." I frown. "That didn't mean anything."

"Didn't it?" He sighs, shaking his head. "You know what, forget it. I have to pack for Colorado. I'll call you later."

The dragon cracks an eyelid. Who does this guy think he is? I met him a few months ago! We spend one weekend together, and all of a sudden he wants to be my everything? I should never have opened up to him. I should never have gone to Thanksgiving with him. I definitely shouldn't have introduced him to Bailey.

Desmond knows my deepest secrets, he knows how hurt and alone I've been for ten years, and he's giving me shit about what I said to my ex? Is he for real?

He's just another man with an overinflated ego that I'll have to bend over backward to accommodate. No, thank you. I did *not* sign up for this.

I push my hip out to the side and cross my arms. "Don't bother calling," I sneer. "If you're going to get all upset over a throwaway comment, I have some things to think about."

His eyes narrow. "A throwaway comment? How hard is it to tell him you're with me? Are you that embarrassed about me?"

"Why the hell is this about you?" I throw my arms out to the sides. "I'm trying to navigate this messed-up relationship with my ex-husband in a way that doesn't traumatize my daughter. Where did your name come up in that sentence? That's right: nowhere."

"So, what, the past couple of months mean nothing?"

"Not in relation to this!"

"Right." He snorts and turns to the door.

"You know what, Des, I can't deal with this right now. I need some space."

"Well, I'm leaving, so you're getting about three states' worth of space from me."

"Good," I spit.

"Good." He repeats. Then the door bangs, and Desmond is gone.

THIRTY-THREE
DES

ANGER BLOWS through me like a gale, carrying me across town and back to my home. But it isn't really home, is it? At least, not for long.

I grit my teeth. Half of me wants to turn right around and make Mia understand what she means to me. I want her to get that when she pushes me out like that, it makes me feel like I'm eleven years old again, being tormented by my aunt's favorite.

Stopping in the middle of the sidewalk, I stare at the gray sky. As the wind cools my skin, reason returns, and I know that Mia is right.

She's dealing with real issues that are happening right now. So what if my teenage years were hell? So what if my old boss decided to give his company to his own son? That's in the past. Mia has to deal with her ex-husband and her daughter right now, and I'm making things harder for her.

My shoulders slump. I know I was wrong. Spinning on my heels, I take one step back toward the barbershop, then freeze.

I need some space.

She was crystal clear about her needs, and I want to rush back there and make her listen to me? No, I'm not going to be that guy. I'm not going to be the oaf who needs to be coddled and included. I'm going to respect her wishes.

Once I get back from Lovers' Peak, she'll understand how I feel. She'll see how much she means to me.

Turning back once more, I make my way to Seventh Avenue and let myself into my building. It's a good thing these properties are sold. It's a good thing I can move into my own place, figure out what's next for me. It means there's space in my life for new things, new people—like Mia and Bailey.

Getting in the elevator, I force myself to be grateful that the buyer wants a quick settlement. They're buying both condos as-is, furniture and contents included. My realtor said the new owner will occupy Unit 312 part-time, and the condo I'm in will be an investment property.

My grandparents are happy, and this way I can start figuring out what to do with my life full-time. Once I'm done in Lovers' Peak, I'll have a lot more freedom to make a plan. I can come back and tell Mia exactly how I feel—no, I can *show* her how serious I am.

I won't be a customer anymore. I won't have to sneak off in the middle of the night. I'll have a place by her side, where I belong. Plus, as soon as her ex-husband is gone, Mia will be calmer. She'll have more time. We'll be able to connect like we did over Thanksgiving. Everything will be okay. By the end of the weekend, I'll be able to call Mia and apologize properly, and she'll have the bandwidth to hear it.

I'll give her the space she needs, but I'm not leaving her.

When I get to the third floor of my building, I'm surprised to see the realtor standing outside Unit 312—and I'm even more surprised to see her standing beside Mia's ex.

"Des!" Samantha exclaims, smiling wide. She's wearing a bright pantsuit with her silver pixie cut styled in sharp spikes. "This is Colin. He just wanted to check a few things in the condo to see what he needed to buy before moving in. We cleared it with Maude."

Her words stop me short. The hallway stretches and stretches and stretches before me, like some awful, stomach-churning optical illusion. Mia's ex turns to face me in slow-motion, his brows arching when he recognizes me.

It feels like five whole minutes tick by, second by agonizing second, but really it must only be a moment. My gaze bounces between the two of them and lands on Samantha. "*This* is the buyer?"

She frowns. "Um... Yes? Is there a problem?"

YES, THERE IS A BIG FUCKING PROBLEM. I swallow the words down. "No." Glancing at Colin, I say, "I didn't realize you were planning on staying long-term. Mia said you were only here for a week."

His eyes light up, and I don't like the curve of his lips. "She didn't tell you?"

I think of the tension in her body just now, when I hugged her in her barbershop, how it felt like she was holding back from telling me the whole truth about her dinner—and how she never answered my text last night.

This is what she was hiding. This is what she didn't tell me. Is this why she didn't want to tell him I was with her today? Because she knew he'd be sticking around?

Even though I already know the answer, I grit out, "Tell me what?"

Colin spreads his arms. "I'm staying."

Two little words, and my whole world blows up. "You're staying."

"Yep." He jingles the keys and turns the lock. "I want to get to know my daughter. She needs a decent father figure."

"And that's supposed to be you, the man who abandoned her before she was born?"

Samantha clears her throat, tugging at the hem of her suit jacket. We both ignore her.

"Who even are you?" Colin sneers. "When I asked Mia, she said she wasn't seeing anyone."

I must make a face, because Colin's expression clears, and he starts laughing as he pushes the front door open. He holds it ajar with his foot and shakes his head. "It was you that was with her earlier, wasn't it? You were the customer in her shop she was talking about." He glances at the realtor. "This shouldn't take long. I just need to see what I need to buy so I can live in this place."

Samantha nods politely. "Of course." She glances at me, then at the apartment's closing door, catching it before it latches. I can tell she wants to say something to me, and I don't want to hear it. I stalk by her and turn into the other condo, closing the door behind me with a dull thud. Then I lean against it and press the heels of my hands into my eye sockets.

Her ex is staying—and she didn't tell me.

Then my phone rings. I see the name on the screen and think about my genius plan to prove myself to Mia...and I know there's no going back.

I'll have to go to Lovers' Peak and finish what I started, whether or not Mia wants me at the end of it all.

THIRTY-FOUR
MIA

EVERYTHING IS TOTALLY FINE. Everything is great. Everything is going to be okay.

Those words have been on repeat for a week and a half, ever since Des told me he was leaving. I'm a Stepford Wife, smiling blankly at the world as it goes by, pretending everything is A-okay in my little fucked-up world.

"The two condos are on Seventh Avenue. Apparently the old couple was desperate to sell. I got an amazing deal. It's a great investment." Colin shoves more food in his mouth and keeps telling me how smart he is.

How did I ever love this man? How did I ever find him attractive? I mean—my God. I *definitely* need to have my head examined.

It's been ten days since Des was at my barbershop, and I've hardly heard from him other than a couple of cagey texts. I suppose I deserve that, don't I? I asked for space.

Now, I'm learning that Colin bought both of the condos Maude and Arthur were trying to sell, which means Des doesn't even have a home anymore.

Everything is totally fine. Everything is great. Everything is going to be okay.

"When do you move in?" Bailey takes a bite of her pizza.

"I close on both properties tomorrow," Colin replies. "I'll move in right away. It's furnished, so all I'll have to do is unpack my suitcase."

Which means Des has already moved out, and he didn't tell me—because I asked him for space. Because I'm so terrified of intimacy and of being abandoned that I pushed him away, like a coward.

Bailey squints. "So you're really staying in Heart's Cove?"

Colin puts his fork down. He meets Bailey's eyes. "Yeah. How do you feel about that?"

"Um," my daughter says, picking a mushroom off her pizza and flicking it to the side of her plate. "I feel okay, I guess. Why are you staying? Don't you have work to do?"

"I'm going to be working from home. And I'm staying because I want to know you better. I missed you growing up."

Oh, barf. That's such a lie. He didn't even think about her, and now he wants an award for showing up after a decade. Missed her, my ass.

Deep breaths, Mia. He's doing his best. Bailey deserves to know her father. Everything is totally fine. Everything is great. Everything is going to be okay.

Thankfully, Bailey is not an idiot. She doesn't look convinced. She just takes another bite, chewing thoughtfully.

Maybe this was a mistake. I should have set better boundaries, told Colin I wasn't comfortable with him staying in town. But it's not like I can control what he does—if he wants to buy a couple of condos, who am I to stop him? I *can* put limits on how much time he spends with Bailey. I can make sure she's comfortable. If at any point she decides she doesn't want to spend time with her father, I can stop all of this, investment properties or no.

"You know," Colin says, flicking his gaze to mine, "you could move into one of the condos. It would be better for Bailey if you lived somewhere a little safer. We could even look at getting you a house with a yard." He glances at Bailey, smiling. "You could get a dog."

Bailey's eyes grow wide. She spins her head toward me, the hope pouring off of her in thick waves. "*A dog?*"

I'm going to kill Colin. Kill him dead. Then I'll bring him back to life just so I can kill him again. And again. And again.

"We'll see," I say, then turn to Colin and give him my best death glare. "That's enough. Let's get the bill."

He throws his hands up. "Look, I'm sorry, I just figured you wouldn't want to raise our daughter behind a barbershop her whole life, is all."

"I will make decisions for *my* daughter, thank you." I stand and grab my jacket off the back of my chair. "Come on, Bailey. You have school tomorrow."

"Mia, wait!" Colin stands and comes around the table. "I'm sorry, okay? I just figured if you needed a place to stay, you could have one of the places I just bought."

Oh, lovely. He's just swooping in to save me—and conveniently keeping me right in his sights.

No, I did *not* spend the past ten years of my life rebuilding everything just to hand it over to my fucking ex-husband. "Goodnight, Colin."

"Can we do lunch this weekend?"

"We're busy this weekend," I answer, then take Bailey's hand and walk out of the restaurant.

When we're in the car and halfway home, Bailey lets out a dramatic sigh. "Why don't you want to get a dog, Mom?"

"Because I'll be the one to take care of it, and I already have enough on my plate."

"What if I take care of it?" She tugs at her seatbelt and leans forward. "I could feed it and everything. And I could pick up its poo even though it's gross. I'd make it sit and roll over."

"Mm." I take the turn onto our back laneway. Is it too grimy? There's a little patch of grass outside our door—and the park is just at the end of the road—but is it really so bad? This is our home. The condo building is bigger, but it's not any better. Especially after all the renovations Des did for us.

"Are you mad at me, Mom?"

I park the car outside our door and turn to face her. "No, honey. Not at all."

"Oh."

I take a deep breath. "Sometimes, it's just hard for me to be with Colin. He hurt my feelings before, and I haven't entirely forgiven him."

"Because he left before I was born?"

I nod. "Yeah."

"I don't want to move to his condo. I want to stay here."

My shoulders relax. "Me too."

"We could still get a dog, though. I bet Mr. and Mrs. Thomas would be okay with it. They always smile and pet dogs when they pass them on the street. It could be the mascot for the barbershop!"

I unlatch my seatbelt and open the door. "We'll see, kiddo."

"That's what Des calls me."

An ice pick lodges itself in my chest. I wince, and it comes out like a huff. "Yeah. I must have picked him up from him."

"When is he coming back? Do you think he'll want to come watch my next basketball game?"

Oh, it was definitely a mistake to get involved with Des. It was selfish and stupid and shortsighted of me. Now my daughter is caught between two men who don't care about her nearly as much as she deserves.

"I'm not sure when he's coming back," I admit. "He didn't tell me."

"Oh." Bailey follows me to the front door. "Okay."

When I open the door she runs inside, and I knock my head on the doorjamb, cursing myself...until the sound of a big engine draws my attention. A huge RV looms at the mouth of the alleyway and starts honking cheerily. My mother pokes her head out of the passenger's side window. "YOOHOO! We're HEREEEE!"

THIRTY-FIVE
MIA

MY MOTHER IRENE is an avid reader, a crossword whiz, and a social butterfly. Twelve hours after she and my father arrive in Heart's Cove, she's already integrated herself into the community better than I ever have.

"And we saw a California condor flying above the Grand Canyon, didn't we, Earl?" She leans toward Dorothy, one of the elderly ladies who owns the Heart's Cove Hotel, and doesn't wait for my father's answer. "They were declared extinct in 1987, but we met some birdwatchers who told us all about the conservation efforts that had been successful at reintroducing them into the wild. Absolutely fascinating!"

"Isn't that something!" Dorothy sips coffee from her cup, her leopard-print kaftan fluttering around her like feathers of her own. "You know, I've never been to the Grand Canyon. Marge, any interest in selling the hotel and buying an RV?"

Margaret, her twin sister, just gives her a flat look. "No."

Dorothy laughs. "Well, a week away at least. We can find a nice, comfortable hotel with a full-size shower."

Her twin laughs. "That's more my style."

I pick at the croissant crumbs on my plate, grateful that the attention is off me, for once. My parents only stayed for a few minutes last night, but it was long enough for an intense inquisition into my career, love life, and goals.

"Here," my father says, pushing his plate over. There's half a bagel with chive-flavored cream cheese smeared on it. "Have the rest of that. You look rail-thin, Mia."

I glance down at all my pudge and frown. "You're delusional, Dad."

He laughs and pats my hand. "Eat, kiddo."

The pet name makes me stiffen. I glance at my silent phone, cursing Des for his silence—and cursing myself for my cowardice. I asked him for space, and I know it's my responsibility to reach out. But what if he rejects me? What if he tells me he'd rather stay in Colorado? What if I pushed him away so well that he never comes back?

"Now," my mother announces. "Who's going to tell me the truth about this Desmond fellow? Bailey wouldn't stop talking about him last night!"

"He is a *dear*," Margaret exclaims, putting a hand to her chest. "He dotes on his grandparents like you wouldn't believe. Orphaned at eleven, worked his way up his company, then dropped everything to come take care of Arthur and Maude. Just an absolute gem of a man."

"Well," my mother exclaims, giving my father a sneaking

glance. "How wonderful! Don't you think, Earl?" She turns to Dorothy. "Do you agree?"

"One hundred percent," Dorothy says with a decisive nod. "And he's easy on the eyes too."

"Well!" My mother lets out a happy little squeak and stares at me, nodding encouragingly. "Bailey sure did sing his praises. When does he get back from Colorado? What did you say he was doing there again?"

Hah. Nice try, Mom.

Before I can answer with something suitably distracting to get her off the scent of my pitiful love life, Colin breezes through the door.

My father's bushy eyebrows draw down over his eyes. He straightens in his chair, angling his body almost as if to shield me. Colin spots us all at our table and changes his trajectory. When my mother spots him, she lets out a surprised and slightly horrified gasp but recovers quickly.

"Colin! What a lovely surprise!" She stands up, shooting me a questioning glance before turning to give him a kiss on each cheek. "Mia told us you were in town."

"Here to stay," he answers proudly.

"That's a surprise," my father mumbles.

Colin extends a hand to my father, and they shake. I grab the bagel and stuff it in my mouth so I don't have to talk to anyone or do anything specific with my expression. I endure my mother's polite conversation until Colin begs off to get back to work.

Sighing, I lean back in my chair, exhausted. My life as a barbershop hermit was much easier than this.

"I always liked him," my mother says wistfully. "So charming. It's a shame about him being such a cowardly turd."

Coffee singes my nostrils as I explode into a laugh at the worst possible time. My father pats my back and says, "There, there," while my mother jumps up to find some napkins. I splutter, coffee streaming out of orifices that it definitely shouldn't, and finally dissolve into laughter.

Margaret dabs at my face with a scratchy napkin and winks at me. Dad tosses the coffee-covered bagel remnants and orders me a brownie. My mother's eyes glimmer.

Maybe my parents aren't so bad, after all.

THE NEXT DAY, I'm at Four Cups waiting for my coffee to be prepared when Maude and Arthur walk in. Fiona gives me an opaque glance. She knows as much as I do about why Des left and how long he'll be away. Believe me—I asked. The gossip network is seriously coming up short on this one.

At the end of my rope, I texted Desmond last night, but our conversation was short and stilted. When I asked him what he was doing, he wrote, *Taking care of a few things. I should be back in Heart's Cove within a week or so*, like that was an actual answer. I didn't respond, and that was the end of it. I reread the texts a dozen times, trying to divine some hidden meaning, to see if he was still giving me space or if he was just sick of my mercurial moods.

Maybe I'm meant to be alone.

"Mia!" Maude comes shuffling toward me, one hand on Arthur's elbow. She deposits him at a nearby table and turns to face me, beaming. "You look beautiful, my dear. Have you heard from Desmond today?"

I frown. "Um, no, Maude. I've barely heard from him since he left town."

"Well, isn't that strange?" She clicks her tongue. "He must be busy, what with everything he has to do."

I exchange a glance with Fiona, then say, "What is it, exactly, that he has to do?"

"He didn't tell you?" She seems surprised.

I shake my head.

Maude beams at me, clutching her heart. "Well, I can't ruin the surprise." She pats my cheek, then goes to order at the counter.

Frowning at Fiona, I lower my voice. "A surprise?"

Fiona shrugs. "Maybe Des is planning something for you."

"Fiona, Des and I aren't even dating for real. This was all based on a fake date. He paid me to go to Thanksgiving, remember?"

She cringes. "And you don't know when he's getting back?"

I shake my head.

"Maybe you should call him. Straighten this out."

Inhaling deeply, I nod. She's right. No more ruminating over three or four text messages. No more being stuck in my own head. I raised Bailey on my own, damn it. Pushed her out of my body and got my vagina cut open in the process. I am strong. I can't let the fear of being rejected hold me back from knowing the truth. Time to put my big girl pants on and have this out with Des, once and for all.

There's no time like the present—if I wait until I'm alone, I'll lose my nerve. A quick glance at Maude tells me she's on her way back to her seat, so I pull out my phone and dial.

It rings...and rings...and rings...and rings...

When it finally disconnects, with no option to leave a message, I frown at my phone. "No answer."

Fiona plants her fists on her hips. "That's odd. You didn't want to leave a message?"

"There was no voicemail."

"Huh."

The young lady behind the register calls Fiona's name, so she squeezes my arm and hurries away. I'm left standing on my own, utterly confused, when my name is called and my coffee is ready.

I wave at the Thomases, intending to avoid them as I walk out of the coffee shop, but Maude calls me over to her table with a smile and a wave. "Mia!"

Forcing my lips to curl, I grit my teeth and cross over to where she and Arthur are sitting.

"Arthur and I were just talking, and we want to have you and Bailey over for dinner this week. How's tomorrow night for you?"

Suddenly, I'm weary. I don't want to spend an evening with Maude and Arthur, pretending that Des has some amazing, romantic surprise for me. I don't want to confuse Bailey any more than she already is. I need to start planning an exit. All signs point to this whirlwind romance being over already. Real, lasting relationships can't be built on shaky foundations like the one Des and I have. Maybe it's time for me to face the music: Des doesn't have feelings for me the way I have for him. If he did, he would've reached out by now. He would've stayed. He would've told me how he felt.

"Tomorrow isn't great," I start gently, then stop.

How do I tell this sweet old lady that her grandson doesn't actually care about me?

"Sunday. I'll make a roast," Maude says with a decisive nod. "If Des isn't back by then, we can all video call him. I'm sure he's desperate to hear your voice. He must miss you something awful, our Desmond."

I can't take this anymore. My filter dissolves to nothing and I blurt, "Desmond doesn't care about me, Maude."

She looks at me like I'm insane. "Mia! Don't say that."

"Maude, he doesn't."

"Stop it." Her lips pinch. "You stop that right now. I saw the way he looked at you at Thanksgiving. That boy is in love with you."

Oh my God. I'm going to explode. Between her insistence, Des's disappearance, and Colin sticking around like a bad smell, trying to turn my own daughter against me, I feel like I'm losing my fucking mind. My body is a pressure cooker with a broken valve, and I'm going to explode.

"Now, don't be ridiculous. You'll come to dinner, we'll call Des and put him on video, and you two lovebirds will be able to speak. Really, he should have called you already. I don't understand what goes through that boy's head sometimes. So moody! You'd swear he never grew out of his teen years, and—"

"Maude, *it was fake!*" The words blow out of me like bullets, echoing around the room at the exact moment the espresso machine stops whistling. All heads turn toward me, but I can't stop myself. "It was all fake! He told me he'd give me free rent for three months to go to Thanksgiving with him and try to win that stupid race. None of it was real. He doesn't care about me. He doesn't care about Bailey! He never did! He doesn't want to talk to me. He doesn't want to do a video. He hasn't called because *he doesn't care.*"

Maude's mouth opens and closes. Her hand presses against her chest, kneading gently at the soft pink knit of her top. She gasps, blinking—then goes limp and keels out of her chair.

I leap, catching the old woman around the shoulders and bringing her to the floor as gently as I can. She lands on top of me, her mouth open, her eyes closed. Arthur cries, and chairs all around us push back as people react with shock and dismay.

I blink, confused, as my swirling world comes into focus again. Maude is completely still in my arms. I'm lying on the floor, holding her to my chest—and, oh my God, I think I just killed Desmond's grandmother.

THIRTY-SIX

DES

RITA'S BAR & Grill is moderately busy, but I still manage to get a seat on the covered patio near one of the heat lamps. I order a burger and a beer and let the cheerful atmosphere soak into my pores. Across from me, my brother David leans back in his chair.

"House is finally sold, huh. I never thought you'd go through with it. That house was a big deal when you bought it."

"First thing I did for myself," I agree.

"The Webbers happy?"

I think of the joyful look on Mr. Webber's face when he and his wife signed the papers. "Ecstatic," I tell David. "They finally have a home to call their own."

"And you've cut your final tie to this place." His smile is understanding. "I think it's a good thing. Have you told Mia everything went through?"

I grimace. "I haven't actually told her about the sale."

"You haven't told her at all? About any of it?"

I shake my head. "I wanted it to be a surprise."

David blows a raspberry, then lets out a chuckle. "Not how I would have done it, but you know the woman best. She'll be pretty happy when she finds out."

I shove my fingers through my hair just as the waitress drops the burger and beer in front of me.

My house was the last tie I had to this town. The last chain to break so I can finally move on and find somewhere I can truly call home. The money cleared from the escrow account this morning, and I called my grandmother right away. She said she'd already done the paperwork on her end, so now I'm finally ready to start my new life in Heart's Cove. Finally ready to show Mia how important she is to me.

A wriggling earthworm of worry tunnels its way through my heart at the thought. What if this is a mistake? What if I was too impulsive? What if this all blows up in my face?

I take a bite of juicy burger, chew, swallow, and finally admit, "She hasn't called."

David glances up from his own food, brows arched. "Since you left Heart's Cove?"

I nod.

"So you haven't talked to her at all? Why didn't you call her?"

Sighing, I wash down my food with about a quarter of my beer. I've spent my entire life feeling like I'm on the outside, never belonging, and I just can't bear the thought of being that pathetic, clingy sod who doesn't know when he isn't wanted.

I left Heart's Cove so quickly, resolving to give her some space...but was that the right move? Did she need space, or did she need affection? I've been so focused on proving myself that I haven't stopped to wonder if I'm going about it all wrong.

After another bite of my hamburger, I finally answer David's question with one of my own: "Why didn't she just tell me her ex-husband was staying in town? She had the chance. We were in the barbershop together and I asked her what was bothering her."

David lets out a long sigh. "How did the conversation go? Maybe you missed something."

I take a gulp of beer and stare at the condensation on the side of the glass, replaying our final conversation over in my mind—and realization hits me.

She didn't tell me, because *I said I was leaving*. I thought she needed space, but she really needed reassurance.

I sit up straighter, meeting my brother's gaze. "Oh, shit," I whisper. I messed up—bad.

"What?" He sips his beer, frowning.

"I was so focused on this stupid plan being a secret until it was done—and then I was angry about her ex sticking around—that I didn't realize when she went cold on me." Horror spreads through me like ice forming on the surface of a lake. Slow, inexorable, undeniable. "She didn't tell me because she thinks I'm not coming back."

"What?" David looks shocked.

I fumble for my pocket, and—"My phone's dead."

"Use mine."

"I don't know her number!" I shout the words, half-standing. "I don't know anyone's number! Everything's saved in my cell phone! The only number I know by heart anymore is our old landline from when we were kids." *Fuck.* Oh, no. I need to talk to

Mia. *Need* to talk to her, explain that the whole reason I left town was for her. For this stupid surprise that I don't even know if she'll want.

Damn it, why didn't I memorize her number? I could... I could call her barbershop!

I shove my chair back, and David fumbles with his own phone. "Call Grandma. She'll be able to get in touch."

"Yeah. Yeah. Okay." Grandma first, then the barbershop.

But when I dial our grandmother's phone number, it rings out. They still have a landline, so I try the house—no answer. My grandfather doesn't have a cell phone, and no one answers at the barbershop. Why does no one answer at the barbershop? She should be there. David doesn't have anyone else's number in Heart's Cove. I could call the hotel, maybe? Four Cups?

"I need a phone charger." I glance behind me, at the bar lining the far side of Rita's. Someone in here will have a charger, and I'll be able to call Mia and explain everything.

But I've only taken a single step toward the bar when Vince walks through the door.

"Here we go," David mutters behind me.

Vince's smarmy smile spreads over his lips, and he strides toward us. "Well, if it isn't Mr. Faker. I fucking knew you paid her to show up to Thanksgiving. A woman like that doesn't voluntarily spend time with a guy like you."

I freeze, the panic in my veins solidifying to something much, much worse. "What?"

David, who had stepped around to my side of the table, spins to face me. "What?"

Vince just laughs. "It was all a lie. All those daddy-daughter moments you had with Bailey—fake. All those moments of PDA and Des being the gallant hero carrying Mia inside after they fell in the pond—fake. The touching—fake. The kisses—fake. The moon-eyes—fake, fake, *fake*. Every bit of it." Vince leans in, his face growing hard. "And now Grandma is in the hospital because of you, you asshole. Because you didn't have the balls to just show up to Thanksgiving alone like you should've."

This time, both David and I speak at the same time. "*What?*"

"She passed out when she heard you lied to us all, Des, and now she and Grandpa are both admitted to the hospital. You probably gave her a heart attack. Mom's blowing her lid."

I don't even answer. I just grab my jacket, toss a few bills on the table, and take off at a sprint for the nearest taxi. All my stuff is in the hotel room. Doesn't matter. I'll deal with it later—somehow. The whole point of coming to Lovers' Peak one last time was to sell the house and organize shipping for all the belongings I'd kept in storage, but none of that matters now.

All that matters is getting on a plane and getting back to Heart's Cove.

Because I messed up bad. I messed up so bad, I might not be able to fix it again.

THIRTY-SEVEN
MIA

I'VE BEEN SITTING in the hospital waiting room for hours. Des's phone is still going straight to voicemail, and I don't have anyone else's number. Arthur was so distressed by his wife's fainting spell that he had to be admitted to the hospital too, so I had to take Maude's keys, go to their home, and rifle through their things to find Wendy's phone number. Then I came back here and started my long vigil, feeling like the worst person in the world.

I caused this. A nice old couple is in the hospital because of me.

A commotion happens down the hall, and I stand up from the uncomfortable waiting room chair to take a look—and my heart stops.

Des comes striding down the hallway like a runaway train. Nurses and orderlies scurry out of his way and scowl as he passes, but the force of him is too strong to be stopped. I grow roots and stand where I am, ready to be chopped down like an old tree.

I deserve whatever anger he has for me. I deserve it all. I hurt his grandparents—me. Because I was too much of a coward to face him, because I couldn't look him in the eyes and tell him I cared and I didn't want him to leave.

Des comes closer, his dark eyes terrible. His jaw is covered in scruff, like he hasn't shaved since the last time he was in the barbershop. That's crazy. It means it's been nearly two weeks since he shaved, when he's usually clean-shaven. He looks angrier than I've ever seen him. His jaw is tight and a muscle in his cheek jumps. His shoulders are larger than life, his body looming larger and larger with every step.

Finally, when he's three feet away from me, I find my voice. "Des, I'm so sorry—"

His lips collide with mine, those big, warm hands curling around either side of my neck. I'm so surprised that I let out a squeak against his mouth, eyes widening as he kisses me harder. Then he pulls away, gaze flicking between my eyes, and says, "Are you okay?"

My head is spinning so hard I don't know which way is up. "What? Yes, I'm fine. But Des, your grandmother—she—I—it was my fault, because I said—I told her, and you were gone..."

He kisses my forehead, and I snap my lips shut.

What in the world is going on?

A door closes behind me, and we both turn to face the doctor exiting Maude and Arthur's room. The doctor is a tall woman with dark-brown skin and hair streaked with silver. She studies Des for a beat. "Are you the grandson?"

He nods. "Are they okay?"

"They're fine. Your grandmother had a shock, and she experienced what we call vasovagal syncope. Essentially, her heart rate and blood pressure dropped suddenly, and she fainted. Your grandfather needed to be sedated. We're keeping them both here for observation overnight, but they should be fine by morning."

He lets out a long breath, his big body trembling beside me. "Can we go in?"

The doctor nods. "Maude is awake, and she was asking about you."

"I'll wait out here," I tell him with (what I hope is) a brave smile.

"Like hell you will," Des says, then clamps his hand around mine and drags me to the door.

Oh, dear.

Fear starts beating a drum inside me as we approach the door. I haven't seen Maude since I made her pass out from shock. I haven't had the guts to face her. And now Des is here, and my heart feels like everything is okay, but my brain is all muddled.

Is he angry with me? But then if he is, why did he kiss me?

Where has he been? Was I wrong about everything being fake? Why did he come back?

Maude lies in her hospital bed, looking paler than I've seen her. No one looks good when they're wearing a hospital gown and they have tubes sticking into their veins—but Maude still smiles at the two of us and beckons us closer.

"Desmond," she croaks. "You're back. Did you get everything sorted?"

"Yes," he says. Then, when his grandmother's eyes narrow, he sighs. "I had to leave all my stuff behind. I rushed here."

"Well, that was silly."

Des arches a brow at his grandmother, at the beeping machines, at Arthur sleeping in the next bed. "Was it?"

Maude waves a hand—and then her eyes land on me. "Desmond," she starts, holding my gaze, "will you explain to this young lady what you were doing in Lovers' Peak?"

Des squeezes my hand. "Grandma, let's just talk about you, okay? I want to make sure you're okay."

Her gaze narrows, and Desmond flinches. This big, strong man *flinches* at the look his grandmother gives him. "Did you lie to me, Desmond? When you took Mia and Bailey with you to meet our family, was that all a lie? You didn't care about them the way you made us believe?"

"Of course not," he answers, and it's my turn to stare at him. He glances at me, frustration making a vein pop in his forehead. "It wasn't fake," he insists.

Relief starts to sweep through me, but I can't quite believe it—not yet. "Des, you gave me three months free rent for me to go to Colorado with you. You said we should pretend to be together. It *was* a lie." Apart from all the kissing and touching we did beforehand...

"Absurd," Maude huffs, crossing her arms. She scowls at her grandson. "I'm disappointed in you, Desmond."

"What else was I supposed to do? She hated me!"

"I didn't hate you," I say, even though, yeah, I kind of did.

Maude arches her brows at him as if to say, *You see?* "This young lady believed you didn't care about her. Now, I've had a few hours to think about it, and I want to see you two fix this. Right here and now. Tell her what you were doing in Colorado."

"Grandma, I don't want to do this now."

"Well, tough shit," Maude says, swearing for the first time I've ever heard. I'm so shocked I just freeze. "Tell her."

Des sighs, turning to face me. He rakes his hand through his hair. "I was selling my house."

"Okay..." I frown. Good for him?

There's a pause, and Maude clears her throat.

"Look, Mia..." He exhales in a huff, then stares at the ceiling. "That house was the first place where I felt like I belonged. It was my first home, apart from the house my parents had, which I barely remember. I sold it because it was also a chain that held me back in Colorado, and I didn't want anything in my way when I started a life here."

Blood pounds in my ears. I grip the end of the hospital bed to steady myself, the hard plastic smooth against my palm. "You're staying here? You're not leaving?"

"No, Mia," he says on an exhale. "I'm not leaving."

The plastic beneath my palm creaks as I grip it harder. "Oh," I manage to say, my throat clogging.

Des takes a step closer and lifts his palm to touch my cheek. "It was never fake for me, Mia. From the very first moment, it was you."

"Even when I was angry and awful to you?"

His lips tilt. "You were never awful to me. And your anger just made me want to stay even more. It made me feel like you cared—like I belonged here with you."

I inhale shakily, wanting so badly to believe him. But—who

actually *likes* my temper? Is it even possible for someone to appreciate all my flaws?

"Oh, tell her the rest," a raspy voice says from the other bed. We turn to see Arthur with eyes slitted open, scowling at us. "It nearly killed us to go out and do the paperwork this morning, so she might as well know the whole story."

Des goes still. "You already did the paperwork?"

"Of course, darling boy," Maude says, smiling. She gestures to her purse, which is sitting on a table beside her bed. "It's all there. We were just getting a coffee after going to the lawyer's office this morning when Mia tried her best to give me a heart attack. Cheeky girl."

"But I haven't transferred any money—"

"Call it an early inheritance," Maude says. "Plus, you'll need your own money to start your life here, don't you think?"

Des stumbles over his words, staring at his grandmother.

I shift my weight from foot to foot. "Um. Anyone want to explain what's going on?"

Des blinks, then walks to the purse. He pulls out a green file folder and flips it open. Blinking, he huffs and shakes his head. Then he closes it again and hands the folder to me.

It takes me longer than it should to realize what I'm looking at. It's a property transfer deed, and it has my name on it—and the address of both the barbershop and the attached apartment. Des planned on buying the barbershop and apartment from his grandparents to give to me. He sold his house to get the money, not knowing Maude and Arthur would gift it to me anyway.

It's too much. My hands start trembling, my eyes go blurry, and it's impossible to read any further. I drop the folder onto the end of Maude's hospital bed, bury my face in my hands, and burst into tears.

THE HOUR that follows is a blur. I know that, from their hospital beds, both Maude and Arthur alternated between comforting me and chiding me for being silly. Des dithered and worried about me like a ginormous mother hen.

By the time the nurse kicked us out of the room, I felt like I was living in a dream land. Des had come to the hospital in a taxi straight from the airport, so he gently extricated my keys from my hands and told me he'd drive.

Now, the car is sliding into the parking space behind the apartment. Yellow light spills out of every window, and when Des cuts the engine, we just sit there in silence for a while.

His hand covers mine, squeezing gently. "I love you, Mia," he says simply.

I turn to look at him, throat tight. "Really?"

He smiles. "Yes."

"You didn't have to give me a whole property to prove it, you know."

That just makes him laugh. He lifts my hand and places a kiss against my palm, then leans in to kiss my lips. It's slow, tender, and it consumes me from the inside out. He tastes like home, like happiness, like everything I've denied myself for a decade.

When our kiss ends, I rest my forehead against his. "I love you too"—I touch his beard, combing my fingers through the coarse hair—"but you need a shave."

His laughter is the most beautiful sound I've ever heard. He kisses me once more, then exits the car and helps me to the door.

It's only when the door opens that I remember who's watching Bailey.

My mother is in the kitchen, putting foil over some kind of casserole she made for dinner. My father is sitting at the table across from Bailey, frowning at his cards when Bailey crows, "Go fish!" with a triumphant smile.

Bailey jumps out of her chair. "Mom! Des! You're back!" She runs toward us and, expecting her to hug me, I spread my arms—but she goes straight to Des.

She flies into his arms, wrapping her arms and legs around him, and he lifts her off the ground with a delighted, surprised chuckle.

"Hi Mom, Dad," I say, crossing the room to give the two of them a peck on the cheek. "Thanks for watching Bailey."

"Anytime," my father answers. "But I don't think I'll be playing cards with her again."

"How are Maude and Arthur?" my mother asks, even though I already texted her that they were fine when we left the hospital. "Is this Desmond?" my mother asks as Des sets Bailey back down on her feet.

"Yep," Bailey says, taking his hand and tugging him inside. She shows him off with a sweep of her other arm. "He likes the L.A. Lakers, but I still like him."

I snort—and there's a knock on the door. I walk across the room, open it, and see my ex-husband standing on my doorstep.

"Mia," he says, sounding relieved.

"Hi, Colin," I say, just as Des steps into view behind me.

Colin's gaze jumps over my shoulder, then back to me. "I didn't know you had company. I was just stopping by to make sure you were all okay. I heard you were at the hospital with some friends."

"We're fine, dear." My mother comes bustling past us and hip-checks me out of the doorway. She grips the doorknob with one hand and the jamb with the other. "Is anything wrong?"

"No, no. I just wanted to make sure Bailey was okay, you know, with everything going on."

It must be divine intervention that allows me to not roll my eyes. Father of the fucking year here, swooping in to make sure everything's okay. What a freaking hero.

Giving this man the benefit of doubt is not in my skillset, apparently.

My mother gives him a smile that makes me think of the Big, Bad Wolf. "Bailey is perfectly fine. Thank you for stopping by. Bye-bye, now!" And she slams the door in my ex-husband's face.

Sometimes I love my mother more than usual.

She spins on her heels, gives me a curt nod, then strides to Des and pats him on his big barrel chest. "Now. Des." She points at the table while grabbing his elbow, the other hand still smoothing his pectoral muscle. "You sit down and eat something. I'll fix you a plate."

Des, looking completely out of his depth, follows my mother's commands and sits at the table. Bailey jumps up beside him, legs swinging off the chair. "Are you staying here tonight, Des?"

"Um." Des's panicked eyes meet mine.

"Of course he is," my mother interjects, placing a plate full of warmed casserole in front of him and another plate in front of an empty chair. She looks at me and gestures to the chair. "Where else would he stay?" She pats his shoulder and hums to herself as she heads back to the kitchen to clean up.

Exchanging a grin with Des, I take a seat at the table and eat my dinner. Under the table, Des reaches over to squeeze my knee.

"Is it okay if I stay tonight?" he asks quietly when my mother has moved to the living room to sit next to my father on the couch.

"Yeah," I answer. "I'd like that."

"You can make pancakes for breakfast," Bailey informs him, then squints. "You can cook, right?"

Des grins. "Yeah," he says, "I can cook."

Oof. My poor ovaries. Did I ever stand a chance against this man?

"Good. Because sometimes Mom's food is not so good. Maybe you can take over."

I snort, shaking my head, and Bailey scampers away. Des and I finish our dinner and wash the dishes, but before we can go around the corner to join the others in the living room, he curls an arm around my waist and tugs me close.

"Love you," he whispers. "You have no idea how good it feels to finally say that to you, or how good it feels to have dinner with you and your family."

"I love you too." I touch his cheek, heart full. "But to be honest, Des, I think they're your family too now."

Des's answering smile and kiss send my heart thumping—then we go join the rest of the family in the living room to wind down for the evening.

Later, when Bailey's in bed and I'm guiding my parents through the barbershop to head back to their hotel (they're treating themselves to a real shower while they're in town), my mom stops and gives me a tight hug. "I like him," she whispers in my ear.

I smile. "So do I."

"Good." She hugs me once more, then threads her fingers through my father's and heads across the road to the hotel. I walk back through the barbershop and into my home, and I find Des alone on the couch, reclining with one arm curled around his head. He shifts on the sofa to give me enough space to lie down in front of him, and I find myself wrapped up in his warmth—and I know I'll never be alone again.

EPILOGUE
DES

AFTER SO MANY years as an outsider, I never realized how good it would feel to have a home. And when the holidays roll around, I find myself surrounded by dozens of people who treat me like one of their own.

Mia, Bailey, and I arrive at Grant and Fiona's house bearing bottles of wine and bags of snacks. We're ushered inside with hugs and kisses, into the chaos of the gathered crowd.

Along with everyone who was in Lovers' Peak for Thanksgiving, there's Dorothy, Margaret, and their partners Eli and Hamish. There's Lottie, the Viceroy women's mother, there's Mia's parents, and all the children. For the first time in my life, I find it easy to talk to various people. I don't feel like I stick out at this gathering, like I don't belong.

We eat way too much food, and I spend more time than I'd like to admit just watching Mia interact with her friends. She's bottled sunlight. She's energy and fire in human form. She's magic.

"I've always wanted a man to look at Mia the way you're looking at her," Earl says, taking a seat next to me with a slight grunt of effort. He puts his drink down on the floor beside his leg, smiling at me. "You care about her."

"Yes, sir."

"She's more fragile than she looks, our Mia," he says, eyes drifting toward his daughter. "You sure you can handle her temper? You can treat her right even when she infuriates you?"

I huff, meeting Mia's eyes from across the room. She smiles at me, and it's like the warmth of the sun's rays on my skin. "Is it crazy to say that her temper is one of the things I like most about her?"

Earl barks out a laugh. "Yes, son. It is."

I chuckle. How can I explain to this man that when Mia is angry at me, when she's snippy and sassy, it's a reminder that I exist—that I matter. I've spent so many years drifting through life, being on the outside, but that's impossible with Mia. She drags me by the collar and forces me to be present, to be here—with her.

"You'll take care of her," Earl says, and it isn't a question.

"I love her," I reply.

He smiles softly at me, then shakes my hand. "Welcome to the family, Desmond."

"Des! Yoohoo! Des!" Irene pokes her head around the corner of the kitchen and beckons me. "We need someone nice and tall to get something from the upper cabinets."

"Duty calls," I tell Earl, who just laughs.

In the kitchen, I find Irene, Dorothy, Margaret, Lottie, Agnes, and my grandmother crowded around the island. I'm put to work opening a cabinet over the fridge, where the bottles of alcohol reside. I pull them all down as Dorothy hoots and starts hunting through cabinets and drawers for a cocktail shaker.

Irene giggles, then pats my arm. "Thank you, honey."

I'm run out of the kitchen shortly afterward, but my chest still feels warm. That has never happened in all my childhood at my aunt's house. No one would ever specifically search *me* out and ask *me* a favor. As I wander back to the living room and take a seat next to Mia, slinging an arm behind her shoulders, I start to wonder if that's what belonging is all about.

It's not just accepting affection from others—it's being seen. It's being important enough that someone is angry with you. It's doing favors for people. Being here is being part of something bigger than myself.

Mia puts her hand on my thigh and leans into me, then turns her face to mine. I lower my head and kiss her softly, my heart growing three sizes in my chest.

"Ew! Mom! Des! Don't be gross!" Bailey comes stomping toward us and throws herself on the sofa beside Mia, scowling at us. "Kissing is disgusting."

"You won't always think that," Mia warns.

"Yes, I will," Bailey replies emphatically. "I'm never going to kiss anyone, ever."

I chuckle, letting my thumb stroke over Mia's shoulder. A kid comes running into the living room and calls Bailey's name, and she's off again.

"Will you sleep at our place tonight?" Mia asks quietly.

I've gotten a small rental apartment in town, because it

seemed too soon to move in with the two of them. "Sure," I say, smiling.

"Good," Mia answers with a nod. "Bailey wants pancakes tomorrow morning."

I laugh, happy to be of service.

A WEEK LATER, on the first of January, I glance at myself one last time in the mirror, straighten my bowtie, and put on the black suit jacket I've recently had dry cleaned. A dozen roses wait for me near the front door, and I slip my feet into gleaming black dress shoes before taking the flowers and heading out.

Tonight, to go along with the first day of the New Year, Mia and I have special plans—our first official date. Bailey is having an overnight sleepover at Trina's place, and Mia will be all mine.

My nerves are wound up tighter than ever by the time I make it behind the barbershop and knock on the door. My palm sweats around the rose stems, and I touch my bowtie for the thousandth time to make sure it isn't crooked.

Then the door opens, and everything is all right in the world.

Mia is radiant. She smiles at me in a plunging black gown, her feet clad in strappy, rhinestone-encrusted shoes that are not at all season appropriate. Her gaze drops to the flowers, and she glows.

"No one's ever bought me flowers before," she admits.

I store that tidbit away for future use. "They won't be the last you get from me," I answer, handing them over. I enter the space and watch her fuss with the roses as she puts them in water, positioning the blooming red roses in the center of the table with a happy smile on her face. Her blond hair gleams, falling in delicate tendrils around her face. She's beautiful. She's mine.

"Okay," Mia finally says, throwing a wool jacket over her shoulders. "I'm ready."

I extend my arm and lead her to my car. When she's safely seated inside, I jog to the driver's side and get in. We spend the evening watching a show at a nearby theater—a romantic musical that makes me want to put my arms around Mia and never let go. Then I take her to the restaurant for a do-over.

"Dolce Vita," Mia says with a laugh as we pull into the parking lot. She grins at me. "I hear the cannolis are divine."

"I wouldn't know," I answer. "My last date walked out on me before I got to try any of the food."

She laughs, then takes my arm. We enter the restaurant together, then have a beautiful meal with delicious wine. All those weeks ago, this is what I craved—but the reality is better.

I'm not pretending to be anyone other than who I am. Mia sees me—all of me—and loves me for me. So, after the waiter brings out our cannolis for dessert, I clear my throat, reach into my breast pocket, and stand up from my chair to get down on bended knee.

Mia has a mouthful of creamy, crunchy cannoli, and she stares at me with wide eyes. I flip open the ring box to show her the diamond ring I picked out the day after I got back to Heart's Cove. She stops chewing, a bit of creamy filling dotted on the corner of her lip.

I reach over, pick it up with my thumb, then lick it clean. Then I smile and say, "Mia. I know it's soon, but no matter how much time goes by, I'll always know you're the one for me. I love you so much, looking at you feels like staring directly at the sun. Please, make me the happiest man in the world and be my wife."

It takes a while for Mia to chew and swallow. She throws me a few glares, eyes shining with tears, and finally swallows her dessert before saying, "You couldn't have warned me about this before I stuffed an entire cannoli in my mouth?"

I laugh, plucking the ring from its velvet embrace. "Is that a yes?"

"Insolent man," she grumbles, but she reaches her hand forward anyway. A tear rolls down her cheek as she meets my gaze and says, "It's a yes."

"Yay!" Bailey's voice echoes in the restaurant as the rest of the dinner patrons applaud. Bailey comes sprinting over from the hostess's stand where she'd been hiding and crashes into her mother's arms. Mia snorts and sniffles, surprised, delighted, happy —and mine.

I stand up and wrap my arms around the two most important ladies in my life, before leaning down to kiss Mia's cannoli-flavored mouth. "I love you," I whisper.

"I'm very angry at you," she whispers back, not looking angry at all, "and I love you too."

MIA

WE DECIDE to set the date of our wedding for a full year later, to give us time to plan the biggest, most wonderful party this town has seen. Des and I are both loners, but our friends and family in Heart's Cove have dragged us out of our shells kicking and screaming, and the wedding is a way for us to show how much we appreciate it.

In between wedding planning, I run my barbershop, I spend time with Bailey and Des, and I make sure to stop in at Four Cups at least once a day to see the girls. The library above the café becomes a sanctuary for me too, and when Georgia hears about her sister's adventures in Lovers' Peak (and her hot, infuriating new boss, Rhett Baldwin), I'm the one who ends up falling on the floor because I'm laughing so hard. The girls were telling the truth. It really is more fun from this side of things.

Des ends up working with Grant as a project manager to help

with a lot of the in-office work while Grant manages the construction crews. The two of them build a friendship as well as a partnership, with Des eventually buying into the business so they can expand, using some of the proceeds from the sale of his home.

Surprisingly, Colin sticks around. He rents out the condo Des had been living in and spends about six months of the year in Heart's Cove. Bailey develops a relationship with him but decides she doesn't want to call him Dad. That honor goes to Des, bestowed upon him a week before the wedding. She says it while they're watching basketball on the couch, casually saying, "Hey, Dad, pass me the remote."

Later, in bed, Des tells me it was one of the best moments of his life. We both end up in tears, arms wrapped around each other, elated and emotional and overwhelmed.

After the wedding, Des moves in with us. The apartment is small, and Des is very large, but it works. I think, because of the way he grew up, Des's definition of home is different from most people's. He doesn't need a big mansion on a mountainside, or even a yard to call his own.

He just needs us.

A week later, we get a dog. He's a tiny black-and-white chihuahua with a sausage-like tail that wags nonstop. Bailey names him Dunk and does indeed take over most of his care, even picking up his poo (even though it's gross).

Want more fake dating heat...with a cozy mystery twist?

*Check out the Four Groomsmen of the Wedpocalypse series with
Book One: CONQUEST!*

351

EXTENDED EPILOGUE

MIA

PEOPLE SAY you're supposed to be more modest for your second wedding.

I say who cares?

The conference room at the Heart's Cove Hotel has been transformed into a winter wonderland. The centerpieces are delicate pine wreaths with fat, white candles in the center. The chairs are draped with gauzy material. White roses are dotted across the room in delicate arrangements.

Wearing a white silk robe and slippers, with my hair and makeup done, I give Fiona a nod. "It looks amazing."

"Good," she smiles. "I'll tell the wedding planner you're happy. Now go finish getting ready."

I shuffle back down the corridor and run into Simone and Jen, who are pushing a trolley carrying the cake. It's a three-tiered cake with naked sides that Jen toiled over all week. Fresh flowers are clumped artistically at various points, with gold leaf and other decorations accenting the tops of the tiers. It looks amazing, and it's my favorite flavor: vanilla. I can see the specks of vanilla bean in the frosting and in the cake.

My mouth waters. "Wow," I breathe.

"She did good," Simone says with a nod.

"I'm hoping the buttercream holds up to the heat in here." Jen frowns. "Maybe I can get Margaret to turn on the A.C. in the room."

"I'll go ask her," Simone says, letting Jen push the trolley down the hall. She links her arm with mine and bumps me with her hip. "You're looking fab," she says. "Where's the dress?"

"Upstairs," I answer. Dorothy and Margaret rented Des and me one of the suites for a ridiculously low price. My dress is currently hanging in the closet in all its ivory glory.

"Mia!" Trina comes hurrying toward us, a broad smile on her face. "Come, come. Let's get you dressed." She grabs me from Simone's arms, who waves at us and peels off to go find Margaret about the air conditioning. Trina guides me to the elevators and chatters excitedly about my hair and makeup.

"The stylist did an amazing job on your blowout," Trina notes, looking at the soft, voluminous waves that are falling down my back. "It's going to look great with the veil."

"I hope so," I smile.

We reach the room, and the rest of the gang is waiting inside, along with my sister Ria, my mother, Lottie, Dorothy, Agnes, and Maude. They all cheer when I enter, and I'm engulfed in a group hug, followed by individual hugs.

"You'll ruin her hair!" Trina cries, batting them away from me. "You can hug her after the photos."

I laugh, taking a seat at the vanity and letting the stylist smooth my hair out again. My mother hands me a glass of champagne, and I'm surprised to see tears in her eyes.

"Mom," I chide softly. "Don't cry."

"My baby is finally getting married," she says. "Of course I'm going to cry."

"You didn't cry when I married Colin," I note with a wry twist of my lips.

She clicks her tongue. "Can you blame me? He doesn't look at you the way Des does."

My chest warms at the thought of my soon-to-be husband.

"There you go," the hair stylist says, arranging the hair at my temple oh-so-carefully. "You can put the dress on now."

A hush enters the room as I slip into the suite's bedroom and put on the dress. Trina helps me with the zipper at the back, then steps back with her hands clasped at her breast. "Beautiful," she says.

She opens the sliding pocket doors that lead to the suite's living room, where the rest of my girlfriends and family are waiting.

My gown is floor length and trumpet-shaped. It has a form-fitting bodice with thin shoulder straps and delicate lace detailing all over. The train is scalloped and glamorous, and the back dips low to reveal half of my spine. I feel beautiful.

"Oh," my sister says. "You look incredible."

I touch the skirt, arranging it so it falls more prettily around me. "You don't think it's too much?"

"No such thing," Trina answers.

My mother approaches with the veil. It's the one her grandmother wore at her wedding, passed down to my mother and sister. I didn't wear it when I married Colin, because we had a super simple ceremony and it didn't seem appropriate.

It's appropriate now.

The lace trim of the veil matches my dress, and my mother slides the veil's comb into my hair. I turn to look at the mirror, and my bottom lip trembles. "Oh," I say. "I'm getting married today."

My mother kisses my cheek. "Congratulations, honey."

DESMOND LOOKS AMAZING. He's wearing a black tux with a white shirt, and the same bowtie he wore to our first date. A white rose is pinned to his lapel. His eyes are dark as they sweep up my body, his hands slowly falling to his sides.

Thunderstruck is the word I'd use to describe his expression. He stands utterly still as my father walks me down the aisle. My father pats the back of my hand and says quietly, "That man loves you, Mia."

"I love him too, Dad."

Bailey stands on the dais, beaming at me. She wanted to wear a tux just like Des, so she's there with her hair in a high ponytail, pink lipstick on her lips, and a smart black tuxedo. She looks quintessentially like herself—and she looks amazing. I wink at her, and she winks back. We reach the end of the aisle, and my father turns me to face him. He's crying, which is also something that didn't happen the first time around, all those years ago. He squeezes my shoulders. "I don't want to mess up your hair," he whispers.

"Come here, Dad," I laugh, and hug him tight.

He steps aside as I turn to face my fiancé, and everything else falls away.

We found each other despite fighting our feelings every step of the way, but that's over now. There's only the future to look forward to.

Bailey steps forward with the rings, smiling at the two of us.

And the moment we're pronounced man and wife, Des doesn't waste a second. He hooks an arm around my waist and kisses me as hard and as passionately as ever, then murmurs, "I love you, wife."

"I love you, husband." I smile against his lips, the cheers of our guests finally filtering through to my consciousness.

Then we pull away, lift our clasped hands, and lead our guests to the reception hall.

What follows is a party like no other. I dance in my husband's arms, I laugh at my daughter's antics, and I let my happiness buoy me to heights I didn't know existed.

A year and a half ago, this wouldn't have been possible. I had few friends, had no community, and was on the brink of disaster. Now, I have a husband, friends, a thriving business, and stability. I have a home—all because Des saw the real me hidden beneath the scaly, fire-breathing exterior.

LATER, when my feet are sore from dancing and my cheeks ache from laughing, I slip my hand into my husband's and let him take me away from the reception and up to our suite. It's been tidied since the tornado of women getting ready hit it, and the staff sprinkled rose petals on the bed. A chilled bottle of champagne waits for us near the door—something I'm sure Des organized personally.

Kicking off my heels, I smile and accept a glass. "We did it," I say.

"We did," Des answers. "No going back now."

Laughing, I sip my champagne, then decide there are more important things than bubbly drinks and set it aside. I wrap my arms around Des's neck and pull him down for a kiss. "I love you," I murmur. "Now take me to bed."

"Yes ma'am," he answers, then hauls me up over his shoulder and carries me to the rose-petal-covered bed.

I land on the soft mattress, bouncing twice, giggling like a madwoman. Des moves very slowly as he strips off his tuxedo jacket, undoes his cuffs, and loosens the bowtie. Mesmerized, I watch him, heat coiling in my core.

When his shirt is off and his belt has been slipped out of its loops, Des kneels on the bed, making it dip and shift beneath me. He slides my dress up, up, up, letting out a low groan.

"I'm going to enjoy this," he says, lying down so his shoulders push my thighs apart. "So don't you dare tell me to stop."

Smiling, I wiggle on the pillows and make myself comfortable. "I won't," I promise hoarsely.

We don't speak for a while after that, and it's perfectly fine by me.

ABOUT THE AUTHOR

Lilian Monroe adores writing swoonworthy heroes and the women who bring them to their knees. She loves making people laugh and is eternally grateful to have found people who share her sense of humor.

When she's not writing, she's reading (or rereading) a book, walking, lifting weights, or attempting to play the guitar with very limited success.

She grew up in Canada but now lives in Australia with her Irish husband. He frequently asks to be used as a cover model for her books, and she's not quite sure whether or not he's joking.

Dirty Little Midlife Dilemma

Dirty Little Midlife Drama

Dirty Little Midlife (fake) Date

Brother's Best Friend Romance

Shouldn't Want You

Can't Have You

Don't Need You

Won't Miss You

Protector Romance

His Vow

His Oath

His Word

Enemies to Lovers/Workplace Romance

Hate at First Sight

Loathe at First Sight

Despise at First Sight

Secret Baby/Accidental Pregnancy Romance

Knocked Up by the CEO

Knocked Up by the Single Dad

Knocked Up...Again!

Knocked Up by the Billionaire's Son

Yours for Christmas

Bad Prince

Heartless Prince

Cruel Prince

Broken Prince

Wicked Prince

Wrong Prince

Lone Prince

Ice Queen

Rogue Prince

Fake Engagement Romance

Engaged to Mr. Right

Engaged to Mr. Wrong

Engaged to Mr. Perfect

Mountain Man Romance

Lie to Me

Swear to Me

Run to Me

Doctor's Orders

Doctor O

Doctor D

Doctor L

MISTRESS OF CINDERS

If they never look your way, they never see you coming....

The Kingdom is the world's most exclusive VR platform where the rich, famous, and evil can cavort in a utopian fairy tale world. Little do they know that the code beneath their feet grows weak. The only thing keeping the platform-and all their secrets-secure is the tireless and unsung efforts of a single Plaxis employee and sole remaining Purusha Prime language programmer, Cindira Tieg.

For her part, Cindira couldn't care less if the Kingdom went permanently offline tomorrow. Only, the same source code that makes it possible also powers Plaxis's original VR platform, Gaia. There, war is waged virtually, saving the planet and humanity from ruin. It was the greatest legacy her mother left the world, one she intends to defend and sustain.

But when a detective from Authority shows up at Plaxis, demanding access to the source code, Cindira fears an enemy at the gate. In the real, Francisco Batista is a mystery, untraceable and without public record. The only way to discover his true identity and intentions is by going into the vreal herself. But when the coder confronts her mother's creation, she'll discover there's a lot more at risk than legacy. Making the wrong move could defragment the vreal and lead to her very real downfall.

PRAISE FOR KENDRAI MEEKS

A charming adventure into the digital landscape, full of mystery and political intrigue. Complete with ALL the Cinderella tropes we each know by heart. For the tech savvy, there's plenty of IT-geared explanation to satisfy the reader who wants to know HOW it all works. Made sense to me, and my job is literally waging war in simulated environments.

-ROD A. GALINDO, AUTHOR

An exciting read I did not want to put down. Meeks has created an incredible worlds and explored the ramifications of what technology like this would cause - both in the gritty dystopian real world and the gilded virtual world. Lots of fun Easter eggs throughout. A rich plot with well drawn characters - the kind you love or hate, they might frustrate or infuriate you, but they are never bland.

-VINE VOICE REVIEWER MAJORIE

I absolutely loved this Cinderella retelling! Kendrai's version of this well known story is just brilliant. The way she weaves in parts of the original tale with this new one blows my mind. I was quite impressed that 2 wholly different story lines could have such similar foundations.

-THIS LITERARY LIFE